FROM THE HOOD WITH LOVE 2

BRIANN DANAE

*This book is dedicated to my baby, LeGend.
I love & miss you so much. Continue to watch over
your mommy.*

*To my sister, I love you for life. You gave strength a
new meaning for me. Know that it's okay to not
always be strong. God will carry you on those days.*

Chapter One

"Loriana, you need to eat something."

Food was the last thing on her mind. Could food cure this excruciating sadness that was suffocating her heart? Would food bring her mother back? Was food going to stop her tears from falling? Every answer to her nonverbal questions was no. Nothing in this world would make her feel better.

Sitting in her mother's bed with her comforter wrapped around her, tears dripped from her face. Loriana was numb. She'd never in life felt this type of pain, and this was only the beginning. Hours had gone by since the paramedics confirmed that Linette had indeed passed away. Watching them carry her mother out of the house ripped Loriana's heart in two.

Her screams and cries had the entire neighborhood on alert. Once that door to the ambulance closed, everything after that became a blur.

Thankfully, Ms. Mable from next door was able to contact Aunt Peaches and let her know what had happened. Never in a million years did she expect to receive a call about her baby sister passing away. Peaches couldn't wrap her mind around it, especially when she'd literally just seen her the day before. For her niece, though, she had to be strong. Loriana was going to need all the support she could.

For hours, she sat crisscrossed in her mother's bed with her thoughts running wild. She didn't understand how such an amazing night turned into the worst of her life. The thought of having lost both Projex and her mom had Loriana sobbing into her hands once more.

Soothingly, Nyree rubbed her back. There were absolutely no words she could utter to make her friend stop hurting, so Nyree made sure her presence and love were felt. Even though she and Akira weren't friends, when she texted Nyree saying something was going on at Loriana's crib, Nyree didn't hesitate to drop everything she was doing. She'd already been on edge because Loriana had seemingly disappeared after prom. With her phone off, the people close to her had to find a way to reach her.

Even more heartbroken, Greg stood perched against the dresser, drenched in sadness. He knew something was wrong with Linette yesterday. Still, he had chalked it up as her being nervous about Loriana going to prom. Seeing his baby girl cry her heart out had him shaking his head and heading for the door. He couldn't watch her like this.

"Please try and get her to eat something," Greg urged Nyree.

"She'll let us know when she's ready to eat something."

Nyree was hoping that was the case. Loriana hadn't uttered a word since everyone arrived. She was afraid that if she spoke, it'd make this all too real. In her mind, she was playing the lead role in a horrible nightmare. One that seemed to stay on loop. Watching everyone hug her with sad eyes, ask if there was something they could do, or if there was anything she needed, was all *so* much. What she needed was her mother; the one person she knew wasn't coming back.

"I can't believe this," Loriana muttered, speaking for the first time.

Nyree exhaled as tears pricked her eyes. "I know. I can't either."

"L-Like. This is so fucked up. She was just here a-and now she's not. Both of them."

She sniffled and shook her head, trying to rid the fogginess in her brain.

Both of who? Nyree wondered. Before she could ask Loriana who she was talking about, commotion coming from the front of the house grabbed her attention. Loriana didn't make a move while Nyree stood up to see what was going on.

In the front room, Mhyale was pulling her hair into a ponytail. One thing she didn't play about was her respect, especially when it came to her family. They were already dealing with enough, and the fake love Akira showed up trying to give wasn't needed.

"I don't think now is the time for you to be here," Aunt Peaches stated, pushing Mhyale back.

"Nah. She came here trying to be funny. The way I'm feeling, I'll kill this hoe." Mhyale was seething and hurting.

"We ain't about to have none of that up in here," Ms. Mable fussed with warning in her tone. "Young lady, if you came over here to start mess, you need to leave."

"I didn't. Ms. Linette was like a mother to me too. I just wanted to check on Loriana."

Mhyale smacked her lips. "Like a mother? Bitch, my auntie didn't even like you."

"Mhyale! That's enough!" Aunt Peaches shouted.

It was one thing for her to be upset, but Peaches didn't play that cursing shit around her and other grown folks. She'd let her get off with calling Akira a hoe, but that was as far as she was letting it go.

Akira blinked back tears. The family was staring at her like she was an outcast, and she was. Loriana hadn't made it known that they weren't friends anymore, but it was obvious Akira wasn't welcomed there. With her arms crossed over her chest, Nyree stood mugging her. She was so glad Loriana had finally come to her senses and stopped fucking with her. Akira showing up to prom with Keith, then here like everything was good, is what got her. The girl was clearly losing brain cells.

"Can I at least give my condolences?" Akira muttered uneasily.

"I don't need them."

All heads turned toward Loriana, who'd just stepped into the room. Everyone gulped and watched her every move as she made her way deeper into the living room. Tiredness leaked from her pores, and pain coated her body like a blanket of snow in the middle of the winter. It was unmoving, would be difficult to melt away, and caused chills. Her family ached for her. Linette was Loriana's everything.

Her moves were unhurried. She had nowhere to be. The closer she got to Akira, the longer everyone held their breaths. When she walked by her, Peaches exhaled, but a bit too soon.

"Loriana I—"

Bam!

The words couldn't escape Akira before Loriana had punched her dead in the mouth. So caught off guard, she stumbled right back out of the door on her ass where she should've stayed.

"My goodness," Ms. Mable gasped.

A blank expression was plastered on Loriana's face as she looked down at someone she used to consider a friend. Anger boiled in the pit of her stomach, ready to do more than just punch her, but she had no energy to do more. Quite frankly, Loriana wasn't giving her that satisfaction of whooping her ass. Knowing the real type of person she was, Akira would just try and use this moment against her.

"I should've listened to my mama when she warned me about you. Don't come back over here. You're not welcomed."

"And you knew that, so get on up," Mhyale added, walking toward the door.

Greg stood off to the side, shaking his head. This was all too much. He thought his daughter and Akira were still friends and clearly had missed everything that had gone down before prom yesterday.

"Mhy, leave that girl alone," Memphis told her.

Not giving her any room to try something, Mhyale kept shoving Akira right on down the steps until she was away from the door.

"You can stop touching me," Akira hissed, jerking away from her.

"I ain't touched you yet. You lucky I'm trying to respect my auntie's house, or I'd dog walk your ass. Stay from around here. My cousin doesn't fuck with you, and the next time, we ain't letting you just walk away."

Akira's jaw flexed. There was nothing she could say. She'd gotten herself into this situation and couldn't place the blame on anyone else but herself. Back inside the house, Mhyale's eyes scanned the semi-crowded apartment for Loriana. Walking out of the kitchen with a bottle of water in her hand, Mhyale followed Loriana back into her mother's room. It felt weird being in the same place she last was, but

Mhyale wasn't going to voice that opinion. She knew Loriana being in her room more than likely brought her a sense of comfort.

"You need me to do anything?" Mhyale asked.

Loriana drank some of her water and shook her head no. "No. I'm fine. I mean, I'm not, but you get what I'm saying."

"Okay. Let me know if you change your mind. Where's Projex at? I see the rental parked outside."

When Mhyale saw her eyes begin to water, she got upset all over again.

"What did he do?"

Loriana shook her head, wiping more tears. She wished she could stop crying. Nyree looked on with a confused expression. She hoped like hell Projex hadn't played her friend. That was the last thing she needed right now.

"Nothing," Loriana mumbled, sniffling.

"Don't make me call Memphis in here, Lori. What did that nigga do?"

"I don't know," she cried. "One minute we were in the hotel, the next I'm getting a call from his sister saying something happened to him."

"Wait. He wasn't with you at the hotel?" Nyree questioned. Shit wasn't adding up.

"No. I mean, yeah. He was at first, and then he

left and now," she paused, and they hung on to her every word waiting to see what the hell was going on, "now he can't even be here for me."

Mhyale and Nyree glanced at one another, trying to piece together what she may have been hinting at. Mhyale, being who she was, pulled out her phone to see who she could call. Loriana wasn't giving her enough details, and had Projex done something to her, niggas would be on Projex's doorstep. There'd be no need for all of that, though. Projex wasn't there.

H ours Before...

T his was part the part of the game Projex hated the most. *I should've just put some money on his head,* he thought while eyeing the home they were parked across the street from. Getting payback for Chevy in blood was the only revenge he wanted. He'd dreamt about it plenty of nights, and finally, that time had come. He didn't think it'd be on the night of Loriana's prom, nor would it be hours away from their hometown.

Like the pussy he was, Eric, Chevy's killer, had

fled to another city almost three hours away and had been ducked off. Had the police given a fuck, they would've known that and put effort into catching him. Since they hadn't, Projex wasn't going to give them any more time to.

With his gun in his lap, Projex's eyes were trained on the two-story home Eric was in. It was damn near in the middle of nowhere which was fine with him. They'd practically spent the night on his block thanks to Bo, but it'd be all worth it. Projex knew he could've easily ran up in the crib, but he didn't know who all was inside. That'd be a dummy mission, and he didn't like those. It was the quickest way to get caught slipping if he wasn't careful.

"You sure it's just him and this bitch inside?" Projex asked Bo from the backseat. Sneaks was in the driver's seat with his head leaned back.

"Yeah, and a little kid. She should be leaving out for work any minute now."

Like clockwork, five minutes later, the garage door opened up, and Eric was walking out with a car seat clutched in his hand. Behind him, a young girl who looked no older than twenty-one, hit the unlock button to her car. While they carried on saying their goodbyes, Projex eased his mask over his face. The second she backed out of the driveway, he was out of the backseat and clutching his gun.

Too comfortable knowing he was a wanted man, Eric took slow strides back inside the house through the garage. Leaving it open with plans to come back out and smoke his morning blunt like he always did, Projex walked right in behind him. Hearing the door open behind him, Eric turned on his feet, caught a glimpse of Projex, and took off running toward the back door. Letting off two shots, Projex sent a bullet into his shoulder and another through the wall, but that didn't stop Eric.

On the back patio, he hopped over it with Projex right on his heels. Chasing a nigga down wasn't in his plans this morning, but it wouldn't have been the first time. With adrenaline pumping, Projex bobbed and weaved through the wooded area, getting annoyed. With no gun on him, Eric didn't have a chance. He was out of breath and hiding behind a tree, further pissing Projex off. When he tried making a run for it, Projex sent a bullet straight through his neck, dropping him instantly.

Breathing hard, Projex quickly jogged over to him and flipped him onto his back. Lifting his mask with glove-covered hands, Projex smirked as Eric struggled to breathe. Life was quickly fading from his eyes, but he wanted to be the last person Eric saw before he closed them. No need to prolong his demise any further; Projex pulled the trigger once more, placing a bullet into his head.

On the ride home, Projex was silent. His thoughts were everywhere, especially after a kill. It'd been a while since he had to take it there, and no matter how many times it'd happened in the past, this one felt different.

"You straight?" Bo questioned, glancing over his shoulder.

Projex nodded his head. He wasn't, though. His thoughts had ventured that quickly to Loriana, and he wondered if she was up waiting on him. The perturbed look in her eyes when he left out of the room was stuck in his head. Projex hated that he had to leave out after the night they shared, but this was one opportunity he wasn't missing. He just hoped she understood because fucking with a nigga like him had to come with some understanding.

"Drop me off at the crib," Projex let Sneaks know. There was no way he was going back inside the hotel like that.

When he made it home, he was surprised to see Joi up. Normally, Joseline would have to go wake her up multiple times for church on Sundays. Joi took once glance at her brother from the mirror in the bathroom and turned around to face him.

"You came home to go to church with us?"

Projex's smirked. "Nah. I should, though."

"You sure should," Joseline added, coming down the hall. "Where you coming from this early? Checkout ain't until eleven."

"You all in my business," he joked, walking into his room.

"Bryshon. I know you didn't leave Lori at the hotel by herself. I taught you better than that."

He scratched his scalp and pulled the shirt over his head. "Mama, relax. I'm 'bout to head back up there in a minute. Lemme' shower right quick."

"Umph. I hope you weren't out on no bullshit."

"You doing all that cussing. It's the Lord's day."

"I'll repent when I get to church, something you should be doing as well."

Joseline was no dummy. She knew her son better than he knew himself. He was just like his father, a hothead who didn't take shit from anyone. Seeing the fresh scratches on his back as he stuffed his clothes into the hamper, she puckered her lips out and grinned.

"You better treat my girl right. I see those marks on your back too."

Projex stayed facing away from her and smirked. "A'ight. You doing too much now."

"Little boy, whatever. You heard what I said."

"I did, and I got you."

He meant that. Treating Loriana right would never be an issue in his book. At least he hoped it never would be. After taking a quick shower, Projex tossed on some Nike shorts, a plain white tee, a hoodie, and some Air Max 95's. With no phone or gun on him, he snatched the keys up to his car and headed out the room.

"I saw you and Lori's pictures," Joi let him know with a smile. "Y'all looked real nice."

"Thanks, sis."

"Was she surprised—"

Rumbustious knocks sounded off at the front door, halting her words and making Projex freeze up. Wasn't nobody knocking that loud at their front door unless it was who he knew damn well it couldn't be.

Damn. I just offed the nigga. How they find out that quick? Projex thought.

"Police! Open up!"

Joi's eyes widened and shot over to her brother. "What should I do?" she whispered, just as Joseline went to answer the door. She cut her eyes at Projex, who of course, had a nonchalant, blank expression on his face. This was like déjà vu for her. Bryan stayed having the police come to their crib when they were together and trying to make it work.

"Can I help you?" Joseline asked.

"We're looking for Bryshon Emery. Is he here?"

"He isn't. Can I ask what for?"

The officer's nostrils flared. "Ma'am. There's no need to lie to us. We have an arrest warrant, and his car is parked outside. Now, we can do this the easy way, or you can make our job difficult."

Joseline wasn't about to let them just snatch her son up. She didn't give a fuck what they were talking about. Thankfully, the situation didn't get out of control. Projex walked to the door, pulling it open. If they had a warrant, there was nothing he could do. Without warning, the officer's entered their home and placed Projex in cuffs. Joi immediately started crying, seeing them handle her brother so roughly.

"He didn't do anything!" she cried, making Projex glance her way.

"Ssshh. I'm good."

"Bryshon Emery, you are under arrest for the murder of Malcolm Green."

As the officer read him his rights, Projex's chest grew tight. Here he was thinking they were taking him in for something recent, and the murder they were talking about had happened a few years ago. The same murder that started his and Kelsi's impromptu sexual relationship.

Rushing behind them, Joi swiped at her face as they placed Projex in the back of a patrol car. Hearing that he may have committed a murder spooked her. She knew from watching way too many crime television shows that murderers were hardly ever found innocent.

"Ma," she choked on a cry facing Joseline, "we have to go bail him out."

"It's Sunday, Joi. We'll have to wait."

Joi wasn't aware how the system worked exactly, but she'd find out. Frustrated and more worried than anything, she rushed to her bedroom. Yanking her phone off the charger, she fiddled with Projex's car keys that he gave her before walking to the door. Going to Loriana's name, she paced the floor in anticipation. When she didn't answer, Joi called right back.

"Hello," Loriana answered softly.

"Loriana," Joi sniffled, making Loriana's heart stutter in her chest. "It's Projex. He was just arrested. Where you at?"

On the other end of the phone, Loriana was losing it. Joi heard her mumbling no repeatedly. She was sure she hadn't heard anything else she'd said.

"Lori!" Joi shouted.

"Y-Yeah? Huh?" Loriana questioned, picking the phone up from the bed.

"Did you hear what I said?"

"Yeah. I mean, kind of. What happened to him? Please tell me he's okay. Did he get shot?"

Joi frowned. "Shot? No. I said he was just arrested. Are you at the hotel?"

Loriana tossed a hand over her rapidly beating heart. Now clearly hearing that he was somewhat okay, she tried to compose herself. Any call concerning him, especially with the way he'd left her in the hotel, was alarming enough. She just knew Joi had called to let her know he had gotten himself killed. That was a pain she wasn't ready to deal with. Not knowing hours from now, she'd indeed be dealing with one much worse.

"Yes. I'm here. Should I come to the house? Can we bail him out?"

Her words were quick and movements quicker. After getting dressed, Loriana tossed everything into her pink duffle bag.

"You can come over. I don't think we can bail him out yet, though."

Her head was so messed up by the news, she hadn't realized what day it was. She wasn't even sure of the time. Hustling around the room, she made sure she had everything. Letting out a huff, she stepped inside the bathroom, and her eyes widened at her appearance. Hair untamed, dried tears on her face, and drier lips greeted her. *I look a mess,* she thought to herself while running a hand through her hair. Spotting a bright red hickey on her neck, Loriana gasped and covered it with her hand.

"What's wrong?" Joi pressed.

Loriana slowly lowered her hand as if that'd make the mark disappear. Projex had definitely left his mark on her, and she just knew there were probably more of them decorating her frame.

"N-Nothing," she uttered. "I'll be there as soon as I can."

Joi told her okay, and they hung up. Tossing the strap of her bag over her shoulder, Loriana grabbed Projex's phone, the keys to the Range Rover, and was out the door. Rushing through the lobby, she dropped the room keys off at the unattended front desk and kept it pushing. Her mind ran wild with thoughts of what Projex had gotten himself into. Grateful it hadn't been him losing his life, Loriana knew her prayers had kept him covered.

While she was panicking, Projex was relaxed while two officers questioned him. This wasn't his first time getting interrogated, but it was the first time he felt like he'd been caught slipping. Being gang affiliated and what they considered a menace to the society, had their noses turned up at him. Projex didn't give a fuck, and it was pissing them smooth off.

The fact that he'd just committed a crime and was being questioned about another was almost comical. The murder in question was Malcolm, Kelsi's ex-boyfriend's friend. It seemed as though the police had finally gotten some substantial evidence, and Projex couldn't help but wonder how.

Unbeknownst to him, some of Projex's reckless, hotheaded behavior would come back and bite him in the ass. The night he'd picked Loriana up for the first time and hopped out on Mark at the light was just enough to force the officers working on the case to bring him in. They were hoping the gun he used that night matched the one used to kill Malcolm. Projex knew better, though. They were going to come up empty-handed.

"So, you're telling me you and Malcolm had no beef?" Officer West questioned.

"I ain't tell you anything."

"So, I'm lying?"

Projex looked him dead in the eyes. "Are you a liar?"

His partner couldn't stop the chuckle that escaped him. "Listen, motherfucka. We have enough evidence to lock your ass up for a long time. I suggest you get to talking."

Licking his lips, Projex yawned while leaning back in his chair. "Nah. I'd rather not. Do y'all moth-afuckin' job since y'all know so much."

When Projex smirked, Officer West's fist banged loudly against the table. They were getting absolutely nowhere now that they had brought him in, and their captain wasn't going to like that. Especially since they'd been given the go-ahead to arrest him. The captain was sure it'd be a breeze with getting him to talk with the way they were boasting and bragging. Things didn't seem to be going that way, though.

Projex wasn't saying shit. Whether he committed the crime or not, he was sticking to the code. They could threaten him until they turned blue in the face; he didn't give a fuck. Their best bet was to take him to a cell because he wasn't saying anything else.

Hours later, Projex finally got his first call after being taken to a holding cell. Dialing his mama's number, she answered on the third ring, and he heard the worry escape her as she sighed heavily. This was no call or situation any mother wanted to get or be in.

"Are you okay?" was Joseline's first question.

"Yeah. I'm straight. You don't need to be worrying. I'ma get out."

"I'll always worry, so don't say that. What do you need me to do?"

"Nothing right now. They gon' probably hold me until tomorrow or Tuesday, so we can play it by ear. Where Joi at?"

"In the living room with your little boo. You better stop sucking all over her neck. That mess is tacky."

Projex's heart expanded in his chest as he grinned. Knowing Loriana was there with two of the most important women in his life made him needy to hear her voice. After talking to Joi and reassuring her that he was fine, she placed Loriana on the phone.

"Hello," Loriana spoke timidly.

"L-Boogie. What's up, ma? You straight?"

The lump in her throat reappeared, and so did those damn tears. She didn't know what the hell her body was going through, but she hated how emotional she was right now. The sound of her sniffling made Projex mad at himself. He knew she probably wasn't ready to be dealing with his bullshit, again, so early on, but what could he do? This was life. His life; not no made-up fairytale love story where shit just worked out. That wasn't their reality.

"C'mon, baby. Don't get on this phone crying. I need you to lift a nigga's spirit. Talk to me."

His voice made her insides quake. It was deeper than usual, thanks to his lack of sleep. Loriana didn't know what to say. She had a million questions but figured they'd all have to wait—all except one.

"What happened to you being safe?"

Projex smirked. She called herself trying to check him, and he knew it. "I was. What, you think I don't listen to you?"

"I know you do."

"A'ight then. Who called you, Joi?"

Loriana looked at Joi and smiled. That was her little sis for real now. "Yes. I thought you were dead. I've been crying all morning."

"I'm still here. Your nose do sound stuffy, though," he joked, making her crack a smile.

Joseline watched her from the couch and shook her head. She knew her son had made Loriana fall in love with him. It was evident in the way her eyes gleamed, the tone of voice she used only with him, and the way she drove like a bat out of hell to get to their crib. It was cute, and cute shit like that made babies, so she was hoping Projex was using protection.

"Shut up. Are you okay in there, though? Do they feed you?"

Projex couldn't help but laugh. Her innocently asked questions did lighten the mood and made him feel ten times better.

"Yeah, ma. They do. What you doing, though? You sore?"

Blushing, Loriana shifted on the couch. Her body was aching terribly. So many unknown muscles had been stretched out when they had sex; she couldn't wait to soak in the tub.

"Yeah. I am," she mumbled lowly. "I'm okay, though. Just wish you were out. We were supposed to go have breakfast."

"I know. I got you when I get out. Whatever you want is on me."

"We're still talking about food, right?" she had to ask.

"*Whatever* you want. Food, clothes, trips. You can have it all, ma."

"Is this jail talk, or you mean that?"

He laughed loudly, making her laugh as well. "Aye. You really funny, lowkey. Talkin' 'bout some jail talk. What nigga you been talking to from jail?"

"None. Just you now, and I don't like it already."

When the automated women alerted them of having one-minute left, Loriana huffed. This wasn't something she wanted to get used to. Hours of them talking on the phone had been spent, and she'd hate for it to be reduced to a limit.

"Tell my mama I'll call her back. Get my keys from Joi and get that bag out of my trunk for me too, a'ight? Don't be crying either. We good."

"Okay. What you want me to do with it?"

"Take it home with you for me. You can leave my phone in my room."

Loriana smacked her lips. "I should go through it."

"See," Projex chuckled, "you on bullshit already. Don't do that, ma."

"Whatever. I wasn't going to anyway."

"Bet not. I'll talk to y'all later."

She sighed, and before she could say okay, the call disconnected. Looking up from the screen, she licked her lips and gave Joseline a small smile.

"He said he'll call back," she told Joseline and handed her the phone.

"Okay. The only thing we can do is wait—no need in stressing ourselves out. I'ma make some calls and then cook something to eat. Y'all hungry?"

"Yes," Loriana answered.

"I'm always hungry," Joi replied.

Joseline snickered, knowing that was nothing but the truth. After calling Grandpa Joe and letting him know what was going on, Joseline prepared them a meal. While they ate, Loriana couldn't help but ask about Projex and what he was like as a little boy. She was more than intrigued now; the young girl was in love. It'd happened so quickly, she didn't know how to manage her feelings. Losing her virginity to him only intensified every emotion she felt for Projex.

It was more than just spreading her legs and giving up her innocence. She'd literally given him a piece of her that she didn't want back. She wanted to share herself with him forever and become full of him as well.

Once she finished eating and finally decided to go home, she grabbed the bag from Projex's trunk like he asked her. Before closing it, she grabbed one of his hoodies and slipped it on, hoping it'd help her conceal the hickey on her neck. Joseline let her know she'd call if things changed, but they more than likely wouldn't. Loriana was hopeful, though. She was expecting him to be out by morning.

What she wasn't expecting was for her world to get flipped upside down when she did arrive home.

Regardless of how comforting wearing Projex's hoodie was, it couldn't hold her tight, wipe her tears, and prepare her for the worst. Him going to jail was nothing compared to losing her mother. It didn't even come close.

Chapter Two

With aching limbs and a growling stomach, Projex was finally released on Tuesday afternoon. With squinted eyes, the rays from the sun beamed down on him. Inhaling, he took in the fresh air with appreciation. Jail was suffocating like a motherfucker, and he'd only been away for less than seventy-two hours. The only thing on his mind was a shower, a hot meal, Loriana, and how he was about to beat this case.

Once Judge Strine confirmed his bond was $250,000, Projex immediately called his mama. Joseline posted the $25,000 bail with the help of Grandpa Joe and waited for him to get released. He couldn't believe he was actually about to have to prove his innocence for some shit he knew should've never resurfaced.

"When's your court date for?" Joseline asked, hopping on the highway.

Head buried into his phone that Joi had charged up for him, he mumbled, "I don't know yet. The lawyer said he'd call me when he finds out."

"Okay. Joe wants you to call him too. Why are they accusing you of murdering that boy?"

Joseline cut her eyes his way. She didn't care that he'd just gotten out of jail or the fact that it was some of his own money he used to bail himself out. She had questions and wanted some answers.

"You know how that go, Mama."

"I do, but not with you. What if you're found guilty, then what?"

His right shoulder lifted. "Then, I'll be in jail. I don't know what you want me to say right now. I'm hungry, and my head is killing me."

"You think I give a fuck about that right now, Bryshon! Huh? Do you? No, I don't. You sitting here all nonchalant like a murder charge is nothing. You're only twenty-one. A murder charge is nothing to play with."

He knew that. Projex knew she was stressing, but

he really had nothing to say. This was how the game went. She knew that too. If anything, she should've learned those lessons with Bryan. Bryan wasn't her son, though. Projex was. When he didn't reply, Joseline shook her head. She felt like she'd failed him, and it was tearing her up inside.

"So, you're guilty? This street shit is going to have you behind bars for life, and you're not going to realize it until it's too late. While you out here playing Grim Reaper, you need to sit your ass down. You think I want to lose you to the system, huh? Answer me!"

"No, Mama."

"Well, act like it then!"

Frustrated and more disappointed than anything, tears stung Joseline's eyes. She could yell until her head hurt and voice was hoarse, but that wouldn't change how Projex felt. There was just some shit he couldn't let slide, and one of them would always be getting revenge for someone close to him. The plan wasn't to go to jail, and he'd been in the clear for a while, but he wasn't invincible. They both knew that.

"When your ass gets locked up again, don't call me," Joseline fussed. "Wanna sit there on that damn phone."

"A'ight, Mama. Remember you said that, too. Gon' be the first one crying."

"Boy. Don't make me pull this car over. Keep on."

Projex tried holding his chuckle in but couldn't. Joseline's fussing was coming from a place of love. He knew that. She always gave it to him real, and for that, Projex would always appreciate her. Joseline knew there was only so much talking she could do. Her son was grown and making grown decisions that came with tough consequences. She just hoped and prayed his actions didn't bring them any harm.

"Yo, Dell. Where you at?" Projex asked once Kordell picked up the phone.

"Posted. Been waiting on yo' punkass to get out. You straight?"

"Yeah. We'll rap when I pull up on you."

"A'ight, bet."

The next person on his list to call was Loriana. He was hoping she was in the car when his mama picked him up but was glad she wasn't. Putting her too much into his business was sticky. The less she knew, the better. If something went down, he didn't want her to get questioned about her involvement with him at all.

When the call went to voicemail, his top lip curled upward. "You talk to Loriana?"

"No. Not since Sunday when she was at the house. Why?"

"She ain't answering the phone."

Joseline shrugged. "She's probably busy. Everyone's time doesn't revolve around you."

It did if you'd been waiting for your man to be released. Projex knew Loriana. It wasn't like her to not answer her phone, so he called back. When Mhyale answered, he got straight to the point.

"Hello," Mhy spoke quietly.

"Yeah. What up. Where my girl at?"

Glancing to her right at a curled-up, sleeping Loriana, Mhyale exhaled. She hated to have to be the one to break the news to him, but she had no choice.

"Um, she's sleeping right now. Did you just get out?" Mhyale wanted to know.

"Yeah, and I'm trying to see her. Tell her to wake up right quick."

Easing off the bed, Mhyale stepped into the hallway and cracked the door. Loriana was finally getting some sleep, and she didn't want to disturb her.

"I know you probably haven't heard," Mhyale started and cleared her throat that began to ache.

"Heard what?" Projex pressed anxiously.

"My aunt passed away on Sunday. Lori found her when she got home from the hotel."

His body stiffened in shock. "Yo, what?" His voice was damn near a whisper. Joseline glanced his way.

"What's the matter?" she asked.

"Yeah," Mhyale breathed, forcing herself to control her impending tears. "So, I'm trying to let her get some sle—"

"I'm on my way over there," he cut her sentence short. "Aye, ma. Slide me by Loriana's crib. I'll be there in like ten minutes."

"Projex. I get you want to be there for her, but—"

"But what!"

He didn't mean to holler, but Mhyale was about to piss him smooth the fuck off. She had no right to try and tell him that he couldn't check on his girl.

"Man, look. I ain't trying to hear all that, Mhy. I get it, y'all grieving, and I'm sorry as fuck about y'all loss, but she needs me. Unless Loriana get on this phone and tell me she don't want me over there, I'm pulling up in ten minutes."

Mhyale knew that wasn't the case. "I guess I'll see you soon, then."

When he hung up in her face, Mhyale couldn't do anything but sigh. Going back inside the room, Loriana was rolling over and rubbing her eyes.

"Hey," Mhy spoke, easing back onto the bed. "You're up."

"Yeah. Who was that?"

"Projex. He's on his way over here."

Loriana yawned. "Oh, okay."

Before today, Loriana would've been rushing to make herself look presentable. She simply didn't care right now. If he couldn't handle her at her worst, she didn't know what to tell him. So much had transpired over the last three days, Loriana didn't care who did what. People had stopped by to give their condolences, sent food, flowers, prayed with her, and all she wanted to do was sleep. Those tranquil hours, which felt like moments, was the only time she felt some relief. Getting to sleep and staying there was the struggle.

While the two cousins sat in silence, their parents were having a heated debate in the kitchen. Deaths in families brought out the worst in people. Emotions were high, and everyone wanted their feelings to be taken into consideration. Right now, the only concern was Loriana's.

"I don't think moving in with you would be a good idea, Peaches," Greg let her know straight up.

The topic of Loriana moving out of the apartment

had come up yesterday, and they were still on it. Even though she was eighteen, living on her own wasn't something either of them thought was the move right now.

"And moving with you would be?" Peaches questioned with spiked brows.

Greg scratched at his salt and pepper colored beard. "I'm her father."

"And she's my motherfucking niece. That's *my* sister's child. It's not your choice to make!" Peaches snapped.

"You want to argue, and I'm not doing that with you right now."

"Well, you gon' listen. *You* left my sister to take care of a child y'all created. While she never once complained and let you move on and live your life, she sacrificed everything. As mother's always do. Linette got the fucking short end of the stick and broke her back to take care of Loriana while you played daddy on the weekends. You may be hurt right now, but what I won't let you do is come up in here and think you're running shit. Linette may have played nice with you, but you know me, Greg. When it comes to that one in there," she said, pointing toward the back room, "I'ma go to war each and every time. So, please don't play with me."

One thing Peaches despised about Greg was how he tried putting on this front. She got it; he wanted to seem like the daddy who came in and saved the day, but she knew better. Yes, Greg did his part financially, but that was it. That's all it'd ever been before their divorce and after. Linette had grown tired of trying to make him a constant in Loriana's life. One thing she didn't do was beg, plead, or force anyone in her child's life. If they wanted to be there, they simply would be.

Greg had come around and started being the father Loriana needed, and Peaches would give him that. What she wasn't about to do was have her niece move two hours away with him, his wife, and little brother. She wanted her close like they'd always been. Days, weeks, and months from now, Loriana would need her. They'd need each other. Ultimately, the decision would be Loriana's, but Peaches was letting him know off rip; he wasn't forcing her to do a damn thing she didn't want to do.

While Greg pondered on her words, a knock from the front door resounded through the soundless apartment. Giving him a stern gaze, Peaches stood from her chair at the kitchen table and went to answer the door. Greg could sit there and look at her like she was crazy all he wanted to, but she meant what she said.

"Hey, Projex," Peaches spoke, holding the door open. He was carrying a vase of flowers and a teddy bear.

He gave her a warm hug with one arm and said, "Sorry for your loss, Ms. Peaches. You know I'm here for whatever."

"Thank you. I appreciate that. Loriana is in the back. The room on the right."

"A'ight. This my mama, Joseline. Ma, this Ms. Peaches, Loriana's auntie," he introduced the two.

"Hi. You guys are in my prayers. Is it okay if I come in? I just want to check on our girl. She tutors my daughter."

"Mhm. Come on in. I'll take those flowers, Projex."

Soon as they were out of his hands, he was down the hall. His heart was beating out of control, not knowing what he was about to walk into. It didn't matter, though. The comfort she brought him when she found out he'd just buried Chevy was a memory he played back in his head all the time. He just wanted to give her that same feeling; to let his baby know she wasn't alone in this shit and that he had her back. He would always have her back.

Soft raps of his knuckle to the door prompted Loriana's eyes to peel open.

"That's probably him," she mumbled with a yawn.

"Come in," Mhyale called out.

There was something about the air when people were grieving. Projex hated it. It was stiff and damn near suffocating. For her, he'd suffer through it. The gloom look on her face and joyless eyes twisted his heart. Strange and disquieting thoughts began to race through his mind the closer he got to her. Projex wanted to take every inch of her pain and make it his.

When she lifted up from under the covers, Projex swooped her up into his arms. Cradling her fragile frame and heart, he hugged her tightly.

"Damn, baby. I'm so sorry."

His voice was low. Words were spoken directly in her ear so only she could hear him. Her pain was radiating off her body as it began to tremble in his embrace. She'd been somewhat okay within the last couple of hours. Hadn't shed a tear since that morning, but it was something about being wrapped in his arms.

Projex provided safety. A safe haven where only they existed, where she could be vulnerable. Where the warm tears soaking his shirt didn't matter. Where every squeeze of her body against his confirmed what he already knew. She needed him.

Loriana's sobs echoed throughout the room, damn

near making Projex's buckle at the knees. This was the type of pain he knew nothing about. The type of pain he brought upon other families. It crushed his soul hearing Loriana cry out like she was. She clung to him, needing him to take this pain away. It was insufferable.

This wasn't the type of wound she could rub cocoa butter on or cover up with a Band-Aid. She couldn't rub some peroxide and Neosporin on like the time she'd had fallen from her scooter, and Linette doctored her up. This wasn't that. This was a life-altering pain that would take God, Himself to help her through.

Hearing his daughter's bellowing cries, Greg rushed down the hallway. Stopping in his tracks right at the door, his heart slammed against his chest at the sight before him. Loriana was literally wrapped around Projex as if she was his child that didn't want to be let down. While he soothingly rubbed her back, calming her as best as he could, Greg told himself to relax. Whatever relationship she had with Projex was new to him.

When her cries finally simmered and she'd caught her breath, Mhyale handed her some tissue. Placing her on the bed, Projex's eyes met Greg's.

"Sorry. I got your shirt all wet," Loriana apologized.

"You good, ma. I ain't tripping off that." Without waiting for Loriana to do the honors, Projex introduced himself. Maneuvering from the side of the bed, he stuck his hand out.

"How you doing? I'm Projex."

Greg took ahold of his hand, respecting the firm grip. "Greg. Loriana's father."

"Hate we had to meet each other under these circumstances."

"Same. Loriana, I'm about to head out, but I'll be back later on this week. You need me to do anything before I leave?"

"Did Elana agree to write up the program?"

Greg nodded. "Yeah. She said she'll be by tomorrow to sit with you and go over it with the family."

With a million and one things to prepare for the funeral service, Elana didn't mind one bit about stepping in to help. She and Linette may not have been the best of friends, but she loved Loriana as if she were her own. She'd lost her own mother when she was twenty-five and knew this pain all too well. Whatever duties she could relieve the family of, she would try her best to. Grieving and planning to bury a loved one wasn't easy at all.

"Okay," Loriana mumbled. "Thank you for being here."

He knew she didn't mean it the way he took it, but Greg felt like those words should've been used on someone else. Not him, her father. Maybe a friend of the family who she hadn't seen in a while. Where else did she expect him to be?

"You don't have to thank me, baby girl. I'm here whenever for whatever, and whoever."

His gaze fell on Projex.

This nigga threatening me? Projex thought. They held eye contact, and Greg broke it first. As badly as he wanted to speak with him in private about his dealings with Loriana, he'd save that for another day. Today had been enough on him mentally, and there was still so much more to do. So much more to process.

"You feel like eating anything today?" Mhyale asked, slipping on her shoes. She was starving and finally had an appetite to eat more than just some snacks.

"Yeah. Nothing too heavy, though. Didn't Ms. Mable bring some spaghetti over?"

"That is right. Let me go fix us some plates. You want one, P?"

Projex shook his head no. "Nah. I'm good. 'Preciate it, though."

When she walked out of the bedroom, silence fell over them. Projex didn't really know what to say. He damn sure didn't want to say the wrong thing or ask the wrong questions. Loriana didn't give him the chance to.

"What happened?" she questioned.

"I'ont wanna talk about that shit, ma. My focus is on you. Tell me what I can do to make you feel a lil' better."

Loriana's bottom lip poked out. "I don't know. Nothing really. This shit is so unreal. I don't even understand how I'm supposed to move on from this. We had so much more to do. I graduate next week, and she won't even be there."

Hardly ever was Projex speechless, but this was that rare occasion. No words could soothe her.

"You'll feel her presence, though. She's gone be so proud of you for pushing through and crossing that stage."

She sighed. "I hope so."

If it were up to Loriana, she wouldn't even walk the stage. She had time to think about it, though.

Right now, she was taking things one day at a time. The hardest day of them all would be the funeral, and she couldn't fathom what'd she be feeling then. Everything was moving so fast. The days didn't seem to slow down because her mother had died. People were still going on with their lives, and all she could think about was how she would go on with hers.

Chapter Three

This can't be my life.

Numb, Loriana stared at the flower-filled casket that held her mother. Damp tissue was balled up in her hand while the other gripped her obituary. She sat in disbelief as the preacher gave his eulogy. Warm tears dripped from her chin. Beside her, Projex hugged her closer to him. He'd been nothing short of amazing the entire week.

Even when Loriana lashed out, he didn't leave her side. Projex had been her saving grace. Doing his best to give her space, too, he tried not to ask questions he knew she wouldn't have an answer to. With everything on his plate, he was still holding her down. At one point, she was blaming herself, thinking had she not gone to prom, maybe she could've been home with Linette.

One thing for sure and two things for certain, God called home folks when *He* was ready. In Linette's case, she was simply tired. Her body had exhausted itself, and Loriana wished she hadn't kept her health issues a secret from her.

When Linette's mother passed away from a stroke, it rocked Loriana's world. She couldn't understand how her granny, of all people, was just gone. Now, her mother was too. The autopsy confirmed that the cause of death was Sudden Cardiac Arrest. While Linette hadn't had a heart attack before, cardiovascular disease did run in her family. The pill bottle Loriana almost tripped over that day in her room was a new medication she was trying out. The only way Linette would've survived is if emergency action was taken as soon as she lost consciousness. Since it hadn't, every minute after decreased her rate of survival.

Even with that being explained to her in great detail, Loriana still hadn't processed it all. It was and would forever be a hard pill to swallow. Surrounded by family, Loriana couldn't help but wonder if they'd all be checking in on her a week from now. Hell, even tomorrow. The one person she knew she could forever count on was gone, and her heart was in the casket with her.

As Greg, Linette's two brothers, Memphis, and two of Loriana's male cousins, carried the casket out, the family was asked to stand to their feet. Behind dark shades she shielded her eyes with, Loriana moved like a zombie down the aisle. Blurred vision stopped her from seeing who all was in attendance, and thankfully Projex was there to help guide her out of the church.

From the family car, through traffic where people pulled over to pay their respects, and now at the cemetery, Loriana didn't speak. Her grandfather tried cheering her up, but it was no use. Loriana wasn't going to put on a front and act like everything was okay because it wasn't. She wasn't okay and wouldn't be for a while. Life was simply fucked up. While people hugged, trying to save face with forced smiles, she stayed in the limo. There wasn't shit to smile about.

She needed a second to gather her thoughts. Taps at her window had her pushing the door open a few minutes later. Outside of it stood her cousins Mhyale, Oni, and Kia. Loriana glanced up at them and blinked.

"Hey, pooh. You ready to get out?" Oni asked.

The cousins had never experienced this type of pain, but they felt it. It was bouncing off Loriana's flesh like a heatwave.

Loriana sighed. "No, but I guess I have no choice."

"We're on your time. Just let us know when you're ready." That was Mhyale.

Nothing was moving without Loriana's say so. Taking a deep breath, Loriana scooted across the seat and climbed out. The crowd of family and friends had gathered underneath the green tent, and with each ponderous step she took, reality was finally settling in. Walking up to her, Projex took ahold of her hand and kissed her cheek. Some men in her family had already introduced themselves to him, and those who hadn't were eyeing them.

"I'ma stand over here, a'ight," Projex told her, and she squeezed his hand tighter.

"Can you stand beside me?"

He nodded, moving closer so more people could stand underneath the tent. She didn't have to ask. Projex was willing to wait on her hand and foot. Whatever she needed, he wanted to be there to provide. After one of her uncles said a few words, her grandfather asked everyone to bow their heads so he could say a prayer. Reaching forward, Loriana grabbed one of the red roses from the assortment and held it close to her chest. With her eyes closed, tears fell from them as everything around her faded to black. Tuning her surroundings out, Loriana tried imaging the rest of her life without Linette. She simply couldn't.

Her nights had been restless, tears stained her pillowcases, and her appetite was nowhere to be found. Flashbacks of all the milestones she'd crossed in her life hit her in waves. Linette had been there for every single one. The most recent being one she couldn't even share with her. Falling hard for Projex and loving him was something she didn't expect. It was the type of experience she knew Linette would be happy yet afraid to hear about. She was really her number one fan and first best friend.

The banquet hall the repast was being held at was decorated so tastefully. Music played softly over the speakers as Loriana took it all in. A slideshow with pictures of her as a young girl all the way up until her last day was on display at the back of the room. Just seeing that smile on her mother's face, knowing pictures would be the only way she'd see it now, pained her.

Family from out of town and from in-state were all in attendance. Loriana hadn't seen most of them in a while, but she was grateful for them today. As miserable as she'd been all week, today had been the only day she cracked a smile. In her mind, she knew Linette was at rest. Selfishly, she wanted her there with her, but that was to be expected. With losing a loved one, especially your mother, there was no right or wrong way to handle it. Taking it one day at a time was all she knew, but Loriana was hoping that one day she felt the weight lift from her shoulders.

As the repast came to an end, Projex had his arms wrapped around Loriana's frame outside of the hall. He'd been by her side the entire day and had some moves to make.

"You sure you don't care if I leave?" he asked, rubbing her back. He was so attentive, it made Loriana want to cling to him. She couldn't ask him to stay any longer than he had, though.

"No. I know you have a life too. Can't be all up under me." She chuckled lowly. The light was missing from her eyes, and even her voice was void of its chipper tone. That had Projex ready to cancel his plans.

"I can be if that's where you want me."

Loriana shook her head no. "Bryshon, I'm fine. I really appreciate you even doing as much as you've done. Seriously. You can take your eyes off me for a few hours."

Projex sighed. His government name spilling from her lips let him know she was serious.

"A'ight. I'ma be texting your phone. Where y'all going when y'all leave here?"

"Probably my Aunt Peaches house. I'm not sure yet. I just want to lay down."

Loriana was tired beyond the physical. She just wanted to rest. Her mind was all over the place and feelings in shambles. She'd gotten hardly any sleep since Sunday afternoon and knew her body would crash soon if she didn't listen to it.

"Let them know that then, baby. I know you trying to be a good hostess and all for your family, but nah. You gotta have time to relax too."

All Loriana could do was nod her head because she knew he was right. Gently, Projex stroked her cheek before kissing her lips. Squeezing him with the bit of strength she did have, Loriana really didn't want to let him go. Not just from her embrace, but to wherever he was on a mission to get to. The last time that happened, her world had come tumbling down.

"You promise to be safe tonight?" she asked, staring him in those reddish-brown-colored eyes of his. She wanted to get lost in them and never escape.

Projex hated making promises he couldn't keep. For his sake and the sake of his pending case, he'd better promise something.

"Yeah. I'm not on no bullshit tonight. Strictly business."

Loriana exhaled, not knowing if she should believe him or not. Not wanting to stress herself any more than what she already was, she told him okay. Loriana was going to place her trust in him until he gave her a reason not to.

"Hey," Nyree called out from behind her. She had been looking for her for the last few minutes. "I was just looking for you."

"I was talking to Projex. He went to go handle some business or something."

From the sound of her voice alone, Nyree knew her friend wasn't too convinced. If she were her, she wouldn't have been either. The paranoia in the air was real. It seemed like everyone was on pins and needles to see what else bad was going to occur.

"I know it's hard trying not to worry about him, but he's grown. Whatever decisions he makes are on him. We're supposed to be celebrating the life of your mama right now. If she were here, she'd be getting forced to dance by Aunt Peaches."

Loriana cracked a smile at that. Peaches was the

more outgoing sister who always dragged the younger one into her shenanigans. If there was one thing Peaches was going to do, it was include Linette. It'd been that way since she was born. Peaches figured since their mother really had another baby, and not a fake one like she thought, she'd might as well do everything with her. Their bond was strong. Them having kids made it stronger, and Peaches made a promise to Linette that she'd always have their back. Even in death, she'd never be left out.

"You're right," Loriana replied as they stepped into the building. "This day is for you, Mama."

T he rainy day Projex never saw coming was here. It'd come, gone, and was right back flooding shit and ruining his day. No matter how long he sat and thought about how he'd gotten into the predicament, nothing was clicking. All the money he'd saved up was spent on bail, and he was right back at square one. Owing his grandfather back was on his mind too. Joe lectured Projex's ear off for two hours straight about getting his shit together. It wasn't anything Projex hadn't heard before, but it was hitting home on a different level now.

The only reason he was able to post bail on a 2nd-degree murder charge was because of his background and not being a flight risk. His lawyer, Ross, was getting paid good money by Joe to defend him. With no serious criminal history but gang ties, Projex knew the police would be watching his every move until his court date.

Regardless of the lecture, him going to jail, and being on borrowed time, Projex was still living life on the edge. He figured why switch up now when everything had already hit the fan? The killing of Eric had the city in an uproar, and Projex didn't see why or give a fuck. He knew others did, though, and that's why he was riding around with his gun on his lap as Kordell pushed his tinted Camaro through traffic.

"Them niggas been talking tough on the net all week," Kordell voiced.

"I saw it."

Projex's line had been buzzing when word got out about Eric's murder. Statuses from his family, friends, and homeboys were all screenshot and sent to him. The most social media shit he did participate in was Instagram, and that was hardly often. All that talking and arguing over the internet wasn't him. It was the quickest way to get caught up, so he paid it no mind. If a message needed to get to him, whoever the messenger was knew it didn't take nothing for it to get to Projex if that's what they wanted it to do.

"They acting like they didn't take one of ours. Niggas is lame, bruh."

Projex didn't have much to say. He never did when it came to the life they lived. It was what it was. Projex saw it like this; it was either get his lick back while he could or keep shit going until they were all dead or in jail. He hadn't thought like that in a while, but after Chevy's murder, the last bit of remorse he had was gone. Projex wasn't giving any more passes.

"That ain't nothing new, cuz."

"I wonder who got at the nigga, though. They saying his body was found in the woods and shit, hours away."

Projex's eyes stayed glued to his phone. "Yeah? That's crazy."

"Hell yeah. You know who did that shit?"

His eyes cut in Kordell's direction. "How would I know?"

"Shit. Them niggas tell you everything like you the general 'round this bitch." Kordell chuckled, but Projex didn't find shit amusing at all.

"I'm just saying, cuz. Them niggas ran straight to you when I got at that nigga, Malik."

Malik, the driver of the car that slid on Chevy the

night he was killed, had been on Kordell's radar. Since he couldn't get at him at the gas station that day, Kordell took it upon himself to send a message their way. Malik survived his gunshot wound but would be struggling to get around for a minute.

"I don't know what for. Y'all niggas gotta chill out for a minute. The city hot right now."

Projex knew he was the sole cause of it but wasn't fazed. All it took was for him to set things off, and the group of rowdy niggas who followed his lead would do the same. It was too much going on right now, and one slip-up would cost them everything. He'd already been racking his brain about this case they were trying to pin on him; Projex didn't need shit else.

Pulling up to Kendric's spot, Projex surveyed his surroundings and hopped out. While he was down on his money right now, Kordell had come through with some bread so they could re-up. Projex wasn't dead broke, but he considered what was in his bank account down bad like a mothafucka. Having to give up all of the cash he had saved to post bail hurt his soul but made him want to grind even harder.

Staying true to his word, Projex sold Kendric his usual and headed back to the ride. When he got inside, his phone was ringing with a call from Laurent. More money hitting his line put him in a better mood, but he was still plotting. Projex had told Grandpa Joe it wasn't about the money, but that's because he had some to his name then. Now, it most certainly was. Until his court date, which he was still waiting to hear back from his lawyer about, Projex was about to be ducked off and off the radar. If it wasn't about money or Loriana, you could count him out.

"Why am I even here?" Loriana mumbled to herself.

Annoyed, she stood behind one of her classmates as their senior class practiced walking the stage for graduation. It was hard enough for her to muster up the strength and get out of bed, let alone participate in something she knew she more than likely wouldn't be in attendance for.

Four days.

That's how many days it had been since she laid her mother to rest.

Loriana was still coming to terms with being motherless. Every single thing reminded her of Linette and triggered her emotions without much effort. Linette's favorite scent was fresh linen, and

Loriana had grown to love it as well. Yesterday during class, one of her classmates used some air freshening spray to enhance the room, and tears immediately came to her eyes as she rushed out of the classroom. It was the little things; subtle reminders that her nightmares were indeed real. She'd been praying for a peaceful dream, one to let her know she'd be okay, but it hadn't happened yet.

As one of the teachers rambled on about them making sure they were in alphabetical order by last name, Loriana decided to make her exit. She couldn't do it. Not today, and definitely not tomorrow, which was graduation day itself. Grabbing her backpack, she stopped to talk to Nyree, who was near the end of the line.

"What's wrong? Why you leaving?" Nyree asked, then quickly chastised herself. Her answer would be the same for a while.

Loriana swallowed the ache in her throat and blinked back tears. "I can't do this. I'ma go back home and finish packing or something."

"I'll come with you."

"No. It's fine. You don't have to, Ny. I'll just ask Principal Roberts if I can still get my diploma without walking the stage. I'm sure she'll understand."

And she would. The staff and administration had

been willing to work with Loriana on whatever she needed from them. She didn't return to school until this week, having her teachers send all homework assignments home with Nyree or simply not giving her any. She'd been passing them all with flying colors, so missing a week wasn't going to hurt her. Especially since it was finals this week. Loriana had taken her finals earlier in the week and thought she could make it through today, but she just couldn't.

"She better, or I'ma have to cuss her old ass out," she replied, serious as hell, making Loriana crack a grin. "Ah. I got you to smile."

"You did. That's why I love you."

"I love you more, girl. How you getting home?"

She hadn't thought that far out. "I'll ask Projex to pick me up."

"Okay. Well, be safe and text me when you get in."

The duo hugged, and Loriana trudged up the walkway of the auditorium. On her way out, she caught Akira looking her way. The two hadn't spoken in person since she showed up at her house. While Loriana had no words for her ever again, Akira seemed to have too many. She'd text Loriana here and there trying to see how she was doing, but Loriana wasn't falling for the okie doke. She may have been blind before about her fake ways, but she'd never let grieving be the reason she became desperate for a friendship with her.

After meeting with Principal Roberts and getting the okay to leave, Loriana waited by the school's front entrance for Projex. Of course, like always, he came through for her. Loriana didn't know if that was a good or bad thing, considering how dependent she now felt on him. *He's my boyfriend, though.* She thought just as he texted, telling her he was out front.

Adjusting her crossbody purse, she pushed through the doors. Unlike the mood she was in, the sun was radiating high in the sky, setting the subtle spring air off with a bit of heat. No matter how good it felt outside, Loriana was cold. Death would do that to you. It snatched the life of the person she loved and took hers right with it. Loriana hated it.

Flopping in the passenger seat, she slammed the door harder than usual. Projex didn't say anything at first but decided to greet her.

"What's up, ma."

Loriana burst into tears. Her shoulders bounced as a hyperventilating cry escaped her. It was forceful, followed by heavy breaths that made it hard for her to even speak. Placing her hands over her face, she leaned into her lap and bawled hard. Every day didn't seem to get better like people said it would, only worse.

Moving her hair from her neck, Projex tried his best to help her calm down. Rubbing her back always seemed to do the trick. Just the touch of him did, honestly. When she felt okay to lift her head, she grabbed some napkins out of his glovebox. Blowing her nose, Loriana didn't care how she may have looked to him right now; she was hurting. Bad.

Staring at him, Loriana blinked her wet lashes. "Hi."

Projex wiped one lone tear from under her eye. "I hate seeing you cry, baby. That shit fucks me up."

"I know." Her lip poked out. "I can't help it, though. That's all I want to do. Everything makes me cry."

"It will for a while too. I ain't gone lie. It may not feel like it's getting better right now, but one day it will."

He knew from experience. Losing Chevy tore him up. It was so unexpected when Projex found himself dropping tears days after his funeral; he wasn't even surprised. His death was still fresh, so he could only imagine how much Loriana was hurting. It hadn't even been two weeks since Linette was buried.

When she didn't reply, Projex shook his head. "Damn. My bad. You prolly don't want to hear that."

Loriana dabbed the napkin under her eyes. "It's okay. I need to keep hearing that as a reminder. So when that day comes, it knows I've been waiting on it."

Not wanting to dismiss her feelings but change the subject, Projex leaned over and kissed her cheek. "And you'll get through that day, too."

Her heart warmed. "Thank you."

"So, you ain't gotta walk the stage?" he asked, pulling out of the school parking lot.

"No. I'll still get my diploma, though. I don't see the point in walking, you know?"

He nodded his head and busted a left at the light. "Yeah. I feel you. Glad they wasn't on no bullshit about it either."

"Had they been, I would've called my auntie."

"Peaches woulda' shut this bitch down."

They laughed, knowing how she got down about her niece. Thankfully, it hadn't come to that.

"And wouldn't have cared. What were you doing?"

"At the crib chilling. My lawyer called with my court date."

Her heart dropped. "When is it?"

"May thirtieth."

Loriana tapped the screen of her phone to check the date. These days, she couldn't keep up with the days of the week at all. Time was just passing her by.

"That's a little over two weeks from now."

"Yeah. I'm hoping it go by slow. I got some shit I got to take care of before then."

Loriana hated how he was talking. She hadn't really had time to just sit and think about what would happen to their relationship if he got locked up. Hearing him talk about it so nonchalantly as if it were just another day kind of bothered her.

"You already know what you're charged with, right?"

Projex nodded his head. "Yeah. I'm innocent until proven guilty, though."

"Are you guilty?"

She wasn't sure if that was an answer she wanted to know but asked anyway.

"You think I'm guilty?"

Loriana shrugged. "I only know what you tell me, which isn't much."

"I'm innocent. Know that. Believe what I tell you, not what I don't tell you."

She pondered over his words, putting together her own meaning behind them. Still, Projex was a mystery to her. Three months in, and Loriana wondered just how many layers of him she'd have to peel back. One she was for sure had been peeled long ago was his soft spot for her. Projex made it his duty to make sure she was taken care of in all aspects of her life even though he was in a tight situation right now.

"What you trying to get into? How much more you got to pack up?" he asked, driving in the direction of his grandma's crib.

Realizing staying in their apartment wasn't the best for her, Loriana made the decision to move in with Mhyale. While Greg wasn't the least bit happy, he was glad that she didn't move with Peaches. The apartment manager was giving her until the end of the month to be out, but Loriana planned to be gone long before then. She hated feeling like she was just boxing up her mother's belongings, but she was suffering being there. For her sanity, she had to leave.

"Not much. My auntie and cousins have been helping me. Just some things in my mama's room are left, and the furniture in the living room."

"I'll buy it from you."

She looked at him. "The furniture?"

"Yeah. One of my homegirls needs some furniture. Her and her little girl just moved into their own place."

"That's so nice of you to do that for her," she gushed. "You don't have to buy it, though."

Projex shook his head no. "Nah. Ain't nothing in life free."

"It is when you want to be a blessing. I remember when I was like seven or eight, me and my mama had just moved into a new place. The people across the hall from us were moving out and gave us their furniture for free. The lady had a daughter about my age, and her mother stayed with her. I'll never forget her telling my mama that 'Us single mothers have to look out for one another.' That made my mama's day. I didn't know we were struggling back then, but looking back on it, we were. My mama just did the best she could."

Hearing her speak on struggling had Projex wondering. His mama went through the same hardships and shouldn't have had to if Bryan would've stepped up to the plate. Projex realized they hadn't ever really discussed the relationship between her and her dad.

"Yo' pops didn't help out?"

"Yeah, sometimes. I only noticed once I got older,

though. He and my mama had gotten divorced, we moved, and that's when everything changed."

"You and yo' stepmoms seem to get along good, though," he pointed out.

At the repast, when Loriana somewhat introduced Projex to the people that mattered, he could tell Elana wasn't the type to fake like a kid because she was married to their dad. Loriana wouldn't have even wanted her there if that was the case.

"Yeah. I didn't at first, but as I got older, we grew a lot closer. I used to blame her for why my parents weren't together but realized them divorcing had nothing to do with her. She was just the woman my daddy decided to be with after it didn't work out with my mama."

"You wanna get married one day?"

She blushed. "To you?"

Projex laughed. "Shit, maybe. I told you you'd be rocking my last name one day."

"You were being corny as hell." She laughed.

"Damn. I was, huh? I was just trying to spit some game to you."

They shared a laugh.

"And now look at you. Can't stop breathing down my neck."

Staring at his side profile as he grinned, Projex

shook his head in amusement. She'd called him out, but that was all good cause she was right.

"Just call me thirsty if that's what you tryna say, ma."

"You aren't, but it is cute. You've really done more for me in the short time that I've known you than people I've known my entire life. Not saying money-wise or materialistically, but just being here. I appreciate that more than you know."

His heart did that weird shit again in his chest, making him clear his throat. The truth was, Projex was new to this. The chemistry between them came so naturally, he didn't know where it came from half the time. So organic and pure, he vibed with it. While he was new to exploring what it was like to be someone's all, Loriana was too. They were experiencing their firsts of a lot of things, including love, together, and it was deeper than they both expected.

"As long as you let me, I will be. That ain't even something you gotta worry about."

And she wouldn't. Loriana had enough worry on her plate. She found comfort in knowing with him, she'd always have him there.

"You ain't answer my question, though," he reminded her as he pulled onto his grandma's block.

"Yeah, I do. I could see myself getting married.

It's not something I dreamed about as a little girl, but I think the idea of loving someone and only that person forever is something I want."

"Even with not knowing if that person will switch up on you or not?"

"I can't base what I want off of what I think that person may do. I can only live in the moment. I feel like, why deprive yourself of the experience because you're thinking too hard of a negative outcome?"

That's where she made him think. Projex wasn't the type to do something, hoping it worked out. If he was all in something, he knew what it was going to be. He'd think himself right out of a situation or opportunity because he always thought about the shit that could go wrong. He was strategic, especially when it came to his heart. Pulling in his grandma's driveway, he placed the gear in park.

"Why not think ahead of the outcome? Sometimes, you can save yourself the hurt and disappointment if you've already made up in your mind that this, whatever it is, could go wrong."

"I guess that's where we see differently. I don't like to assume things. Life is full of surprises, so there's really no way to prepare for anything it throws your way. Especially when it comes to another person's feelings. Why even go into marriage thinking it wouldn't last?"

Projex shrugged. "Shit, cause most of the time they don't. I ain't saying all, but from what I seen, ain't too many two-parent households from where I'm from. My mom's a single parent herself, so that's proof right there. Never even been married. That's just me, though. My mind may change as I get older."

"I would hope so."

He chuckled. "Damn. That was dry."

She grinned. "Sorry. I'm just saying. It's interesting having this conversation with you. I learn more and more about you every day."

"That's a good thing?"

Yeah. More layers are unraveling. "It's always good. We learn from each other. That's the best part."

"Glad I could teach you something. You get to meet one of the ladies who been schooling me for years."

Her eyes widened, and her head swiveled back to the house. "She's here?"

"Yeah. I told her I was on my way to pick you up earlier, and she said she wanted to meet you."

"You want me to meet your grandma?"

Projex laughed. "Yeah, man. What you saying it like that for?"

"Because that's a big step. Niggas don't play about their grandmas."

He couldn't stop laughing. "Man, get out the car. You better meet the lady whose house you was moaning all loud in."

Loriana's jaw dropped as Projex opened the door and climbed out. She couldn't believe he just said that. Then again, yes she could. Some days, he literally had no filter. Most days, honestly. Unlike before, Projex held her hand and led them through the gated fence, up to the front door.

The sweet smell she'd inhaled the first time she visited was no longer present. Instead, it was replaced with memories. Ones that made her think of her mother. Fresh linen wafted through her nostrils, making Loriana inhale sharply. Unlike at school when she smelled the scent, this time, it gave her a sense of peace. A tiny gesture that maybe her mother was right there with her.

"You good?" Projex asked, closing and locking the door.

All she could do was nod, afraid her words would come out in a blubbered manner. The further they ventured into the home toward the kitchen, the smell changed. Loriana's stomach growled at the distinct aroma of chicken being fried.

"Granny, what you in here cooking?"

Loriana couldn't help but smile as the older woman turned their way. Juanita was aging gracefully, as Black women did. Dressed in a lavender Nike active outfit that consisted of capri leggings and a logo t-shirt, she didn't look sixty-five at all. Her burgundy hair was pulled into a bun at the top of her head, showcasing all of her ageless features. Loriana immediately wanted to ask her what she was using on her skin and putting in her body to stay looking so young. Her golden-brown skin was shining.

"Some food for your girlfriend." Juanita smirked. "Hi, honey. It is so nice to finally meet you. I'm Juanita."

With open arms, Juanita embraced Loriana in one of those hugs that made you feel right at home. It was warm, inviting, and just the kind Loriana needed. It was so reassuring that she didn't want to let go.

"Nice to meet you, too. I'm Loriana."

"Such a pretty name for a pretty girl. When he told me he was picking you up, I got excited," Juanita let her know.

Projex shook his head and sat at the dining room table. Loriana followed suit.

"Don't be all extra, Grandma," he told her.

"Boy, hush. I was. Joseline has told me all about

you, and Bryshon always smiles when I bring you up. It was only fitting to meet the young woman who has him sneaking you in my house. Am I right?"

Loriana's cheeks warmed, and she smirked at Projex. "Yes, ma'am, you are."

"And she has manners. I like you already."

"We didn't sneak in. You saw us on camera." Projex laughed.

"Mhm. You heard what I said. You hungry, Loriana? I'm fixing something quick to eat if you have time."

"Yes. I don't have any plans."

"Good. One thing you can count on is getting a good, hot meal. Now, tell me how you ended up in a relationship with my knucklehead grandson? You must be something really special."

She blushed and glanced Projex's way. He mouthed, *you are.* A few girls had met his mama, but he didn't like them enough to meet his grandma unless it was by accident. Their relationships never got that serious. Projex was a family man, so if and when he did bring you around them, that meant more to him than he put out.

"Um, we just kind of clicked, I guess. He was real nice to me."

Juanita looked over her shoulder and grinned.

"Nice? Oh, child, you done stuck my baby with an arrow from Cupid."

"Dang! I'm not nice, Grandma? You being fake right now."

"Am not. Now, I will say you are the most giving person, but nice? No, sir. You're mean as hell like that grandpa of yours. Be talking to people all crazy."

Projex cracked up. "I'ma tell him you said that too."

"I'll tell him myself. He stays calling my phone, wanting to fly me out there to California."

Loriana snickered under her breath. While Projex didn't personally know a married couple today, he had before. His grandparents were married back in the day, but Joe's lifestyle was too much for Juanita. The constant trips, tours, rumors, drama, women, and lies had run their course. There was no love lost, just papers signed. Juanita and Joe were still very good friends to this day, but Juanita refused to stay in a marriage she wasn't one hundred percent happy in. They still shared the kind of love that made Projex believe in it.

"Y'all are too much," Projex let her know.

Piling Loriana's plate with fried wings, hot water cornbread, and some cabbage, Juanita filled her a Mason jar full of an iced cold Pepsi. Loriana didn't normally drink dark pop, but she wasn't going to turn it down. While they ate, the trio made small talk, making Loriana feel as if they'd done this before. Not once did Juanita bring up the tragic death of Linette, ask Loriana how she was doing, or any questions that made her uncomfortable.

She simply made her feel all the love she had to give. Something Loriana would need for days, weeks, and months to come.

Chapter Four

"And for you?" the server asked Mhyale as she glanced over the dinner menu.

With the entrée options consisting of either chicken, steak, or salmon, Mhyale decided to go with a nice medium-well steak.

"Mashed potatoes and asparagus as your sides, okay?"

"Yes. Y'all have some A1 sauce?" she questioned.

"Yes. At the end of the table."

"Thank you."

Moving down the buffet-style line, Mhyale held her plate of food and swayed side to side to the music playing. It'd been a while since she'd gotten out of the house, and she planned on enjoying herself tonight. The upscale birthday dinner for her friend, Rhyli, was the perfect weekend activity. Her boyfriend had gone above and beyond for her twenty-fourth day like she knew he would. Spending money on her was never an issue, and it'd been that way since Rhyli met him when they were teenagers.

"I can't wait until I get a man who goes all out for me like this," Maliya, one of Mhyale's best friends said.

"Me and you both. That nigga, Blayze, does no faking when it comes to her."

"Right. It's so cute too. I wonder where you know who is," Maliya teased as they walked back to their table.

Amiya, Maliya's twin sister, and Mhyale's other best friend, stood to get her a plate.

"That shit looks so good, and I'm starving," Amiya voiced.

As always, when it came to showing support to Black businesses in his city, Blayze had *Evans Catering* provide the food for the evening. While the twins had tasted their food on plenty of occasions, many attendees had not. First impressions were everything, and the way Mhyale just inhaled a piece of her steak and groaned had her making a reminder to grab one of their business cards before she left.

Since she tried to act like she didn't hear her the first time, Amiya asked, "You think he coming?"

"I don't know. Probably."

Mhyale didn't mean to sound annoyed by her question, but damn. She had been trying her best not to let the thoughts of Naaz cloud her mind. He'd been on it and in her dreams since she saw him at the gas station. He'd made his presence known again when he reached out to her when Linette died.

Surprised by his actions, Mhyale tried not to think too much into it. It was just the courteous thing to do, right? I mean, he had met Linette too and had been around her a few times over the years. It was the timing for her. Mhyale was in a vulnerable place. She felt somewhat stressed with Loriana moving in with her, and in a sense, wished he'd done more than let her know she and the family were in his prayers.

Naaz was a praying man. From his lips to God's ears, everything he ever wanted in life was sent from above. Including Mhyale. She used to be his little angel on earth, but one fuck up had turned her into a demon in his eyes. Blayze was Naaz's right-hand man, so she was sure he'd make his grand appearance soon.

While Mhyale and Naaz no longer communicated once he'd moved out of town, she was still cool with a few of his homeboys. Even his younger brother, Dominick, who they called Neeko, still called her his sis. She could still pull up in his hood at any time and get love. It was weird at first, considering how things ended between them, but Mhyale went with the flow. Even his mama still checked up on her from time to time. Her comments on Mhyale's Facebook posts were always referring to her as her daughter. Mhyale knew better, though. Regardless of how cool the family and friends of Naaz kept it with her, she knew there had to be someone else. She was just the first girl he ever loved and gotten his heartbroken by.

That was a pain none of them would ever forget.

"How is everything?" Rhyli asked as she approached their table.

Dressed to the nines, as the birthday girl should be, her long white sleeve, deep plunged asymmetrical dress hugged her slim-thick frame. The feathered details that aligned the hem were an addition by Amiya herself. Rhyli was so thankful to know not one but two Black women who owned their own clothing line. When she received the dress in the mail from an online boutique, she immediately knew something was missing. Thanks to Amiya, the minuscule touch made the dress pop even more. All white was the theme, and her guests did not disappoint.

"Good, but you knew that," Maliya told her.

"I was just making sure. Blayze really went all out for me. I was not expecting all this."

Mhyale waved her off. "Girl, yes you were. He does it big every year."

"Yeah. Trips and gifts. This is more sentimental. He really put some thought into this, and it shows."

Rhyli's face was lit up, and Mhyale loved that for her. When they first met, Mhyale had quickly learned that her past was one she wished on no one. It made them quickly become friends and experience the ups and downs of life together. Dealing with men of Naaz and Blayze's caliber didn't come with a rule book. Back then, their lifestyles were all gas, no breaks, and the women were right there with them. So, to see Rhyli still being treated so well meant everything to Mhyale. She deserved it.

"He did. Even down to the decorations," Amiya voiced.

Most of the décor had the letter R on it. The customized napkins at their table had 'Happy 24th Birthday Rhyli' on them, while all the other decora-tions let you know not a penny was spared for her day. Walking up behind her, Blayze kissed her on the cheek.

"I did good, huh?" he asked cockily, knowing he did more than good.

Mhyale smirked. "You *know* you did. Let me find out I need to hire you for event planning."

The table laughed.

"Shit, nah. I can't take all the credit, sis. You know my boy, Naaz, plugged me in with the right people."

When she rolled her eyes, Blayze chuckled.

"Of course, he did. Anyway, it's really nice in here."

"Don't do my mans like that. But 'preciate it. Soon as her folks leave, we turning this mothafucka up."

"As we should," Amiya told him. "Who has an open bar at a birthday party? This isn't a damn reception."

Laughter escaped them all. In his eyes, it was only right to go all out, so Blayze thought outside of the box. Most of his niggas were there celebrating his baby's day, so providing the liquor was nothing. By nature, he was a supplier... on and off the streets.

"Aye. Just imagine how the wedding gon' be." Blayze smirked and licked his lips at Rhyli. She was just blushing, making his thug ass fall deeper in love with her. "Come on, bae, so you can eat. I'ont need you getting sick later on when you start drinking."

"I'll be back over here later, y'all," Rhyli told her friends, and they strutted off hand-in-hand.

Once everyone had their fair share of food, the DJ had everyone up and out of their seats. While the silver open back heels on her feet weren't giving her any issues, Mhyale's dress was. The mini one-shoulder dress with ruching details and a high split up the side was making it hard for her to drop it low. Most of the party, besides her older family members, had taken shots of Tequila at the bar with Rhyli and were definitely feeling them. When *Mask Off* by Future played, the party went wild.

"Rep the set, gotta rep the set," Rhyli rapped, throwing up Blayze's hood while he and his niggas did the same.

"She's drunk already!" Amiya yelled in Mhyale's ear.

"Hell yeah!"

The circle of family and friends stood around Rhyli as she danced. Making it to see twenty-four may not have meant much to some people, but to her and her loved ones, it meant everything. When the DJ transitioned into *Bad and Boujee* by Migos, it was a wrap. Mhyale, Amiya, and Maliya hyped Rhyli up as she twerked. Blayze just stood back, smirking and shaking his head. This was their crew, and they were going to turn up regardless of who wasn't.

"Aye! Get that shit, Lee!" Mhyale encouraged, calling her by her nickname. Doing a little twerk herself, she held the front of her dress down, not wanting to expose her goodies.

"Damn, Mhy. You ain't missin' no meals."

Facing the person whose voice was a bit too close to her ear for her liking, she grinned when she saw who it was.

"Boy. Don't walk up on me like that."

Giving him a quick hug, Mhyale's face grew warm when his hand dropped dangerously low at the curve of her back. Softly, she pushed him away. Like the smooth nigga he was, Jasheer licked his lips and took a swig from his Styrofoam cup she was sure was filled with a purple beverage with jolly ranchers at the bottom.

"What's good?"

"You tell me," Mhyale flirted with ease. "You walking up on me like your boys ain't standing right there."

"I can't hug a friend of mine?"

Mhyale's full lips tooted out. "Don't play with me."

Jasheer smiled, giving her a glimpse of his gold and diamond bottom grill. She remembered him always talking about getting one.

"You know that's one thing I don't do is play."

"Mhm. Tell me anything. You look nice and high."

He was. With his dreads swinging in a crinkled manner down his back and red-rimmed eyes low, Mhyale was sure he'd just smoked a fat blunt. His cologne did nothing to mask the scent, but he wasn't trying to. Cockily, he brushed the imaginary dust off his white Gucci collar shirt. He paired it with some black jeans and the Pure Money Retro 4 Jordan's that recently dropped. She copped the same pair but wasn't wearing hers for another few months.

"And you looking fine as fuck." He leaned in to tell her. "It's been a while since I saw you."

"Yeah. I'm not trying to get all into that, though. Where the weed at?"

Jasheer chuckled. "Dopehead ass. I got some in the whip."

"Bet."

Turning away from him, Mhyale went to talk to her friends. While her back was turned, Jasheer took in her curves. How she seemed to have gotten thicker since he last saw her was crazy to him. Mhyale was a stallion. Thick thighs matched her fat ass. An ass these new bitches he saw on social media laying out on the table for. Mhyale's was homegrown, and he missed having access to view it whenever he pleased. The thought of the chance happening soon had his dick hardened.

"I'm about to go hit this blunt with Jasheer right quick," she let the twins know.

Maliya gave her a weird look. "You sure?"

Mhyale gave her a confused look right back. "Um, yeah. Should I not?"

"I mean, if you want that nigga, Naaz, to snatch you up on the way out the door."

Nodding her head toward the entrance of the building, Mhyale followed her gesture. Sure enough, Naaz was looking dead in her direction and had been for the last few minutes. Even from a distance, his alluring aura made Mhyale's breathing hitch and temperature spike. It always did. He always affected her. Even still when the feelings she had for him should've been nonexistent.

There was no shaking Naaz. She couldn't back then, and clearly, she wouldn't be able to now. Mhyale was stuck in a daze. Not because he looked so fine decked out in his all-white, but because he hadn't come alone. Not that she expected him to or expect anything from him, but Mhyale knew for a fact he knew she'd be here.

So, why he was standing there staring as if he was waiting for her to come speak like before, she didn't know. He had her fucked up. Her nostrils flared as she focused her attention back on her friends.

"The nerve of this nigga," she fussed.

"Don't tell me you're mad he has a date," Maliya voiced.

"Do I look mad?"

"Uh, yeah." Amiya laughed, and Mhyale flipped her off.

"Fuck you. He knew I was going to be here and brought a bitch just to try and stunt on me. I really need to smoke now."

Jasheer was still standing off to the side, waiting on her, but now on the phone. When Mhyale did wave her hand for him to come on so they could get high, Blayze hopped on the mic. Demanding everyone's attention with the clearing of his throat, they all faced him.

"Look at all you nice folks in y'all all white," he joked, making them laugh. "Before everyone gets too drunk, I wanna take the time and show love to the reason we're here."

"Bitch," Mhyale whispered. "Is he about to propose?"

"I don't know but let me pull my camera up just in case," Amiya said.

"To my lifeline, the real reason a nigga prolly still on this earth, happy twenty-fourth birthday. You deserve the world, baby. I hope you enjoy your present."

With eyes misted over with tears, Rhyli stood waiting to see what her gift was. Blayze always had a trick up his sleeve, so she had no clue what it could be.

"What is it?" Rhyli questioned.

"Right!" some of her family shouted.

Digging in his pocket, Blayze pulled out a key fob. Not caring what type of car it went to, Rhyli rushed him, snatching it from his hands.

"Oh my gosh, where is it?"

Her excitement had him smiling hard. "It's outside. Come on."

As the crowd dispersed, Mhyale took her precious time strutting by Naaz. The woman by his side must've just been some type of arm candy for the night because the way he was staring her down, there was no way Mhyale would've just sat there quietly. Those piercing dark eyes of his made her insides shudder, but she held her head high.

Up close and personal now, she admired the white Versace button-down shirt with the sleeves rolled up. White distressed denim jeans covered his legs, while low-top Christian Louboutin's adorned his feet. The diamonds on his neck and wrist danced as he tilted his head some to scratch his beard. Something about him in all white, looking like a fucking boss, made her knees weak. Naaz's sex appeal was effortless; the nigga just had it. When he licked his lips, Mhyale wanted to drop the front she was putting on and hump his face. He knew it too.

But like before, Naaz didn't bother to utter one word to her as she exited the building. Mhyale was frustrated with herself for even caring, but how could she not? When no man had ever had access to her heart, mind, body, and soul like he had, it was going to always be a struggle while in his presence.

Rhyli's joyous screams echoed in the parking lot as she jumped up and down. Only purchasing the best of the best for his baby, Blayze copped her a coke white 2018 Mercedes Benz E300.

"That hoe clean," one of Blayze's homeboy's voiced.

People in earshot of him nodded their heads in

agreement.

"Thank you so much, bae. I love you," Rhyli spoke against his lips before kissing him.

"I know that's right, sis!" Katrina, Rhyli's older sister, shouted.

While everyone stood around taking pictures of her and her new whip, Mhyale's attention was back on Naaz. His girl, or whoever the fuck she was, was whispering something in his ear, causing Mhyale to roll her eyes.

"I'll beat her ass," Mhyale hissed, making Amiya chuckled. She was with all the fuckery.

"Mhy, please don't start." That was Maliya.

She was the more civil of the two but could turn up when need be. Right now wasn't the time. Some shit simply didn't deserve to be addressed. In her opinion, falling back was all that needed to be done. She didn't want to see Mhyale embarrass herself and wouldn't let her if she could stop it from happening.

"I'm not. I'm just saying."

"Are you going to speak to him? I'm surprised that nigga don't have his fake ass bodyguard with him."

The trio chuckled. When Mhyale called the twins the night she saw him, they had a good laugh about her getting punked by his security. Big man wasn't with him today, but she still wasn't speaking. Naaz was just the type of nigga whose ego would be stroked if she broke first. It was written all over his face.

"Nah. I'ma play it cool today. I'm sure if he wanted us to exchange words, he would've made it happen by now. I'm good."

She meant that. For the remainder of the party, Mhyale paid Naaz no mind. Not even when Blayze mentioned something about her giving his boy a dance for old times' sake. She happily declined. Shot after shot, Mhyale drowned out the voices in her head telling her to just walk up to Naaz's ass and ask him what his issue was. She knew what it was but still needed him to verbally say it.

"Why she keep looking over here?" Mhyale sneered.

"Oh, my gosh. Here we go," Maliya groaned.

"I mean, if the bitch wanted to speak, all she had to do was do that."

Maliya glanced at the table Naaz's date was sitting at and back to Mhyale. "Maybe because you're staring at her like you're crazy."

"I am."

"Oh. Bitch, we know." Amiya laughed. They weren't best friends for no reason.

"Let's go to the restroom. Y'all need to chill," Maliya stressed, standing from her seat.

Her feet were beginning to hurt, and the party was winding down some. After they used the restroom, she was going to tell Rhyli bye and to enjoy the rest of her birthday. Coincidentally, a call came through on Naaz's phone that had him standing to his feet. Telling his date he'd be right back, he walked behind the group to a quieter area of the building. The restrooms were right up front. Looking behind her as if she just knew it was him, Mhyale gave him a once-over and smirked.

"Yeah, hello," he spoke into his phone. His deep, gravelly voice alone had her scurrying inside the restroom. She loathed that she was still in love with the sound of his voice. It was nerve-wracking. It'd been so long since she'd been given the pleasure of hearing it, Mhyale thought about eavesdropping on him. After she peed first, though.

At the sink, after she relieved her bladder, Mhyale tried keeping her emotions in check. The liquor in her system was playing with her mind and emotions. One second, she was angry; the next, tears filled her glossy eyes. When she squeezed them shut, the tears dropped inside the tempered glass sink where suds were.

"No. That's what we're not going to do," Maliya

cooed, rushing to grab her some tissue. She thought she was crying over Naaz, but it was so much more.

Mhyale's tough exterior could only last for so long. With the death of her aunt, watching Loriana struggle to navigate her new life, and past trauma reminding her of her faults, Mhyale wanted to break down. Had she not been drinking, she was sure she'd be just fine. That damn Tequila had her ready to sob.

Her chest heaved, jumping slightly as she cried silently. Holding back the noises she knew would draw too much attention. On each side of her, the twins consoled her. They had only seen her break down once since Linette's passing and were somewhat relieved that she was letting it all out. Bottled sadness only turned into angry actions once released.

Inhaling once her tears stopped rolling, Mhyale stood up straight. "Okay. I'm good now. That shit just hit me out of nowhere."

Maliya cleared her throat, dabbing underneath her own eyes with a paper towel. "That's how it be."

"You have to let those cries out, Mhy. It's unhealthy holding it in."

I've always held them in, she thought to herself. "I see that. I'm good to go back out there, though. Honestly, I'm ready to go."

"Me too," Amiya agreed.

When they walked out of the restroom, Mhyale was hardly expecting for Naaz to still be there, but there he was. Hearing their heels click along the tile floor, his head lifted from his phone. His eyes connected with Mhyale's, and his brows pinched together.

"Mhy-Mhy, you been crying?"

Her red eyes broke his resolve. Mhyale's heart tumbled in her chest, hearing him call her nickname reserved for him. He never pronounced her name like everyone else. It sounded more like Ma-Ma coming from his lips. Like when a child first learns to call its mother. It was spoken slowly, caressing her eardrums with ease.

"No."

Her answer was hard and tough to accept, just like the front she was putting on. When she went to walk away from him, Naaz easily hooked his arm around her waist. Pulling her back, he told the twins he had her and stepped inside the ladies' restroom. Since there was no lock on the door, Naaz leaned against it, hoping no one came in.

His six-foot-three frame made them almost the same height with her heels on. Mhyale was tall, had legs for days, and curved to his frame perfectly. Still in his embrace, Mhyale didn't even feel angry anymore. Her head was beginning to hurt from crying, and all she wanted to do was go home, not have whatever conversation he was going to try and force her to have.

"I'm not even trying to go there with you right now," she spoke calmly.

"Shut up."

She tried holding her smirk back but couldn't. That was just like him to show a bit of compassion and still be an asshole. Checking her with his hand clasped around her neck, Mhyale stood stiffly against him. One wrong move, and she knew she'd be bent the fuck over. Grabbing his wrist, she tried moving his hand, but it was no use. Naaz wasn't letting her run shit. The feel of her he'd missed way too much. Her soft, natural scent intoxicated him. While he placed kisses down her exposed shoulder, he held her firmly at the neck with one hand, while his other pressed against her belly.

Mhyale's eyes had been fluttering to close, at first, but shot open at the moment. Forcing herself out of his grasp, she turned to face him. An angry scowl back on her pretty face. Naaz could stare at her all day. Her clear milk chocolate skin, round stubby nose that fit her face perfectly, and full cupid bow lips were perfect. Back when things between them were good, he'd watch her sleep. He couldn't believe she was his...and then she wasn't. That subtle reminder made his jaw clench.

"Can you move?" It really wasn't a question.

"Our first time speaking in how long and this how you wanna play it?"

Mhyale's head jerked back. "Says the mother-fucka who acted like—" She stopped herself.

With a chuckle, Mhyale shook her head. She wasn't about to argue with him. That's exactly what he wanted. He'd almost gotten a reaction out of her, one she would've regretted later on. Mhyale had become reticent with her feelings since him. They weren't something she was willing to give up so easily, no matter how much he may have thought she should've.

"Naaz, please move. This isn't the time or place to discuss anything with you."

"We got a lot of shit to discuss too. Don't think just because I wasn't here that I don't know what was up with you."

He spoke so calmly, Mhyale wondered what he was really getting at. *Did he know?* She pondered. *Nah. He couldn't have known.* She searched his face for any clear sign of what he was hinting at, but of course, there wasn't one. His poker face was A1.

"Is that supposed to scare me?" she asked genuinely.

"Nah. Nothing I do should scare you. I'm just making you aware, love. I like how that dress fitting you."

His eyes raked her body, drinking her in. Mhyale felt her nipples harden but didn't do anything to cover them up. She did shift in her stance, though. The pulsing between her thighs was a clear indication that they needed to wrap this conversation up.

"Thank you," she mumbled. "Now, can you let me out of here? I'm sure your date is wondering what's taking so long."

Naaz smirked. "Probably. When have you ever known a person to stop me from getting to you?"

"You're so cocky, I can't even right now."

"I bet that pussy wet, though. You standing there playing tough. The only reason why I don't have you bent the fuck over that sink is cause I know how I get."

His eyes turned to slits. Something in him had switched that quickly, and Mhyale's stomach dropped. She wasn't afraid of him at all. It wasn't a look that intimidated her. Naaz used to give her that look when he was pissed off right before he fucked her senseless. Their rough, passionate make-up sex was her favorite. Mhyale was hot-headed, impulsive, and needed to be checked from time to time. Naaz always delivered.

"You know how I get, Mhy," he reiterated as if she hadn't heard him.

"Okay, Naaziq. Anything else you'd like me to know?"

His eyes softened. "Nah. Nothing else."

Stepping aside, he pulled the door open for her. Not knowing if he'd let her pass for real this time, Mhyale held her breath. When she made it over the threshold, she exhaled. Her body responded to him, speaking again as she turned to face him.

"There is one other thing I want you to know, though."

"And what is that?"

"It's yours still."

His heart.

Mhyale's cheeks lifted in a closed-mouth smile. That was the only acknowledgment she was giving his statement. It was facts. *I knew that,* she told herself before switching away. Once she staked claimed to it, it belonged to her. Mhyale didn't give a fuck what happened in the past. They still had their entire future to get shit right… that's if they were both willing.

Chapter Five

W hile staring at her reflection in the mirror leaning against her new bedroom wall, Loriana forced herself to smile. What used to come naturally to her felt strange now. *There's not much to smile about,* she thought to herself before shaking her negative thoughts. If she didn't, she'd be in a horrible mood for the remainder of the day.

With the one month of her mother's death approaching, Loriana tried busying herself with just about everything. Her fear of being alone had her moving into Mhyale's place with a quickness. Once she could no longer handle the silent nights back at the old house and not as many people checked in on her, she knew it was time to make a move. With open arms, Mhyale cleaned out her spare bedroom for her cousin.

Mhyale had been paying the bills by herself for a while now, so she wasn't charging her to stay there. Greg insisted, though. Since she wasn't ready or willing to be on her own yet, he covered half of the bills—rent, electricity, groceries, etcetera. Loriana surely thought her first experience of having a room-mate would be in college. She was okay with Mhyale being her first, though.

A knock came to her door that was slightly ajar. "Hey. You ready?" Mhyale questioned.

"Yeah. Just gotta put my shoes on."

Giving her a smile, Mhyale said, "You look pretty."

"If you say so. Thank you, though."

"I know so. I'm trying to cheer you up. Hmm, I guess I'll have to give you a hug until I see a smile."

Rushing her, Mhyale wrapped her arms around Loriana's body and rocked them back and forth. Annoyingly, she kissed around her face, making Loriana groan.

"Mhy, come on."

"Nope. Not until you smile. Oh! I know what I need to do."

Tickling her sides, Loriana squealed and tried

breaking free from her. Mhyale didn't let up. Any subtle touch from her wiggling fingers had Loriana scrambling away from her with a huge grin on her face.

"Mhy, stop! Okay! Okay! I'm smiling, see."

She showed her teeth. Mhyale faked like she was going to tickle her again, making her jump.

"You better had. We're gonna have a good day today. It's nice out, and we're about to go shopping."

"We're only going furniture shopping."

"So, what. That's the best. Any kind of shopping is, honestly. I think the older I get, the more I love spending money on household stuff. My mama bought me a blender the other day, and I was too hype."

Loriana gave her a soft smile. Any mention of someone's mother, including her own, always saddened her. Mhyale caught on quickly. It was just natural for them to discuss things like this. Every day was a struggle when trying to hold a conversation with Loriana. One wrong word could trigger her.

"I'm sorry. I wasn't even thinking when I said that," Mhy apologized.

"No. It's okay. It's just gonna take some getting used to, you know?"

Mhyale nodded. "Yeah. We'll get through it

together. Now, come on. Oni supposed to be meeting us there."

"She needs furniture too?" Loriana questioned as she slipped on her shoes.

"No. She just wants to hang out. Omari is with his daddy, so you know how that goes. My girl trying to be in traffic for the weekend."

Loriana smirked. That was just like Oni. Since she had her precious baby boy eight months ago, whenever she did get some free time to herself, she wasn't couped up in the house. At twenty-two, Loriana applauded her older cousin. The family was so worried about her having a baby at what they considered too young, but Oni was grown. She took care of her responsibilities as a mother, and they couldn't do anything but respect it.

Soon as they hopped in Mhyale's mustang, Loriana's phone rang. Even that triggered her on some days when she was lost in deep thought. It always brought her back to that night she got the call from Joi. She never knew if the person on the other end was calling with bad news or not. Thankfully, Projex was just hitting her line to hear her voice.

"What's up, ma. What you on?" he asked smoothly, warming her insides.

"Hey. On my way to Furniture Deals with Mhy. What're you doing?"

Projex grinned, loving her proper ass tone. It made him want to pull up on her and be all in her personal space. He was playing her close but still giving her room to breathe. He knew how it felt to be overwhelmed with grief and just want a few seconds by yourself.

"Shit. Chilling. Posted up." He was speaking in code.

"Oh. Okay. Sounds like fun."

He chuckled. "Nah. Ain't shit fun about this. I'ma shake to the studio later on, though. You tryna slide wit' me?"

Had this been the month prior, Loriana would've been ecstatic to go with him. She wasn't in the mood today, though.

"No. Not today. Maybe I can come with you another time."

Projex didn't like her answer. He let it be known too. "You got plans or something?"

"Not that I know of."

"So, why you ain't trying to chill with me then?"

"I just don't feel like being around a bunch of people, loud music, and smoke. You know I always want to hang with you. You're tripping for no reason right now."

He sucked his teeth. "Yeah, a'ight. You hanging out with Mhy, though. I see how it is. Y'all have fun."

"Are you serious right now?" Her voice cracked, making Mhyale glance her way.

"Yeah. I'll hit you up later."

There were no other parting words before he hung up in her face. Loriana couldn't gather her words quick enough to stop him from doing so. Waves of shock hit her at what just transpired. She stared at the screen of her phone, hoping he'd hung up on accident. When thirty seconds went by, and his name didn't flash across her screen, her hands began to tremble.

"You good over there?" Mhyale asked.

I'm not gonna cry. I'm not gonna cry, she chanted to herself. Projex had really just hurt her feelings, and for what? Because she didn't want to go to the studio with him? Loriana found that so childish. With her eyes closed, she inhaled and exhaled slowly.

"I'm fine. He just hung up on me. Should I call back?"

Mhyale chuckled as if that should've been a question. "That's up to you. See me? I'm blowing that line down until I piss you off so bad, you turn the bitch off. But that's the old me. New me is blocking niggas for the disrespect. A nigga ain't ever getting that much energy from me."

All of this was new to Loriana. If she called back and he answered, what was she going to say? If he didn't, then what? She wasn't about to beg him, but damn. Something small put her in her feelings, and now she had an attitude with him when she was happy to hear his voice just minutes ago. Deciding not to call back, she sent him a text instead.

Lori: *Don't ever hang up in my face. That's so disrespectful and uncalled for. Don't try to call back either.*

Projex: *A'ight*

Irritated by his dry reply, Loriana locked her phone. She couldn't believe he was really acting like this with her.

"What'd you text him and say?"

"I just told him he was wrong for hanging up on me. All he said was a'ight," she said, mocking his tone she knew he used.

Mhyale chuckled at his audacity, then remembered how old Projex was. Really, age had nothing to do with it. When men didn't get their way, they wanted to act as if having an attitude about it would make things better. As if everything had to go their way. She learned early on that there was just no pleasing them if it wasn't exactly how they wanted it.

"You're getting your first dose of relationship blues."

Loriana rolled her eyes. "I see. If he wants to be stubborn and not reply, so can I."

It sounded good, but Mhyale would see. Once at the furniture store, Oni showed up ten minutes after them. While Greg had bought her mattress and box spring, he hadn't gotten around to getting a dresser, bedframe, or nightstands. Loriana didn't know how long she planned on staying there, but she wanted to at least make it feel like home. The empty room made her feel as if she didn't belong, even though she knew she did.

Picking out a silver bedroom set, Loriana swiped her card. This was her first big girl purchase, and she was sick seeing the total on the screen. It wasn't necessarily her money since Greg had given it to her, but still. She could only imagine how much it'd cost to furnish an entire place.

"So, the delivery people will be at your place on

Monday morning. Make sure someone is home so they can set it up," the salesman told her.

"Okay. Will I get an email or call saying what time they'll be there?"

"Yes. Anywhere between nine and noon. That's what time you told me."

She nodded her head. "That's right. Thank you."

"You're welcome," the man said politely. "You have a good day."

"You too."

Stuffing the receipt in her purse, the trio walked out of the store.

"They know some of that shit in there is too high," Oni fussed.

"Right, and looks cheap as hell and got the nerve to be overpriced. They be scamming people's pockets," Mhyale added.

"Why y'all let me get scammed then?"

They both laughed. "Girl. We would've told you if you were trying to get some cheap shit. The one you picked out is nice. Kia got the same one in her apartment."

"Oh. Okay. I was about to say. Y'all fake."

"Never that," Mhyale let her know. "Y'all trying to grab something to eat? I'm hungry as hell."

"Me too. I got a taste for some wings. What you wanna eat, Lori?"

"It doesn't matter."

"You always say that."

She chuckled. "Because, I'm not a picky eater."

"Okay. Don't be complaining if we go somewhere you don't like. Oni, you want to follow me?" Mhyale asked, pulling her door open.

"Yeah, I can. This place better have some liquor too."

"You already know I'm not going anywhere that doesn't serve drinks. Whose child am I?"

Oni chuckled. "Don't remind me."

Ever since she could order alcoholic beverages at restaurants, Mhyale didn't eat out anywhere that didn't serve them. She never ordered one trying to get drunk unless that was the occasion. She simply liked to enjoy a nice drink, especially if it was made just right. Pulling out into traffic, Mhyale headed in the direction of *Juvie's Lounge*. Not only did they serve some of the best chicken in the city, but their bartenders weren't stingy with the alcohol. The Black-owned establishment was one of her favorites, and the community made sure to keep them in business.

A few hours later, Oni was headed to her

boyfriend's crib while Mhyale and Loriana swung by Peaches' house. Loriana was texting Nyree, who said she had something important to tell her but didn't want to do it over the phone. They told each other everything, so there was no telling what it was.

Walking inside the house, weed smoke smacked them in the face. The stench was so potent, Loriana began to cough. No matter how many times she'd been around people who smoked weed, her virgin lungs weren't accustomed to it at all.

"Hey, y'all," Peaches spoke.

A wine glass was in her hand, but she wasn't sipping any. These days, wine wasn't doing the trick for her. It wasn't giving her that strong buzz she needed to escape her feelings. Losing her sister had her head so fucked up, she had to take extra leave from work. Thankfully, she knew how to finesse her landlord and the system, so she wasn't behind on bills.

Beside her sat Bo and Sneaks. On the small loveseat, her friend, Deb, was taking a pull of the blunt. She was around the same age as Peaches but looked a little older.

"Hey, Mama," Mhyale spoke. "I bought you some food."

"Damn. You couldn't call and ask if we wanted

some? You know you can't walk up in a black person's house with food for one person," Bo jested.

"The same way you drove over here is the same way you can drive to get you some food. What you think this is?"

Peaches laughed and grabbed the bag. "Say that. Hey, Niecey Pooh. You looking all cute. Where y'all coming from?"

"Thank you. We just left the furniture store and out to eat," Loriana answered.

"Umph. So yo' daddy did give you some money for that?"

"Yeah. Was he not supposed to?"

Loriana was taken a bit back by her tone and choice of words.

"Yeah. I told his ass he better have and stop acting like he was broke. That nigga be doing all that fronting like he living this extravagant life up there with them saddity ass white folks, while you down here in the hood."

"Mama, please," Mhyale urged.

"Ain't nothing wrong with the hood shit," Deb added.

"It's not, but when you can't even pitch in for your own child without making somebody threaten you, that's when I have a problem. Glad he did that for you, though, Niece. Would've hated to have to blast him on Facebook."

Mhyale shook her head. Peaches wasn't necessarily the black sheep of the family because everyone loved her, but she was the one who gossiped the most. She and Linette would sit up on the phone for hours and run down everybody's business as if it were their own. Well, Peaches did. Linette would just listen, chime in if she had something to say, and call her crazy. Peaches didn't care, though. She may have talked her shit, but one thing you couldn't say was that she did it behind folk's back. If she said it over the net or phone, she was damn sure saying it to your face. Mhyale had gotten it honest.

Standing in the middle of the living room, Loriana didn't know how to take what she'd just said. On one hand, she wanted to defend her daddy, but on the other, she knew her aunt was right. There was no reason Loriana should've had to ask for shit right now. Not a damn thing, and Peaches was going to make sure Greg knew that. Before she could think of something to say, the doorbell was ringing.

"I'll get it. That's probably Ny."

"Tell her ass if she ain't bring no weed or no food, she can't come in!" Bo yelled out.

"Shut yo' ass up," Peaches told him.

"We need to shake anyway. I got somewhere to be," Sneaks said, looking at his phone.

At the door, Loriana let Nyree in, and they gave each other a quick hug.

"Ooh. You look cute. You sure you just went furniture shopping?" Nyree questioned with a smile.

Loriana was starting to think they were hyping her head up. She'd heard how pretty she looked all day but honestly didn't feel it. Her exterior was deceiving, while her interior was crumbling. She wouldn't say it was a façade or that she thought she was ugly or anything. She just didn't feel like herself.

"You're like the fifth person to tell me that today. Thank you."

"I think it's your hair. You never wear it down, so it's making you pop. Still cute, though. What y'all in here doing?"

Out of its signature bun, her hair was parted down the middle. Her curls seemed to be bigger and shinier today than they had been in a while. Whatever it was about her appearance today made the compliments hard to accept. She believed them, but Loriana was modest when it came to her looks. In her eyes, she was a regular girl with glasses too big for her face and irritating acne bumps that were outrageous these days.

At eighteen, she was still figuring out who she

was and hadn't tapped into her bad bitch realm yet. It'd happen soon, though. A good girl could only be innocent and unaware of her true beauty for so long. The thing was, her heart was just as beautiful. That's what really mattered.

When they were back in the living room, Nyree spoke to everyone. When she greeted Sneaks and Bo, her face flushed with a look of discomfort. Loriana caught it, but thankfully no one else had. For a few minutes, they all made small talk until Nyree couldn't take it anymore.

"Aunt Peaches, you got some pop in the fridge?" Nyree asked.

"Mhm. It should be some in there unless these niggas drank em' all."

Standing up from her chair they'd brought in from the garage, Nyree told Loriana to come to the kitchen with her. It wasn't unusual for her to ask that. Loriana figured she was ready to tell her whatever she mentioned in her text. What she wasn't prepared for were the words she actually said.

"Why are they chilling over here?" she hissed lowly, with almost bulged eyes.

"Who?"

"Sneaks and Bo. I heard they snitched on Projex. You didn't know that?"

Loriana's face contorted into a frown. "What? No. How would I have known that, and who'd you hear that from?"

"The hood is talking. They saying they had gotten into it and got cool again but were talking to the police. Projex know you know them?"

"Yeah. He knows I know Bo. Why would he hang with them if they snitched on him?"

"Keep your enemies close, hell. I don't know." Nyree shrugged.

This information was new to Loriana. Anything about Projex was, honestly. He was so hush-hush, she didn't even know he was facing a murder case until Mhyale let her know. Yes, the hood was talking, niggas were too, and all she wondered was if he knew. More so if it were true.

"Should I say something about it?" Loriana questioned.

"Say something about what?" Bo asked, making them both jump.

Facing him, Loriana searched for any signs that made him look like a snitch—whatever those signs were. Bo was attractive with his caramel-toned skin, short curls, and tapered fade. Loriana had openly flirted with him on many days but stopped all that when she got with Projex. Now, she was staring at him with disgust in her eyes and anger in her belly for snitching on her boo.

"Why you being nosy?" Nyree sassed, rolling her neck.

"That motherfucka gon' snap one day. Keep on." He chuckled, then focused on Loriana. "You been good? Sorry about your mom."

Her jaw clenched. She didn't want to reply but didn't want to be rude either, so she mumbled, "Thanks."

Were people really sorry when someone died, or was that just the right thing to say? she wondered. She'd heard it so many times it didn't even matter. The ones who cared, she felt. The ones who didn't, well, she felt them too. Their absence spoke loudly.

"I know you fuck with my boy Projex, so I ain't gone try to hit on you no more. We can still be cool, though, right?"

"I didn't know we were cool to begin with."

His head drew back as he laughed in a disbelieving manner. "Damn. I thought we were. I guess not."

"People think a lot of things. You never really know someone, though, right?"

He didn't know what she was hinting at, but her tone of voice let him know this wasn't a conversation she was trying to have. He could be a pest when he wanted to, but a thirsty nigga he'd never be. Bo got the hint.

"Shit, I guess not. Y'all be easy."

Walking out of the kitchen, Loriana watched his back until she couldn't see him anymore. Loriana didn't even feel comfortable not letting Projex know what she'd just heard, but he had pissed her off earlier, so she was going to wait. She knew if Nyree had heard about them snitching, then surely Mhyale had. *My auntie wouldn't have them over here if she knew that, right?* That was all she could think of. Loriana didn't know right from wrong nowadays. Everything in her life didn't make sense, so she didn't expect this situation to either.

"The fuck she keep calling me for," Projex grumbled, declining another one of Loriana's calls. First, it was Kelsi's, then hers, and he was starting to wonder if they had gotten into or something but didn't care enough to find out.

High and slightly tipsy, Projex was in the studio down north vibing out. The terminology of saying *down north* was a Kansas City thing. It only made sense if you were from there. Laurent had hit his line with some work, and Projex was on it. Eyes low, with the room cloudy and music loud from the song Laurent just recorded and played back, Projex had not a care in the world.

When his lawyer gave him his court date, Projex already knew what time it was. He only had a few more weeks to get in as much work as possible. Instead of fucking off like he could've, he tied up loose ends, was making a few bands a day, and getting his stash back right. Grandpa Joe had already let him know his ass was paying him back the fifteen grand plus what he had put up for his bail. Owing another man was never his style, so Projex was getting it out the mud like he'd done plenty of times before.

"You feeling that one?" Laurent asked, swiveling in the chair he was in to face him.

Projex nodded. "Hell yeah. Watch when the bitch drop. Gon' have the city turned up."

"I'm already knowing. I can't wait to be making millions off this shit. Going on tours, fucking all the bad hoes."

They chuckled, envisioning that lifestyle. They'd seen it plenty, been around it not as much.

"It's gone happen."

"Fasho. You gon' be right there with me."

"You trying to get signed to somebody?" Projex questioned, taking a pull from his blunt before passing to Laurent.

He nodded his head. "Yeah. Being independent cool. I got a solid fan base and shit, but I want more."

"I feel you. That shit gon' happen. Your ass bet not sign for nothing less than an M, too, nigga."

Laurent cracked a smile. "You already know I ain't going for nothing less. These niggas be in my DM, emailing me and shit, but my shit too raw for some chump change. My work ethic too different."

Projex knew that for sure. The same way he was in the studio, Laurent was in it two times as more. They'd gone from slanging drugs in the hood, hitting them a quick lick at a store, then posting up on the block. Laurent didn't start taking music seriously until their local radio station played one of his songs and had it in heavy rotation. Then, he was getting booked for club appearances and opening up for the headline artists. He knew then that he had to stop taking his raps as just a hobby. The money he was bringing in didn't change him; it made him want to grind harder.

"Yeah, it is. Shit gon' fall through, watch, and you

gon' blow up. Don't forget about a nigga." Projex smirked.

"Never. You my mothafuckin' dawg. This shit for life, nigga. What's going on with yo' case, though? What yo' lawyer talking about?"

"My hearing on Tuesday. He saying they got a witness and some mo' shit."

"What's that?"

Projex smirked. "Shit, I don't even know. They got something substantial enough, though, talking about second degree. A nigga might really have to sit down and do some time."

"I doubt it. They would've never let you out on bond if it was that serious."

He thought the same thing. The judge hadn't expected for him to post bail, but he had. Projex could only imagine how long he would've had to sit waiting on a trial date had he not been able to.

"Probably," he spoke, clearing his throat. "Ain't shit I can do about it now, though, so fuck it. When yo' next show?"

As Laurent let him in on his moves music-wise, Projex couldn't help but to be proud of his nigga. Even with him being some years older, Laurent didn't treat Projex like an underdog. They put each other up on game, ran that shit, and was running their money up. Before long, Laurent could see them both taking over with their music, but he had to let go of the streets first. Laurent already had but was still heavily connected.

"You know my grandpa be on my ass about this music shit. I'ma give him yo' number so y'all can link."

"Joe a legend. Gon' and text me his info. He stay out in Cali still, right?"

Projex nodded his head just as his phone vibrated on his lap. "Yeah. He still out there. They got a camp coming up for TWC this summer. I'ma fly out there if a nigga ain't in jail." He chuckled, and Laurent shook his head.

"Your ass better not be. That's a crazy opportunity. Shit, tell Joe I'll take yo' spot if you can't make it."

"You for real?" Projex wanted to know.

"Hell yeah. If you cool with it."

"You know I don't give a fuck. Go down there and soak that game up, my nigga. We gon' see how this shit play out next week, but I'm sure he would be cool with it."

"Fasho, fasho. You just got me hype." Laurent grinned as they slapped hands.

"Make me proud, son," Projex joked. "I'ma shake

in a little bit. My girl tripping. Blowing my motha-fuckin' line down."

"I know you ain't talking about Kelsi? That's her hitting you now."

Looking down at his screen, Projex's nostrils flared. He most definitely wasn't talking about her. Clearly, she had something she needed to say to him, so Projex finally accepted her call. Standing from the couch, he told Laurent he'd be right back.

"The fuck do you want?" he spoke harshly into the phone. "Blowing my line down like a crackhead."

"I just wanted to talk. I miss you."

"Man," Projex stressed, scratching at his chin hair. "What the fuck you really want?"

"Can you come see?"

"Nah. I ain't gone be able to do that."

Kelsi sucked her teeth. "And why not?"

"You remember that ass whooping you got, right? My girl ain't going for that."

"You act like she really put hands on me, but okay."

Projex laughed. Maybe Loriana had knocked a bit of sense out of her cause from what he recalled, Loriana had indeed put them hands on her.

"Yeah, a'ight."

"I know she ain't sucking your dick right. Just

come by, so I can taste it real quick. You don't have to stay long."

He was a glutton for some fire head, and Kelsi knew that. His dick grew hard, thinking about her wet mouth and how deeply she could take his dick down her throat.

"A'ight."

She perked up. "For real?"

"Yeah. I'll call you when I'm outside."

"Okay. See you in a little bit."

Sliding his phone in the pocket of his hoodie, Projex went to the restroom across the hall to piss. After washing his hands and going back into the studio to rap with Laurent for a few more minutes, he was out the door and headed to his car. Head on a swivel, he scanned the parking lot. He feared no man but would never be caught slipping by one of his enemies. Projex was on a few people's shit list.

Hopping on the highway, he cruised until he made it to his destination. Pulling onto her block, Projex didn't see a car in the driveway, so he parked in it. Grabbing his phone, he went to her name in his call log and tapped on it. It rang three times before she answered, and he was surprised she took that long.

"Come open the door. I'm outside," was all he said before hanging up.

Climbing out of his car, he made sure it was locked and walked up the few steps that lead to the door. Hands in his pocket, he observed the neighborhood. Cricket's chirped in the distance as the streetlights flickered. When the door opened, his breath got caught in his chest.

"What do you want?"

Projex licked his lips and smirked. She was upset, and it showed all over her pretty face.

"You not gone let me in?"

Loriana rolled her eyes. "I shouldn't. I should've ignored you like you've been doing me all day. You sure you still even my boyfriend?"

His smirk fell. "Quit playing with me."

Stepping over the threshold of the door, he gently pushed her back some and closed it. With a lock, his hand left the nob and was around her waist. Hugging her close, Projex inhaled her floral scent, and his dick twitched.

"You smell good," he complimented.

"And you stink," she barely could get out because he was holding her so tight.

He smacked her booty in the little shorts she had on. "No I don't. You miss me?"

Loriana melted. She missed him but was still mad. Projex just had to come around invading her space, reminding her young heart that there was no escaping him.

"No."

"You aren't a good liar, ma." He chuckled and kissed her neck. "Don't matter, though 'cause I missed you."

She eased out of his embrace and looked him over. His hair was a mess in a pulled-back ponytail because he hadn't been to see Moo all week, face relaxed, and eyes red. She liked when he was high. He was always so focused and paid extra attention to everything. Which, in her case, was good right now because she wanted him to hear and understand her.

"What?" he asked, reaching out to grab her.

Loriana put her hand up to stop him. "No. I want you to let me talk and don't interrupt me." His head tilted forward some, urging her to continue. "Do not hang up in my face ever again. I don't care how mad I make you or whatever the case was earlier. I'm not the chick that's going to grovel at your feet and beg you to tell me what the issue is. I have enough shit I'm dealing with. If you can't communicate with me and under-stand what I'm going through, then we don't need to be together. No use in wasting any more of our time."

"A'ight," he said, and her eyes turned to slits.

"I know that's not all you—"

"No. It's not all I have to say. I'm human too. A nigga be in his feelings just like you. You right, though. I should've never hung up in your face and ignored you. That was some pussy shit. I know what you're dealing with but can't begin to imagine how you feel. That's why I wanted to get you out with me. Clear your head a lil' bit. A nigga ain't used to rejection, especially from you, so it threw me off. I'm sorry. I won't do that shit again, a'ight?

Stunned by his words and more so by the kindness he spoke them with, Loriana blinked quickly. Wetness coated her lashes as she forced the lump in her throat to go down.

"Okay. I guess, I can accept your apology."

His grin was back. "You ain't have no choice. We wasn't moving from this spot until you did. Gimmie a kiss, so I know it's real."

Loriana pulled him to her by the pocket of his hoodie. On tipped toes, she met his bent head and smooched his lips. She thought he wanted a simple one to seal their first argument, but he wanted more. He always did. Sliding his tongue in her mouth, Loriana tasted the peppermint he chewed on the way to her and the flavor of ash from his blunt. Rubbing on her booty, she groaned when his hands tried making their way into her shorts.

"Wait," she breathed, pulling back.

"What's the matter?"

"I don't know where your hands have been."

"They trying to be on you," he replied lustfully.

She smiled softly. "I know. You have to wash them first, though."

"A'ight. Come on."

One thing Linette had schooled Loriana on, like many other things, was that a boy's hands should always be clean before they touched her lady parts. Loriana knew if his mouth tasted like weed, his fingers were covered in the residue from breaking it down. Had he objected, she would've looked at him in a different light.

Once out of the bathroom Loriana and Mhyale now shared, Projex stepped inside her room and closed the door. He knew Mhyale wasn't home but still wanted them to have some privacy just in case she came back. Crisscrossed in her bed that was on the floor atop the box spring, Loriana watched his every move. Since she didn't have a dresser yet, she was using one of her clothes totes in place of one.

Removing his wallet and keys, he placed them next to the lamp she turned on. Next went his gun that was on his hip. Putting it on safety, he placed it atop the container. The sound it made echoed throughout the room as Loriana's eyes stayed glued to it.

"You wanna hold it?"

Her eyes hot up to him. "No. I was just looking."

"I was testing you. You need to get you one. Yo' cousin got one?"

She shrugged. "I don't know. Probably. Why would I need one?"

"Y'all two females living here by y'all self. Shit, somebody needs to be packing. I know yo' cousin gotta have some heat in here."

Loriana wasn't sure, but she didn't doubt it either. Memphis used to take Mhy to the shooting range with him all the time.

"What kind would I get if I did get one?" she asked, watching him pull his hoodie over his head. The quick flash of his lower abs as his shirt lifted, turning her on.

"Probably a Ruger or a baby Glock. Something small that you can hide."

He toed off his shoes and undid his jeans. Eyes trained on him, Loriana licked her lips as he comfortably undressed. Her heart was beating at a different pace now. Looking for somewhere to put his clothes, he hung them over the metal chair she had near the window. Now standing at the side of the bed she was on, Loriana tucked her lips in as a grin covered her face.

Him in her room right now reminded her of when he brought her to his grandma's crib for the first time. Only now, she wasn't a virgin. Her center grew moist at the bulge in his briefs. Projex wasn't super skinny, weighing a buck-fifty if that, but he had muscle. All his weight seemed to reside between his legs. His dick was *heavy*.

"Scoot over," he told her, pulling her pink comforter back. He climbed in and got comfortable. The firmness of the new mattress had him popping the muscles in his back.

"Sorry my bed is on the floor."

"I do not care about that kind of shit, baby. A nigga done slept on the concrete, an air mattress, and all. You good. Everybody gotta start somewhere."

Loriana quickly got into her head, saying *I'm starting completely over.* Before she got in her feelings, she mumbled an okay. Needing to feel his body heat, Loriana wedged herself along his side, tossing her leg over his body. She felt clingy again now that they had made up. An hour ago, she was ready to say to hell with him.

"What kind of furniture you get today?" he asked, stroking her thigh.

"A dresser, two nightstands, and a bed frame. They deliver it on Monday."

"What time? I'll come by and help you rearrange your room."

She smiled against his chest. "Between nine and twelve. You wanna be up that early?"

"That ain't even early, ma," he chuckled.

They sat in silence for a few minutes, just absorbing one another's energy. Projex didn't let her know but ignoring her was hard as hell today. He felt bad for snapping on her, but he was stubborn. He hadn't had to take someone's feelings into consideration in a long time. For her, he would, though.

"I heard something earlier that I wanted to ask you about. That's why I was calling your phone like that."

"What's that?" He yawned, now rubbing on her booty.

Loriana wasn't sure how'd he take what Nyree had told her, but she didn't feel right not telling him. Off top, her loyalty belonged to her man.

"It's something to do with why you went to jail."

His body stilled. A million thoughts of what she may have been about to divulge ran through his mind.

She shouldn't have been privy or hearing shit from anyone about why he went to jail. Her curiosity was going to get the best of her.

"Where you was at early to hear something like that?" he asked, digging for information.

"My auntie's. Sneaks and Bo were over there, and Nyree—"

"Remember what I told you the other day?" he questioned, cutting her rambling sentence off.

"You told me a lot of things."

"What I tell you about believing me?"

"Believe what you tell me and not what you don't."

"Exactly. Believe what *I* tell you. If it didn't come from me, anything a mothafucka putting in yo' ear don't matter."

"But what if—"

Projex sucked his teeth and sat up, forcing her off his chest. "Man. Take these off." He tugged at her shorts.

"What? Why? We're talking."

"Nah. *You* talking too much, and I'm 'bout to shut yo' ass up."

Keeping it gangster with her, Projex did exactly that. Once her shorts and panties were tossed to the floor, he made her straddle his face. Like in the car, but with more room now, Loriana spread her legs and balanced herself above him. Calloused hands gripped her soft ass as his tongue explored her pussy. When his tongue flicked hard along her clit, Loriana gasped, and her forehead bumped the wall with a gentle thud.

"Mmm," she moaned, pressing her hands firmly against the wall.

Projex spanked her ass and gripped her hips. Coaching her, he nonverbally taught her how to roll her hips. The friction made her needier. With each roll of her body, Projex tongued her pussy with so much passion she could cry. He couldn't get enough of her taste. Two thick fingers slid inside her, massaging her pulsing walls. Knowing he'd been the only one inside her, his dick grew harder.

Loriana's back arched when he sucked on her clitoris. "Baby," she whined, trying to lift up.

"Un, un," he mumbled, mouth full of her.

Quicker flickers, his swirling tongue, cushiony lips, and a firm grip on her ass had her climaxing in minutes. She slapped a hand over her mouth, not knowing if Mhyale was home or not. Projex didn't care either way.

"Br-Bryshooon," she cried. His arms held her in place.

He continued to kiss her middle, lazily gliding his

tongue over her slick folds. He always ate her like he was starving, then licked her slowly like she was something sweet he had to have after every meal. Loriana was a five-star course, top-of-the-line, exquisite dish that only he could afford. When her body leaned to the side, having had enough of the pleasure, Projex pulled her onto his lap.

"Man, yo' pussy so good. That shit crazy," he said, lost in his own world.

Atop him, Loriana lowered her face to his, and he grinned before they shared her taste. What she thought was nasty before wasn't anymore. Lying flat along his chest, she grinded slowly, feeling his erection through his briefs.

"Where you going?" Projex asked as she moved down his body, stopping at his thighs.

She popped the band of his briefs. "Take these off."

He choked on a laugh. "Aye. You can't say that to me. I ain't no little hoe."

"But I'm yours?"

"Nah, baby. You ain't no hoe. I can fuck you like one, though."

She didn't know exactly what he meant by that, but it didn't matter. All she wanted was for him to free his dick so she could enjoy examining it with the lights on. Slipping his briefs off, Projex laid back on the bed while she sat up on her knees between his legs. She ran her palm along his pubic hairs, intrigued by how much there was.

"Can you get this waxed like mine?"

"Hell nah, girl. I ain't getting it waxed. I do shave it low sometimes, though."

"Oh, okay," she murmured.

Tracing her hand up the backside of his dick, his stomach caved a bit at her touch. Her eagerness to learn him made Projex want her even more. The patience he exhibited calmed her nerves. Projex wanted her to be comfortable not just sexually with him but in all areas they explored. Her inexperience wasn't a flaw, it was simply a gift; his to unwrap and orchestrate to their liking. He was a leader before anything, and Loriana took pleasure in that.

"It's so warm," she said, now stroking him.

"Spit on it, ma."

She let a sliver of saliva drip from her mouth onto his tip, and he groaned. "That's enough?"

"Y-Yeah."

Watching him grow and harden fascinated her. When she did watch a porno, half the time, it wasn't to touch herself. Loriana was studying. Her inquisitiveness had her looking up the craziest categories in the search bar. Not that crazy because whatever she typed in popped up.

"Fuck, that feels good." His grumbled voice made her mouth water.

Lowering her head, she swirled her tongue around his tip, showing him how thirsty she was to taste him. She couldn't quite place what he tasted like, but it wasn't bad. The way the women on porn was sucking dick, she thought it may have tasted like candy or something.

"I kind of know what to do, but I don't," she told him, looking into his eyes.

He didn't really know how to teach her but would try. "Just don't use no teeth when you sucking. Your mouth gon' get wetter the more you suck, but that's a good thing."

"Okay. What if I gag and stuff?"

He smirked at her naivety and freakiness. "Keep going. Don't hurt yourself, though. It might feel good to me, but if you uncomfortable, you can stop."

She nodded and got right back to the task at hand. *No teeth, keep going if you gag. Got it,* she said to herself.

Covering the head of his dick with her mouth, her teeth slightly scraped him, and Projex flinched.

"You gotta tuck your lips, ma. Like, make em' cover your teeth while you doing it."

Being the quick learner she was, Loriana did as he instructed and made a smooth glide down his shaft. When she gagged, her head shot up from his lap. Eyes watering, she tried again. One hand stayed firm around the base of his dick while she bobbed up and down at an easy pace. She was trying to figure out how to breathe while doing all of this. Her chest heaved as she came up for air.

Sniffling, she said, "Am I doing it right?"

"Yeah, baby," he answered with a lazy drawl from pure bliss. "You doing good. Keep going. Try to breathe through your nose, okay? I'ma hold your head."

She nodded, and Projex placed his hand on her silky black bonnet protecting her hair. Like before, she tucked her lips. Covering him with her warm mouth, she mimicked her movements from before. Projex thrust his hips up slightly, catching her off guard, but she kept going. Wetter, her spit slid down his dick and onto her hand. Remembering one girl from a video twisting her fists, she copied her and smirked when she heard Projex cuss.

"Fuck, ma. Yeah. Just like that. Keeping sucking my shit just like that."

His words encouraged her. She was doing something right. When she made a loud slurping noise before taking him back into her mouth, his hand fell from her head. Projex's toes were tingling. Feeling like she was back in control, Loriana tested her newfound skills and tried to take all of him down her throat.

The first try was a fail, but she wasn't a quitter. On the second attempt, she felt like she had to sneeze. The third one, she relaxed and told herself she could do this. Accepting the challenge, his dick touched her tonsils, and ironically, she found herself breathing through her nose. It didn't last for long, thanks to Projex trying to slide down her throat. Violent coughs escape her, and tears filled her eyes as she pulled her mouth off of him.

"Whew," she chuckled, wiping at her face, "I think I got it."

"You do. No more practicing down there. Time for a new lesson."

Picking her up, Projex made her straddle his lap. He laid her against his chest and smacked her booty with his hardened member before sliding it along her slick lips.

"Damn, you wet," he groaned before sliding inside her.

"Ughh," she moaned, squeezing her eyes shut.

She lost her breath while he was losing his mind. He wasn't even fully inside, and Projex was already trying to think of everything but how tight her walls were. Loriana lifted her upper body some, trying to get away but knew better. Savagely, Projex smacked one ass cheek and held her around the waist.

"No running," he spoke against her ear.

Spreading her legs at the knees, Loriana sank further onto him and held him tightly around his neck. She didn't move for a good ten seconds. How she was supposed to move was the real question. Ever observant, Projex caught on to her hesitance.

"Ride it like you twerking, ma."

While he lifted the tank top she was wearing over her head, she danced on him to her own beat. It was slow and meticulous at first, taking him only as deep as her body would let her. Then, it sped up as his mouth covered one of her nipples. Which one, Loriana didn't know. Her body was in sensory overload.

When she felt comfortable enough to go all the way down, Projex wanted to scream. Instead, Loriana did it for him.

"Oh, my gooosh," she moaned loudly.

Figuring out her groove, she placed her hands on

his chest and moved her body in a back-and-forth motion. Projex helped her, gripping her ass and making sure she took all of him. Her body was on fire. From the way he tweaked her nipples, smacked her ass, and spoke to her, had Loriana delirious. Her eyes rolled to the back of her head as she came.

Legs trembling, Loriana pulled at her bonnet, snatching it off. She was losing her mind as he continued to pump inside of her. She looked so pretty riding his dick, Projex almost nutted. He didn't want to yet, though. Flipping them over, he placed her ankles on his shoulders and fucked her hard. Her dainty hand came to his waist.

"B-Bryshon! You're too deep," she cried, thrashing her head against the pillow.

He dug deeper, making her pussy fart. "Nah. No, I'm not. Move your hand."

When she obliged, her eyes opened and stared up at him. His contorted face was filled with ecstasy. Testing how far he could go, Projex gripped her neck. When her eyes brightened before lowering lazily into a submissive daze, his heart skipped a beat. *Yeah. She with all this shit.*

Leaning over her, Projex kissed her lips. "Why this pussy so wet, ma? You keep cumming on my dick."

"Mmm," was all she could reply.

The friction along her clit had her seeing stars on her ceiling like she was in a Rolls-Royce. Fucking him back, Projex slammed into her with a neediness that not even he was used to. It was as if he was trying to climb inside her body; live in her limbs and make it home. He was home and never wanted to leave.

"Aahh. Keep fucking me," she spoke into his ear in the sexiest moan he'd ever heard.

Projex couldn't control his nut if he wanted to. "Fuuuck!" he croaked, placing his head in the crook of her neck. "Damn, baby."

He was wheezing almost, struggling to catch his breath. Loriana and her greedy pussy had sucked the life out of him. If it was his turn to die, he'd happily go out buried inside her walls. At least he went out a mothafuckin' G.

Lifting off of her, Projex stared down at her like she was the best thing that'd ever happened to him. Quite frankly, she was. Her hair was wild and sweated out, body glistening with sweat, and mouth slightly open. Her eyes, though. They twisted his heart, making him want to snatch that bitch out and hand it to her on a silver platter or with a bow tied around it.

Loriana was staring at him like the night of her

prom when he chin-checked Camron for pushing up on her. Like he'd delivered the stars and the moon to her doorstep. This time, it was the sun too. Where there'd been dark days in her life, Projex was that one thing that shined bright, tanning her melanin skin. He almost hated that she looked at him in this manner because he knew he'd eventually bring the rain soon.

There was nothing but cloudy skies and gloomy moods when that happened. No one lasted when it rained, and Loriana was sure to drown without a life jacket. Fuck an umbrella.

Chapter Six

Ny: *Hey. Was just calling to check on you. Sending you all my love & hugs. I'm here if you want to talk. Love you!*

In the backseat of Greg's truck, Loriana read over the text Nyree sent her. Her brain was saying thank you, but her fingers couldn't move to type out the two words. She'd been shedding tears all day and hardly had enough strength to get out of the bed. It'd been one month since Linette passed, and Loriana didn't know what to do.

She was so lost without her mother, and no matter how much she tried to convince herself that she was okay, she wasn't. The truth was, she would never know what to do. Not immediately, and that was okay. Things would feel overwhelming hard, sad, and scary as hell for some time. Learning to navigate life without her just wasn't fair.

"You wanna get out first?" Greg asked.

Neither of them had moved yet. Nodding, Loriana unclicked her seatbelt and without hurry, exited the truck. In her hand were an assortment of artificial flowers and a teddy bear. Her mouth watered, feeling as if she were on the verge of throwing up. She hadn't been to visit yet, and now she knew why. Linette wasn't here. This was just simply a shell of the woman she was. Her soul was present with the Lord.

Warm tears slid down her cheeks as the late May winds blew her hair. Her legs almost gave out the closer she got. The headstone hadn't been set yet, but Loriana didn't need it to know where she was going. Linette's now permanent place was embedded in her mind.

Standing tall in front of the silver nameplate, Loriana shook her head. Her shoulders jumped in the same manner as her chest, as she began to sob. Doubling over, she held onto her knees for support. Her body was giving out on her. She couldn't believe her life had come to this. Loriana hated her life right now. She despised everyone who still had their mother.

While they could call on theirs, her only option

was to visit her at a cemetery. In her dreams, she waited to see her face. In her prayers, she begged God to return her for just a little while longer. Loriana promised and pleaded to be a better daughter. She'd do absolutely anything to have her mom back. Desperation seeped from her pores as she fell to her knees. Hunched over, the stem of the flowers dug into her palms as she grieved. Wailing, she left nothing to the imagination of how she felt. She was broken. Completely fucking broken, and nothing could piece her back together.

"I need you," she cried. "I need you so bad."

Her body trembled, eyes were burning, and her soul depleted. Loriana was drowning. It didn't take whatever Projex was going to send her way for it to happen. She was struggling to inhale air and take back control of her life.

"I don't understand. Help me understand, Mama," she whined, desperate for an answer. One would never come, and understanding wouldn't either.

Heart out of her chest, Loriana banged on the prickling grass, frustrated and devastated. Her world had gone from what every young teenager dreamed of to one the devil hand-delivered to her doorstep. One minute it was all good. She had so much planned. They had so much planned. A trip to Florida over the summer was her graduation gift because Loriana always wanted to go to the beach. Linette was going to do that for her. She was going to surprise her baby on graduation day and couldn't. The plane tickets had turned into credits through Southwest Airlines.

Loriana's chest was so tight, she didn't care if she died right here. Anything would be better than the agonizing grief coursing through her body. Mourning was sick. Physically, mentally and emotionally, it drained her young body. There was no pick-me-up or energy drink that could revive her.

You have to be strong for you.

Her eyes slowly peeled open, and her head lifted. As it pounded, she looked to her right, thinking Elana had gotten out of the car and was speaking to her. She hadn't, though. The words she heard weren't in the physical but in her mind. She couldn't make out the voice but was okay with that. Something was telling her that it was Linette's anyway.

Her heart calmed, and chills covered her body. For a month straight, she wanted a sign. There'd been subtle ones, but this was the one she needed. Sniffing hard, she cleared her throat and removed her glasses. Wiping her eyes, she put them back on with a clearer vision now.

"I miss you, Mama." Her voice cracked.

Loriana wasn't sure if she wanted to say more. She'd never had to visit someone's grave before.

"So much has happened, and I can't even tell you. I mean, I guess I can right here, but it's not the same. I hope you're not mad that I moved out of the apartment. I couldn't live there without you. Mhyale let me move in with her, and it's different. Not in a bad way, though." She sighed.

"A lot of people stopped checking in on me too like they said they would. That kind of hurt my feelings, but I guess that's life. People make promises and break them. Projex has been there with me, though. Him and Nyree. I forgot to tell you he was my boyfriend now."

She smiled at the thought and a memory of them on Facetime together. Linette was just a grinning as Projex complimented her beauty. He was a charmer for sure. More than anything, he was a protector and provider. He'd introduced Loriana to a type of stability that she never wanted to go without. She hadn't let him know, but she was scared of what his outcome in court would be in a few weeks.

"It's crazy how things happened that night. He went to jail a-and you passed away. It still feels unreal. Like, how am I experiencing this right now? I like Projex a lot, Ma, but I'm scared. I'm so scared he's going to have to leave me like you, and then what? I can't take having my heart broken a second time. It's barely there as it is."

Loriana took a deep breath. Getting all of this off her chest was therapeutic, and she hadn't realized it until now. Her high school counselor had suggested therapy. As young as she was, Loriana needed someone she could vent to that wouldn't judge her or knew her situation. She'd thought about it but then just ended up crying because of the reason for needing it.

"I really don't know what else to say. Coming out here was hard for me, but I feel a little better now. Even though you're not here physically, I know you're still listening. I love you, Mama. I'll be back to see you later."

Shoving the flowers into the ground as best as she could, Loriana stood to her feet and dusted off her blue denim. She gave her mother one last glance and walked back to the truck. Climbing in the back, she closed the door and exhaled.

"Can I give you a hug?" Ethan asked, making her crack a small smile.

"Of course."

Eager to ease the sadness on his sister's face, Ethan scrambled across the seat. His arms that seemed the be growing longer every day, wrapped around her and squeezed tight. When he let go, Loriana kissed his forehead as he grimaced.

"Thank you. You give the best hugs."

"My mama does too. You know she's your mama too, even though Ms. Linette is gone. You still have one. I don't want you to be sad. It makes me sad."

Loriana's bottom lip poked out. "It's okay to be sad."

When she saw him wipe at his face, her chest caved. "She was always nice to me."

In the front, Elana was facing the window, holding her tears back. Greg sat in the driver's seat, blinking his eyes. Hearing their conversation put one thing in perspective for him. Regardless of them not being together, they were still a family. Linette treated Ethan no different just because he wasn't hers. Same with Elana. The fact that Loriana already considered her a mother made Ethan's statement that much more heartfelt.

When the trio got out to visit and place their own flowers down, Loriana stayed in the truck and replied to a few text messages. It was Tuesday afternoon, so she didn't have anything planned but to go back home. Being tucked inside her room for the day, or days at a time, was where she found solace. Even though she had people in her corner ready to help her heal in whatever capacity she'd let them, doing it on her own for now was her preference.

Loriana's mood swings changed by the minute. She questioned God so much, she was sure he'd stopped listening. Some days, she didn't want to be bothered. Other days, she appreciated Mhyale's contagious laugh and nosy personality. She'd come into her room just to see what she was doing and end up in there for hours just talking.

Other days, Loriana locked her door and screamed at the top of her lungs. On those days, Mhyale didn't bother her. She let her know to release whatever she needed to. As a woman, she knew all too well about suppressing her feelings. She didn't want Loriana to be the same way.

Back inside the truck, Greg turned on 107.3 and headed toward the restaurant they'd chosen to eat at. Grateful that they had come down to be with her on today, Loriana figured she could spend a few hours with them before going back home.

The wait at Texas Roadhouse wasn't long, and she was grateful. All that crying had her starving and a bit dehydrated. When their food was ordered, casual conversation around what her plans were for college came up. Greg understood why she didn't want to attend graduation, but not college. Loriana had already made up in her mind that she'd sit out the first semester.

"That's seven months of doing nothing," he said, trying to understand.

"I wouldn't call grieving doing nothing."

He sighed. "You know what I mean, baby girl. Being here is only hindering you. Making you depressed. Going out of state is something we've always discussed. A goal you always had."

"I just need a break. It's not like I can't play catch up over the summer. I'll try to get my scholarships for the spring semester. Plus, living in state will be cheaper if I can't."

"So, you don't want to go to a college out of state anymore?"

Loriana shook her head no and shoved a forkful of rice in her mouth.

"Is it because of that boy?"

"Greg," Elana began, not wanting him to go there.

Loriana stopped chewing. "You think I don't want to go out of state because of Projex?"

"And other reasons, yes."

She scoffed in disbelief. Of all things to assume, he had to make Projex out as the bad guy. He didn't say it, but Loriana knew he felt that way. It was all in his tone. Projex may have been labeled as a menace to his neighborhood, but he was Loriana's person. She knew without a doubt that he would always have her back. If Projex fucked with you, his loyalty ran deep. His was pumping through Loriana's veins.

"I'll let you think that." She wasn't about to go back and forth about his opinion. She simply didn't care, and her decision had been made.

Greg placed his fork down. "No. Don't let me think anything. You gotta tell me something. College has always been a dream of yours, so I can't see you throwing it away behind some nigga."

Ethan's eyes shot up from his iPad while Elana grabbed her glass of lemonade to sip from. Sudden anger lit Loriana's eyes.

"I'm not," she said with gritted teeth.

"Then, what's the real reason?"

As much education as her dad had, Loriana was beginning to think her Aunt Peaches was right. Maybe he was a bit slow.

"If you haven't noticed, my mama just died. The one person I knew who had my back in this world is gone. So, no. I'm not going out of town to an entirely new state just to fall into a deeper depression and probably kill myself. It was never behind a *nigga*, and even if it was, that's my decision, not yours."

Greg didn't know what to say. There was nothing he could say. His fleeting embarrassment quickly turned into a wave of sadness. Hearing the defeat yet stern tone in his daughter's voice broke him down. Here he was worried about her education when she'd lost her mother. He wasn't trying to be insensitive at all, but he just wanted to know. Unbeknownst to Loriana, Greg had peeped Projex's car parked at Mhyale's house on more than one occasion.

The privilege to try and dictate how she ran her life was lost the second he moved out of their home. Yes, she was still his child, but the respect she had for him wasn't where it used to be. She loved him but, in her eyes, only her mother could tell her what to do, and since she was no longer able to, Loriana was abiding by her own rules.

They sat in an uncomfortable silence while finishing their meal. When they dropped her back off at home, Loriana thanked them for getting her out and told them she loved them. It was the truth, and sometimes you just had to let people know their place in your life. Greg was doing way too much for someone who couldn't keep his first family together, and Loriana didn't like that. She wasn't going to hold it against him, though. It was life, and both of them were still learning it.

Peeping the Audi parked on the street, Loriana realized it was the same car Mhyale had dragged her over to that night at the gas station. When she opened the front door using her key, Mhyale was walking down the hallway from her room with Naaz right behind her.

In some black leggings and a cropped white tank top that showed off her pierced belly, she was dressed comfortably. Behind her, Naaz coincidentally matched. He rocked black Nike shorts, a white tee with an iced-out chain hanging from his neck, with a black pair of crew socks and Air Maxes on. Mhyale smiled when she saw her.

"Hey, cousin."

She's in a good mood, Loriana thought, giving her a soft smile.

"Hey."

"What's up. I'm Naaz," he spoke, giving her a head nod.

"Hi. I think I've met you before. It was a long time ago, though."

"Yeah. I remember you. You still look the same, just a little taller."

"How was dinner with your folks?" Mhyale asked.

Loriana shrugged. "Annoying but needed. I had to check my daddy."

"About what? You know what…don't even tell me. I can only imagine why he pissed you off. I'm glad you're here, though. Naaz brought you a gift."

The spot between her brows pinched. "A gift? For what?"

Naaz smirked. "I'm just the delivery guy. It's a gift from Projex."

Her heart stuttered. "Oh, okay. What is it?"

"Hold on. Let me go grab it from my room," Mhyale shuffled slowly back down the hall.

A gift? Projex had texted her this morning, asking if she wanted to be bothered with his presence, and she didn't. Not today. He respected her wishes, told her to hit him if she needed him and let her be. His hearing was today, but he was still making himself available to her. She appreciated his understanding and was now wondering if he'd gotten her a gift to try and cheer her up. Little did she know, it was going to do much more than that.

"Okay," Mhyale breathed out. "Here you go."

Handing her the blue velvet box, Loriana eyed her cousin suspiciously. As nosy as Mhyale was, she knew she'd already looked inside to see what it was.

Nervously, she opened it and her eyes misted over while an almost inaudible gasp slipped from her lips.

"Oh my gosh," she whispered in awe. A gentle smile lifted her cheeks.

"It's nice, isn't it?" Mhyale questioned, and she nodded.

It was more than nice. The white gold angel-winged piece hung from a rope chain that Loriana was sure cost a grip. Each way she turned the queenly custom piece, it sparkled. The diamonds weren't what had her hands shaking, though. In the middle of the wings was a picture of Linette. Loriana remembered the exact day the picture was taken. Memphis had just bought Peaches her digital camera, and she came to their house to show it off.

"Come on, sis. Smile for my camera. I'ma send this picture to those niggas locked up. Let them know you single and ready to answer their jail calls."

Loriana and Mhyale cracked up laughing.

"You better not do that mess, Peach. Now, come on. I'm trying to cook."

"Give me a real smile. Smile like you just hit the lottery or something, shit."

That got a big grin out of her then.

"That money talk gets you to grinning, I see," *Peach clowned.*

"Whatever. Let me see it."

They hovered around as she flicked through the camera roll. Peaches was snapping any and every-thing, but Linette couldn't lie; she'd captured a good one of her.

"That's cute, Mama," Loriana let her know.

"Thank you. When you get my age, you gone look just as fine as me."

"Me too, hell. You see she already got my grade of hair."

They looked at her and cracked up again. Peaches didn't have but a snap of hair by choice but could grow it long if she wanted to.

As the memory replayed in her mind, she sniffled. The memory wasn't from that long ago, and that's what hurt the most. Lifting it up, she looked on the back and knew today was going to be the day she told Projex she loved him. Engraved on the back was a message she needed to see, especially today.

A Mother's Love Never Dies

"H-He bought this for me?" she choked out, looking at them with teary eyes.

"Yeah. I made it, though. He said even though you didn't want to be bothered, he was still getting you this necklace. Luckily, I had to swing by and get your cousin in check for ignoring my calls."

Mhyale rolled her eyes playfully. "Is that what you call yourself doing?"

"You ain't grinning and walking funny for no reason."

She slapped him in the chest. "Shut up. See, that's why you ain't getting any no more. Talk too damn much."

Naaz's knuckle flicked at his nose as he smirked. The taste of her pussy was still on his tongue and lips. "I'll let you believe that. I hope you like it," he said, now talking to Loriana.

"I love it. Thank you so much. When you say you made it, you mean designed it?"

"Yeah. I'm a jeweler."

"Wow. That's a nice job to have," Loriana said.

"Yeah. Especially when I put smiles on people's faces like yours. Ya moms was always nice to me when I saw her. Know for a fact she gon' always be with you right here," he said, tapping his heart. "She's your angel now."

That right there was why Mhyale had fallen in love with him. Loriana stared at the necklace for a few seconds longer before closing the box.

"She is. Thank you again so, so much. I'ma go call him now."

"Fasho. Don't hesitate to call me if you need

something too. Your cousin loves the hell out of you, so that makes you family these ways."

She grinned. "Okay. I didn't know you two were dating like that. Seems serious."

"It's not, but he's right. I do love you and know I got your back through whatever, baby," Mhyale told her.

"I know you do."

"Don't listen to her," Naaz told her with a chuckle before smacking Mhyale on the ass. "Walk me to my car and come get this money."

"Yes, daddy," she joked, making Loriana gag and snicker as she headed to her room.

Rushing to locate her phone in her purse, she pulled it out and Facetimed Projex. She knew he was a giver without being told to give, but this? Loriana was just elated he had thought of her enough to do something to place a smile on her face. When he answered, she had her lip poked out.

"Babe," she whined before he could get a word in.

"What's wrong, ma. Somebody fucking with you today?" he asked, sitting up in his bed. He'd been lying down since he left court earlier this morning and was trying to get some sleep.

"No. Naaz just gave me my gift from you. I love it. Thank you so much."

The fiery in his eyes vanished. Projex thought he was going to have to whoop someone's ass today. He didn't like hearing her whine, but he was starting to differentiate between the one dedicated to him. Sheepishly, he grinned.

"Good. That's why I was trying to see you today. Wanted to see your face when you opened it. You see the back?"

"Yeah. You thought to put that on there yourself?"

He nodded and wiped at the crust in his eye. "Yeah. It's the truth. I hope you having an okay day, baby. I just wanted to brighten it up a little bit."

"You're so sweet. I don't know why people think you're this tough-ass person."

He cracked up. "Man, you say anything. I ain't tough with you; that's all you need to be worried about."

"It is. Why are you in the bed? How did it go today?"

He shook his head. "I was taking a nap right quick. And not the way I expected for it to go but fuck it."

He lost his hearing and was given the decision to take a plea deal or go to trial. Projex saw no need to take a plea, so trial it was. His head was fucked up that things had even escalated this far, knowing he was innocent.

"So, are you going to jail?" She wanted to know.

"Nah. I gotta wait until trial now. It's a whole process, ma. I'ont wanna talk about that, though. You just got home?"

She nodded, now moving about her room. Her furniture had been delivered earlier that week, and she was glad. No longer did it look like she was moving out instead of in. Slipping her shoes off, she put them in the closet.

"Yeah. Just came from seeing my mom and out to eat with my daddy nem'."

"How was that? Where y'all eat at?" he clarified. Projex didn't want her to relive her first visit to see her mom. If she brought it up cool, he'd listen, but until then, he wanted to carry their conversation in a different direction.

"We went to Texas Roadhouse. He asked why I wasn't going away to college this year as if that were a trick question," she said, rolling her eyes.

"You not?"

"No. I don't feel like I'm ready anymore, and he kind of tried to make me feel bad about it." She wasn't going to tell him Greg thought he was the reason why. There was no need to light fire to an unlit match.

"Don't. If you not ready yet, shit, that's what it is. You don't need all the pressure on you anyway, ma. Fuck what he talkin' 'bout."

She snickered. "I knew you'd agree."

"Yeah, but you going second semester. I'ma make sure of that."

"Mhm. Says the person who didn't go himself."

"You already know why I ain't go. You don't have an excuse after the fall."

"And you don't have an excuse as to why you can't take off with your music writing."

Projex got quiet.

"Nah. Don't be all hush-hush now."

He cracked a grin. "You swear you stay checking shit. I hear you, though, and you right. It ain't no real reason. That's why I'm trying to put myself in a position now to make sure I'm straight when that time comes."

"I'ma make sure too. We gotta hold each other accountable."

His heart did a somersault. "I'ma forever hold shit down on my end when it comes to you, ma."

"Promises, promises. You know I believe you, right?" His actions matched his words so far.

"As you should. Lying to you don't benefit me in no way."

Loriana smiled. She knew it didn't, but Projex was still a young man. They lied. Maybe not intentionally, but they just did. For some, it was second nature. Loriana hoped he wasn't just talking a good game like everyone else who'd made her promises. The place she was at in her life; if you weren't all in with her, then you weren't in at all. That's just how she was coming, and she'd hate if Projex got left behind for false intentions.

Chapter Seven

"**D**o these jeans make my butt look big?" Nyree asked Loriana.

While she turned her hips from side to side, Loriana glanced her way. "Um. It looks how it normally looks."

"Then, it looks big then," Nyree confirmed, smacking her own ass. "Remember they were telling us about the freshmen fifteen?"

"Yeah."

"I think I'm already gaining it."

Loriana chuckled. "No, you aren't, Ny. Maybe it is the jeans that got you looking a little thick. Or, it could be something else."

Her hint had Nyree smirking. Out of the house and chilling with her girl for the night, Loriana sat in the middle of Nyree's bed while she went through her wardrobe. It was a rare occasion for her to be off work on a Saturday, so they were taking advantage of it. With a closet full of clothes she knew she wouldn't be packing up to take to college, she decided to get an early start on decluttering. Preferably the items she could no longer fit but had attachment issues letting go of.

"Something else like what?" Nyree faced her.

"I don't know. You tell me."

The friends held a staring contest for all of five seconds before laughing.

"I don't think that's it. I don't even do it enough to be gaining anything."

It being sex. She and Coop had only messed around a few times since prom, but it wasn't something Nyree could see herself doing all the time. As good as her cousins and other associates made it seem, Nyree didn't see what the hype was all about. She definitely didn't see how her cousins claimed to be getting thick from sex.

"Maybe the jeans are just too small. You can get a ycast infcction likc that."

"Ew, no." She grimaced, unbuttoning them and sliding them off her legs. "I will not be walking around with one if I can prevent it."

"How much are you taking with you anyway?"

"I don't know yet. That's why I wanna go through some now. I'ma get some new stuff too, but I honestly have enough clothes. You can have whatever I don't keep if you want it."

Loriana shrugged. "That's cool."

"Nyree!" Nakita shouted from the bottom of the steps.

"Yes!"

"You been smoking in my house again? Don't make me beat you."

Her eyes widened before she and Loriana snickered. She'd gotten high in the basement like she always did but didn't have any more odor eliminator. Nakita wasn't supposed to be back home for another hour, so she thought that was plenty of time to air the basement out. Clearly, she was wrong.

"I wasn't!" she shouted, hoping she didn't come up the steps to confront her. Nyree's eyes were bloodshot red, and she had a gang of snacks sitting on her dresser.

"I thought she was going to get her hair done?" Loriana whispered as if she could hear them.

"I did too. She'll be fine." She waved her off and popped an Oreo in her mouth. "I see you got your toes done."

Examining her peach-colored toes, Loriana wiggled them and grinned. Projex had picked the color out for her when they went to get a pedicure last week. After being in the studio all night, he went to the crib to shower and take a nap before calling her and telling her to get dressed and be ready in thirty minutes. Giddy, not knowing what he had planned, Loriana did as he asked.

When he picked her up, he had a pack of her favorite candy—peanut M&M's in the seat. Instead of a song he'd written, the instrumental to a beat he had produced was floating from his speakers. He was playing around on his laptop at first, faking like he knew what he was doing, but it came out better than he thought. When Laurent and a rapper named, Ayo, approved and immediately began to freestyle over it, he knew he'd just tapped into something special.

After taking his boo to breakfast at *Grandma's Kitchen*, a Black family-owned restaurant that served the best cinnamon rolls in the city, they slid by Moo's shop for a self-care day. Projex knew she was stressed, and a day out of the house to keep her mind off what she couldn't control was his remedy. He was stressed and needed it too.

"Yeah. My nails too," she replied, looking at her

coffin-shaped gel nails. They were the same color as her toes. "Me and Projex went the other day."

"That shit is so cute. What nigga you know get his toes done?"

"Mine." She laughed.

"Okaaay! I heard that. I need to get me a nigga who spoils me, shoot."

"I thought you and Coop were on good terms."

Sucking her teeth, Nyree rolled her eyes. "I mean, we cool. I'm just not trying to get *too* serious with him because I'm leaving for school. I'm just having fun for now 'cause I know if we stay in a relationship, he's either gon' cheat on me, or I'ma cheat on him."

"Why would you think that? He seems faithful."

"They all do until you're not around. I could be wrong, though. I know one thing; them college niggas are top tier fine, and I don't trust myself. So, I'd rather just be single."

Loriana's head cocked some to the side. "Makes sense. Have you broken up with him?"

"No. The man's birthday is coming up, and that'd be so wrong."

"No, it wouldn't. Do it now, so you won't have to buy a gift."

Nyree cracked up. "You shol' right. Let me get my fake cry together."

"I can't deal with you." Loriana laughed just as her phone rang.

The name on her screen made her top lip curl. "What is she calling me for?"

"Who?" Nyree swiveled around and asked.

"Akira. I haven't talked to her in who knows how long."

Nyree rushed to the side of the bed. "Answer it and put her on speaker."

"I don't wanna talk to her." Loriana was frowning.

"So, what. See what she's calling for before she hangs up."

"Ugh," she groaned, answering the call right before Akira went to hang up. "Hello."

Akira hesitated. "Loriana?"

"Uh, yeah. What's up?"

"Hey. I was just calling to check on you."

Nyree sucked her teeth. She hadn't been calling, and now all of a sudden, she wanted to "check on her." Something was up, and she knew it. A bitch like Akira only wanted to keep tabs on whoever she could, liking that she still had access to them. Loriana was about to end all of that real quick.

"You know we aren't friends, right? I'm not sure why you're calling me."

"I know, and that's my fault. I should've never done you how I did," she spoke in a regretful tone.

Nyree's hands flew in the air as she spat, "This bitch."

"Yeah. But, what's up, though?"

"I was just calling to see when you were going away to school. I'm pregnant and wanted you to be here for my baby shower."

Nyree busted out laughing while Loriana's face held the same expression.

"Why would I come to your baby shower, Akira? Like, I don't know what's not clicking, but we aren't cool. How you expect me to come to something for you when you haven't even been there for me? Not like I want or expect you too but come on now."

Trauma was making Loriana wiser. She no longer gave people the benefit of the doubt just because anymore. That didn't matter when it came to her healing. Akira trying to finagle her way back into her life because she was pregnant meant nothing to her. Because she had no one else, not a friend like Loriana, Akira figured she'd try to work things out between them. All that was left of their friendship was ashes from the bridge she'd burned. Loriana wasn't about to send her a damn boat so she could cross her again. Akira was liable to drown her this time.

"I did try," she plead. "You told me not to reach out to you."

"Because you let me get jumped!" Loriana spat angrily.

She wasn't even mad that Akira had pursued Keith. She wasn't falling out and tripping with her over no dick. It was deeper than that.

"What kind of friend does that? That's fake as hell, and you not the type of person I want in my life anymore. It's really that simple. What, I'm just supposed to forgive you because you're having a baby?"

"No. I mean, I thought we could sit down and talk things out. I don't have many friends, and my mama talking about putting me out in a few months. Tre is acting like—"

Loriana cut her off. "I don't care. I really *do not* give a fuck what you're going through. I *just* lost my mother, and you're sitting on this phone talking about you! Girl, fuck you and that baby."

Nyree's eyes widened. "Damn."

"That was wrong, Loriana, and you know it. My baby didn't do anything to you."

"Girl, I don't care. You were wrong. The way you

got that baby, whoever it's by, was wrong. So, what? We're just two wrong people. I'm done with this conversation. We aren't friends, never should've been, and let's keep it that way."

When Loriana hung up, Nyree stared at her in disbelief with a pleased smirk on her face. "Now, that's how you clear a bitch. She's really pregnant. Wow. That's wild."

"No it's not. That's right up her alley."

"I wonder who the daddy is."

"I don't. Ny, I'm not sure what's happening with me, but I seriously have no energy to focus on anyone else. Like, I care about the people close to me, of course, but anything else doesn't matter. Is that wrong?"

Nyree's head shook from side to side. "Un, un. Not at all. It's a good thing, honestly. You gotta focus on you, boo. Everyone else's issues aren't yours. Especially right now. Don't ever feel bad for looking out for you 'cause at the end of the day, it's your happiness that matters. You aren't responsible for theirs and anyone who thinks differently, fuck em'. You don't need them type of people near you."

Loriana released a heavy sigh, taking in her heart-felt words. One thing she could count on Nyree to do was make her laugh and keep shit all the way one hundred with her. Loriana didn't owe anyone a damn thing. Not even a stick of gum. She surely wasn't obligated to accept or listen to Akira's watered-down midlife crisis story. She could keep that shit to herself.

"You're always right and get me together. That's why I love you."

"I love you more, friend. That's what I'm here for. Now, help me figure out how to break up with Coop."

Loriana's head fell back into the plush headboard as she laughed. "No. You can't do it today. I thought y'all were going to the movies later on?"

"Fuck. That is right. I could do it afterward, though. Call Projex and see if he wanna go. We can double-date and if he starts acting crazy, have him knock that nigga out."

The serious expression on her face had Loriana giggling. "My man is only knocking niggas out for me."

"Yeah, yeah. Call the man and see 'fore I say forget it and send Coop a text."

Not wanting her to do that and end things badly, Loriana went to her call log and tapped Projex's name. While she did that, Nyree hopped on Facebook to see what everyone was on for the night. When he didn't answer, Loriana sent him a text.

Lori: *Hey. You busy later on tonight?*

"He didn't answer," she told Nyree.

"Okay. We'll wait until he calls back. This girl stay arguing with somebody on here," she commented about this girl she knew from around the way Facebook status. Nosily, she read through the comments to see what was going on. No matter if she knew them or not, Nyree was gone get to the bottom of some drama on Facebook. It was always something messy going on, and she loved it. When ten minutes went by, and Projex hadn't called back, Loriana hit his line again.

"I wonder why he's not answering," she mumbled.

That was unlike him, especially during the middle of the day. It wasn't just that he hadn't answered; he hadn't replied to her text either. A slight panic rose in her chest as she willed herself to calm down. Just when she went to text him again, Nyree spoke.

"Oh. I know why he's probably not answering."

Loriana's head snapped her way. "Why not?"

"They're celebrating Chevy's birthday. Everybody down at SouthPark, it looks like."

Hovering over the phone screen with her, Loriana watched as her thumb swiped upward on an array of pictures Chevy's cousin was posting. She didn't see Projex in any of them yet, but she knew he was there.

"Ooh, he brought the niggas out today. Look at Juice, fine ass."

"Who is he?"

"He SAG. My big cousin, Wayla, used to fuck with his daddy."

Loriana frowned. "His daddy? How old is Wayla, again?"

"Girl, she in her thirties. Everybody ain't Akira."

They chuckled as Nyree came to the last picture. Projex was posted up with a little girl in his arms as she clung to his neck with a huge smile on her face. His muscles were on display thanks to the wife-beater he was rocking. The single braids in his head were covered by a blue KC fitted hat flipped to the back.

"We should pull up over there," Nyree suggested.

"We weren't invited."

"So, what. SouthPark is a public place. Plus, no one is really ever invited. You just show up."

Loriana scratched her scalp. "I don't know, Ny. Maybe we should just chill."

"No. I'm tired of chilling. It feels so good outside, too. Your cousin probably already out there."

Of course, she was. Mhyale didn't miss a function if she didn't have to. Having grown up in South Ave all her life, Mhyale knew almost everybody from there. They were one big family, and Chevy's death, though not the first of SAG, was felt. So, coming out to show love for his born day was a no-brainer. Nyree wanted to be right where everyone was.

"Fine. I'ma text her and see. Your mama gone let you drive her car?"

"I'ma ask and see. I can't wait until I get my own."

Loriana couldn't either. She didn't bother to drive her mama's, so her grandpa stored it in his backyard until she was ready to do something with it. While Nyree rummaged through the gang of clothes she already had out, Loriana pondered on what she was about to put on. Not thinking they'd be getting out of the house, she was simply dressed in a white cotton dress that came to her ankles.

"That's what you wearing?" she asked Nyree, who laid out some cheetah print biker shorts and a white bandeau top.

"Yeah. You wanna change? Your dress is perfect for the park and your booty sitting all up. Hips poking out," she hyped her up. Loriana smirked.

"I guess, I won't now. Let me do something to my hair," she said, climbing out the bed.

While Loriana had just the perfect amount of ass and wide hips, Nyree, on the other hand, wasn't packing much. She was slim with a little booty, had a beautiful toffee brown complexion, stood about five-seven, and always rocked her hair in different styles. Right now, it was in a flowy short bob that reached just below her earlobes. Next week, she'd probably have box braids. Nyree liked to switch it up like that.

Once she was dressed, she looked on as Loriana stood in the bathroom mirror, contemplating on how she'd wear her hair. It was hot out, but she didn't want to wear it in her signature bun. Undoing the style, she ruffled her hair, flipped it back and forth a few times, and sighed.

"Part it down the middle. It looks cute that way," Nyree suggested.

Grabbing a rattail comb, she parted her hair, making sure it was straight, then applied some Eco Style gel. Putting on some gloss, she rubbed her lips together.

"I'm good?"

"You fine, girl," Nyree said, making her snicker. "Let's go 'fore my mama try to dip out again."

Downstairs, Nakita was in the kitchen fixing her a plate of food. She'd just gotten her hair done and being at the beauty salon all day had her starving.

"Ma, can I see your car?"

She turned away from the stove with her phone pressed against her ear. "You just knew I'd say yes, huh? Girl, yeah. Nyree asking to see my car but already dressed. I should tell her no."

Behind her back, Nyree rolled her eyes. "You not even going nowhere else today."

"You don't know that. I ain't get my hair done to sit in the house, Nyree. I got a life too. I thought y'all were chilling for the night anyway. I was gonna order some pizza and wings."

"We are. It's a birthday party at SouthPark, though."

"SouthPark? Oh, hell nah. It's for little Chevy's birthday?"

Nyree sighed. "Yes. How you know?"

"That's where my man is at. I should get dressed and ride y'all down there to meet him."

"Oh, my gosh," Nyree groaned.

Taking their bickering in, Loriana felt herself getting in her feelings. These were moments she and Linette would never be able to share again.

"Oh my gosh, my ass. Who y'all know down there?"

"It's a lot of people we know down there. Mhy there. She'll make sure we good."

"Mm. I guess, Nyree. It's the summer, and these niggas be out here doing the most. Especially at the park. I don't know why everybody wanna have gatherings there. Mhm. She lucky I don't ride with them," she said, talking to whoever she was on the phone with.

"So… that's a yes?"

"Yes, child. You better text me when y'all get there and when y'all leaving."

Nyree grinned, snatching her keys up from the table. "I will. Thank you. Love you!"

"I love y'all too. Lori, girl. What you gon' do with all this pretty hair?" Nakita asked, following them to the front door.

"I don't know. Can you save me some of what you were cooking?"

Nakita smiled. "I sure can. You know if I don't do nothing, I'ma feed y'all."

"And get on our nerves," Nyree mumbled, walking to the driver's side of the Chevy Malibu.

"What was that?" Nakita asked. "Don't get hurt."

"I was playing, Mama. See you later. You better go inside 'fore Mr. Henry from next door come out and start flirting with you."

They all laughed. Mr. Henry was an old man who stayed pulling younger women, but Nakita wasn't going.

"His old ass." She chuckled. "Let me get in here. Girl, yeah, he be trying to put his game down."

Nakita's voice carried into the house as the screen door closed behind her. Loriana climbed in the passenger with her purse in her lap and buckled her seatbelt. For some reason, she felt weird about popping up on Projex without letting him know first. It felt even weirder because he'd yet to call or text back. Either way, she had tried to reach him.

"Alright." Nyree clapped, doing a jig in her seat. "To a safe, fun night with no drama."

Would the night be fun? Yes. Would it be safe and filled with no drama? Probably not, but they were hoping for the best.

Don't hop in my ride, bitch, if you don't smoke
They be like is you gon' let me drive yo' Escalade? No
These hoes ain't never been around no real money
I'ma superstar bitch, your boyfriend a crash dummy

The classic *I'mma Superstar* by Messy Marv bumped loudly from a tan old school Cadillac Eldorado with fifteen-inch silver rims as Projex walked by it. He tossed his head upward at the owner and kept it moving. High and a bit sluggish from the liquor he'd been sipping all day, his head bobbed to the beat before his ears were graced with another song coming from the heavily tinted Tahoe he made his way to.

SouthPark was packed. Chevy's family and friends had shown up and out for his birthday, though he wasn't there to celebrate it. He would've been twenty-two this year, and it was tearing Projex up that he had to bring it in without him. To ease the pain, he'd been consuming substances that had him moving in slow motion. He wasn't tripping about their enemies sliding through and being off his square. He had a gang full of rowdy niggas that'd pull some triggers for him and get ghost. He was still playing it safe today with his Glock 17 on his hip just in case he had to take it there.

"My phone ring?" he asked the girl sitting in the passenger seat.

"Mhm. Here," she said, handing it to him.

When he saw the missed calls and texts from Loriana, he sucked his teeth. "Why you ain't answer? She gon' think I was ignoring her ass."

"You the one said you were coming right back. I just got in here. Yo' girlfriend gone make you be in trouble, huh? That's cute."

Projex smirked and mushed her head. "Shut up. You supposed to be my best friend and don't even got a niggas back."

"Boy, whatever," Yari replied, not paying him no mind. She didn't have time to be answering his phone and arguing with his girl about why she had answered. When he called her back, Loriana and Nyree were already pulling into the park with all eyes on her mama's car.

"It's so many people out here. Where are we going to park?" Loriana questioned.

Taking in her surroundings, her eyes roamed the grass-filled area where there seemed to be over one hundred people. Cars were parked in the grass, going up and down both sides of the street and even on the hill up the next block. They'd definitely came out to show love.

"That truck is moving from under that tree right there," Nyree told her, driving onto the grass.

As soon as she parked, Loriana's phone rang with a call from Projex. She wanted to be annoyed but realized he may have been having a bad day today, considering what day it was. That still didn't mean he had to ignore her like she thought he was.

"Yeah."

Projex's head jerked back. "Yeah? The fuck you answering the phone like that for?

"Don't curse at me. You saw me call and text you."

"My phone was dead. I just saw yo' missed calls and shit when I came to get it off the charger. What's up? What you doing?"

"At SouthPark trying to find you."

His eyes immediately began to scan the vicinity for her. "You doing pull up's now?" He chuckled, making her do the same.

"Yeah. I guess so. We just got here. It's crowded like crazy."

"I know. I'm by this yellow Tahoe near the swings. What you got on?"

Her eyes scanned the park for the distinctive colored truck. "A white dress."

"Yo, Loriana. What's up!" a guy's voice shouted from the side of her.

"Man, who you know out here?" Projex was now walking away from the truck in search of her.

"Nobody. This your cousin."

Kordell walked up on her with a grin. "What's good. You looking for your boy?"

She nodded her head. "Yeah. He said he's by a yellow truck."

"Come on. He over here."

Loriana didn't even tell him she was hanging up, figuring she'd see him in a few seconds. As they made their way across the park, curious eyes of those who didn't know them followed them. Kids were running around playing while four grills were going. The enticing smell of barbecue made Loriana want a plate. When they made it to Projex, who was standing in the middle of the street, he grinned lazily and licked his lips. The niggas standing around watched as they walked by, wondering who this girl with the tight body, big hair, rocking glasses was. They wanted to know who Nyree was too.

"Damn," Projex murmured, wrapping an arm around her shoulder and pulling her into him. "You look good as fuck, ma."

Kissing her lips, he raunchily slid his tongue inside her mouth while gripping a handful of her booty. Tasting every bit of the liquor he'd been drinking, Loriana was caught off guard. She knew he didn't mind a bit of PDA, but in front of all these people? When her knees buckled, she pulled away and looked up into his dazed eyes. His bushy eyebrows were relaxed and lips soft.

That juicy bottom lip of his was her favorite. The gold fronts in his mouth made her want to lick all over them. She'd never seen him wear them before. Projex was so fine to her, and his intense gaze caused Loriana's skin to flush.

"You okay?" she asked.

His kiss seemed urgent. Needy, as if he missed her, and he did.

"Yeah. You?" Her head bobbed. Projex smooched her lips again. "Good. I like your chain."

Grinning, Loriana ran her hand over his gift to her. "Thank you. It's packed out here."

"Hell yeah. What's up, Nyree?"

"Hey," she spoke back.

Projex's eyes did another appreciative sweep over her body. "You hungry?"

"A little. You been drinking all day?"

He looked inside the almost empty cup in his hand and smirked. "Yeah. Come over here, so I can introduce you to some people."

Loriana's head shook from side to side. "You don't have to do all of that."

"Yeah, I do. What, you ain't tryna meet my folks nem'?"

"I wasn't planning on it."

He drank the rest of whatever was in his cup. "I wasn't plannin' on you being here, but you are. So, come on. Don't be tryna act shy. You got this dress on showing off your body and shit." He hugged her waist and whispered against her neck. "And you smell good."

"You do too," she said, inhaling him. Even though he'd been outside, his musky scent still intoxicated her. It was a combination of weed and him. She loved it.

"Man, you niggas too lovey-dovey for me," Kordell chimed.

Projex's head lifted. "Nigga, mind ya' business. Come on. Nyree, who you know out here?"

"A few people."

"You know where my cousin at?" Loriana asked.

"Who? Mhyale? She was around here somewhere. I saw her like fifteen minutes ago."

"Yo, Projex. You got that on you?" someone yelled out as they walked by.

"Yeah! Come see me."

Curious, Loriana asked, "Got what?"

"There you go being nosy. Acting like that nigga, Kordell."

"No. I'm trying to keep you out of trouble. That's what I'm doing. I won't ask anything else."

"Yo," he stressed, stopping their walk. "Chill out, ma. I was playing with you."

"Well, laugh next time then."

Projex just blinked at her. He didn't know if he was tripping, but it sounded like she had an attitude, and he wasn't feeling that.

"Let's make you a plate first. Yo' ass too grumpy," he told her, now headed toward the two long wooden tables where aluminum pans sat over burners.

Behind them, Nyree snickered. Loriana was a totally different person when she hadn't eaten. While she told him she was only a little bit hungry, clearly her appetite had increased. When they made it to the table of food, they sanitized their hands and picked up paper plates. There was so much to choose from, Nyree grabbed two. She hated when certain foods of hers touched.

"Why I feel like everyone is staring at us?" she whispered to Loriana, who was scooping some baked macaroni and cheese onto her plate.

"Probably because they are."

Granted, the people who were staring didn't know every single person from the neighborhood they grew up in or know the connection Loriana and Nyree had to Chevy. The ones staring knew they didn't know him personally and was wondering why Projex was chauffeuring them around.

"Who are they?" one of Chevy's cousins, Keisha, asked.

"Projex's girlfriend and her friend," Yari answered.

She'd walked over from the truck a few minutes ago, feeling some type of way. Even though she knew who Loriana was through Projex, he still could've introduced them.

"Girlfriend? When the hell my little boo get a girlfriend?" she asked as they chuckled. "Y'all know if he was older, I'd tie him down."

"You'd tie anything down, so I believe you," her friend said.

"Girl, whatever. She's pretty, though. Looks a little young to me."

Yari nodded her head. "Mhm. That's what I said. I think she just graduated high school."

"Lemme call him over here and see. Projex, come here!" Keisha yelled.

Hearing his name being yelled yet again, his head swiveled. Seeing Keisha wave, he shook his head, already knowing she was about to try and get in his business. He looked toward Loriana and Nyree, who were finishing up fixing their plates, before walking over to the table of women.

"I know he doesn't think we're about to walk over there," Nyree sassed.

"I'm not. Let's go find us somewhere to sit."

Loriana wasn't about to stand in the grass and eat. Thankfully, on the slab of concrete, there were a few empty spots. Walking over, Loriana laid her jean jacket across the bench so nothing would get on her dress. Nyree sat beside her after grabbing them drinks out of the coolers on the other side of the table.

"What's up, Keisha?" Projex asked.

She smirked, admiring his muscular physique. "You tell me. Why you didn't bring your girlfriend over here to meet us?"

"Why would I do that?" he asked plainly with a blank expression.

Their table laughed, but he didn't find anything humorous.

"Damn. We can't meet her? What she too young or something?"

"Nah. Y'all too messy. She don't need to be getting any ideas from none of y'all."

Yari smacked her lips. "Boy. You acting like she an angel or something."

"She is."

The glimmer in his eyes when he said that didn't go unnoticed. When he smirked, Yari shook her head.

"You love her?"

"Man. Y'all not about to interrogate me like y'all the mothafuckin' feds."

"Niggas always think when someone asks them a few questions that they the feds," Keisha said in jest.

They all laughed, including Projex, because that was the truth. There was a two to three limit set of questions you could ask a Black man from the hood before he started looking at you like you were wired up. It didn't matter if they were moving around illegally or not.

"Shit, you never know. I'ma fuck with y'all in a minute, though."

Tugging upward on his slightly sagging shorts, Projex headed to where Loriana was sitting. She was smashing her plate of food, making him smirk as he took a seat on top of the table next to her, facing the street.

"You good now?" he asked her.

Loriana nodded with her mouth full. When she finished chewing, she said, "This food is so good."

"No, for real. Fire as fuck. I'ma make me a to-go plate," Nyree added.

"Jasmine, Chevy's aunt, cooked most of it."

"Is that who you were gonna introduce me to?" Loriana questioned.

"Yeah, and a few of my niggas that you ain't met yet."

She nodded her head. While Projex had a gang of

family members, he only looked out for those who looked out for him, Joi, and Joseline. Jasmine was one of those people. When Chevy was alive, she never hesitated to treat Projex like he was her blood nephew. On some nights when Joseline worked late, Joi would stay over at her house and chill. Them taking Chevy from her was deeper than anyone knew. He was the son she hadn't birthed but took care of as such.

While everyone had come out to help turn his birthday into one he knew Chevy would've loved, Projex knew some people were just there to be seen. Chevy had looked out way too many times for people to not have even called and checked in on Jasmine or his siblings. When he died, social media was flooded with posts of him, but hardly anyone was making a peep now—everyone except Projex.

He didn't have to show or post what he did for his nigga and never would. Jasmine and his sibling's pockets were getting lined with money from him every other week just because had Chevy been alive, they wouldn't have wanted for anything. Projex knew Chevy would've done the same had their situations been reversed. It was a loyalty thing with Projex. Always would be.

While he watched Loriana eat, the presence of

someone stepping up and in between his legs almost caught him off guard.

"Aye, what you on," he said, pushing the girl out of his space. Loriana turned her body to see who he was talking to.

"Dang. I can't say hi."

"Yeah, but you don't gotta be all up on a nigga. What's up?"

The way she was eyeing him, Projex knew what was on her mind, and he was hoping she didn't start yapping off at the mouth. From the glossy texture of her eyes, he knew she was a bit buzzed. She licked her lips and eyed between his legs.

"You know what's up. I go back to school tomorrow, and I'm trying to see you before then."

"See you for what?" Loriana asked Projex, giving him an evil glare. Nyree was staring the chick down and was on whatever type of time Loriana was.

"Sweetie, was I talking to you?"

Loriana's head snapped her way. "Was I talking to you is the real question. I was addressing my man, but since you want to feel important, how can we help you?"

Projex grinned, feeling his dick harden from how she just bossed up. "Yo, Brittany. Watch out. She wasn't talking to you, so ain't no need to speak to her. Ever."

"Oh." Brittany chuckled. "I see what this is now. Got you. Remember this conversation, too, Bryshon."

Bryshon? Loriana thought to herself. She never heard anyone call him that except his mama and grandma. When Brittany smirked mischievously before walking away, Loriana almost stood to ask what she meant by that and who she was to him. Loriana pushed her plate away from her. Her appetite was ruined.

With each passing day, she was learning more and more about Projex. Seeing him in his element with his people and how they showed him love intrigued her. What made her nostrils flare and temples throb were the girls always vying for his attention. It made her blood boil, especially now that her heart was involved. She didn't even want a bitch to breathe in his direction, let alone speak to him. She wanted them to act blind when they saw him.

"Who was she?" Loriana asked, wasting no time.

"Nobody important."

She scoffed. "Yeah, okay. Let me see where Mhy is," she mumbled.

"For what? Y'all ain't about to be out here fighting."

Her mean mug took him aback. "Who said anything about fighting? Especially behind that. It's clear you have this secret life or whatever, so I'ma just play the background."

"Man. What is you talkin' about? You asked me who she was, and I said nobody. The fuck you want me to say?"

Loriana stood from her seat. "Nothing. You don't have to say anything else to me while we're here."

"You got me fucked up," he grumbled, hopping down from the table to follow her.

Frustration clouded his vision as niggas gawked at Loriana. She was being difficult for no reason, and Projex didn't know why. Explaining who Brittany was, was irrelevant. It didn't matter if it was irrelevant to him; it was the principle for Loriana.

As she made her way to one of the many trash cans, Mhy spotted her and was walking over. Dressed like she'd been waiting for the sun to pop out all year, Mhy rocked a short, black dress that scrunched on the sides with a black pair of high-top Hidden Heart Chuck Taylors. She was comfortable, cute, and giving the crowd whiplash as her thick thighs and ass jiggled.

"There you are. What's wrong with you?" she asked, noticing the annoyed look on Loriana's face.

"Him." She tossed her thumb over her shoulder at Projex.

"Now you snitching. It ain't even that serious, Loriana."

She tossed her plate in the trash and shrugged. "Okay."

"Huh. Drink one of these," Mhy said, handing her a drink pouch full of some type of green drink. "It'll relax those nerves."

"Shit, I need one too. She about to get on mine."

"Okay, Bryshon. Stop talking to me."

His jaw clenched, and his eyes darkened. "I'm not about to do this with you today. Quit playing and drop yo' lil attitude."

"Yet here you are *still* doing this with me. Just leave me alone. I'm good."

He reached out to grab her, and Mhyale blocked his hand. "Aht. None of that. You can talk without using your hands, or you got a problem?" Her head cocked to the side.

"Man, y'all really trying me. Ain't nobody putting they hands on her. I'm just trying to get her to come here and stop trying to show out."

Loriana punctured the unopened hole in her pouch with the straw and took a sip. "Ooh. This is good. Calming my nerves all the way down."

Projex chuckled. "Yeah. You really on some bull-shit right now. I'ma walk-off 'fore I embarrass both of us."

"You already did, so bye."

He stared at her like she had two heads sprouting from her body. This Loriana was different and way more outspoken and feistier like the one he'd ran into at *Freddie's* that day. Projex didn't know if she was tripping on him because of the heat or because she just wanted to argue. Either way, he wasn't about to feed into her shenanigans. If she wanted to have an attitude, he was going to let her. When he walked off, headed back to the truck he'd been posted by, Loriana rolled her eyes.

"This relationship thing is for the birds," she complained.

"Trust me, I know. I didn't know you was coming out here. You could've rode with me."

"I didn't either. Nyree dragged me out of the house, and I'm glad. It's like I get to see him in a different light every day. If all of these girls on him like this in public, I can only imagine what his phone looks like."

Mhyale shook her head. "Don't even think like that. You gon' drive yourself nuts. Projex is young and bossed up. It's inevitable for girls not to be on him to some extent. Just cause he's approached doesn't mean he's cheating or doing you foul behind your back."

He's doing it in my face, she thought. It wasn't him holding a conversation with Brittany that pissed her off; it was him not explaining who she was. Let a nigga had walked up to her and done the same thing, she was sure Projex would've knocked him out.

"I know. It just frustrates me how different our worlds are sometimes. I be trying to get in his head, but he only tells me things on a need-to-know basis. I don't like that."

Mhyale chuckled. "That's just how men like Projex are. They love hard but don't trust easily. Not saying he doesn't trust you, but some things just aren't meant for you to know, and it's better that way."

Loriana thought differently. "If you say so. Who are you out here with?"

"My homegirl, Zoe."

"You and your millions of friends." Loriana chuckled as Nyree walked over to them.

"I don't have a bunch of friends, honestly. I'm cool with a few, associates with others, but only rock for real with a handful."

As Mhyale got older, she realized each of her

friends served a different purpose in her life, as she did in theirs. Some only called to party, one texted her scriptures every other morning, while others called to get money and talk business. One of her older friends was married and had kids. Her circle was well balanced, and she liked it that way.

"Nyree is my only one."

"Only what?" Nyree questioned.

"My only friend. You're my sister for real."

"That's cool too. You don't have to have a bunch of friends. Just solid ones. Not like that hoe Akira, though. I heard she was pregnant," Mhyale said.

"Mhm. We did too."

Loriana kept her reply simple. She didn't like discussing folks she didn't care for. What they had going on was no concern of hers. Especially not now.

"I'm glad you got out of the house. Got your curves and shit all out. Let me find out you like wearing less and goin' out more."

Snickering, Loriana waved her off. "Will you stop? I can't stand you."

"I'm just saying. Let's go over here right quick. I see some of Naaz's people."

"Ooh. There go Juice," Nyree whispered closely to Loriana's ear.

"Is that the guy you showed me earlier?"

"Mhm. Fine ass. I bet I leave here with his number."

Loriana smirked and shook her head while Mhyale encouraged her. "If you don't, you owe us five dollars."

"That's a bet. If I do, y'all owe me ten apiece."

Loriana frowned. "Un, un. How I get in this? That's between y'all."

"Nope. Just be ready to pay up."

Nyree was all down for a bet, especially one she knew she was going to win. She hated losing at anything, so the pressure was on and about to be applied. Mhyale stepped to the group of men first, and they all showed her love with hugs and jokes about her being ducked off.

"Yo' ass wanna pop out now that Naaz back. You ain't low," Neeko, Naaz's brother, joked.

"Right. Her ass ain't ever been outside this much," Juice added. Nyree was staring him down.

"Y'all swear. I been outside. Stop playing with me like Naaz running something."

Neeko smirked. "You got it, sis. I ain't even gone do you like that in front of yo' peoples. What's up, ladies."

"Hey."

"What's up."

Loriana and Nyree spoke in that order. Juice inhaled the blunt deeply and looked Nyree in the face. "Who you?"

"Nyree. Who are you?"

"Shit, you know exactly who I am the way you staring."

"Boy," she waved him off, "wasn't nobody staring at you."

"Boy?" Juice ashed his blunt. "I ain't been a boy in a long time, baby."

Nyree's nipples hardened, and she knew they could probably be seen thanks to her not wearing a bra. Juice was just the type of fine Nyree loved. His cinnamon-colored six-foot frame, clean-cut fade with deep waves, and light brown eyes looked even better in person. She'd seen him out and about a few times but hadn't said anything to him, just observed the way he moved.

"So, what are you then?"

His niggas laughed at her questioning him.

"All man. Fuck with me and find out."

"Nah," Neeko spoke up. "I think Nyree and Neeko got a ring to it. What you think?"

Nyree watched with smug delight on her face. Unlike Loriana, who was just coming out of her shell, Nyree had always carried this confidence about her that made her attractive. It wasn't snobbish, but she knew she was the shit and went after anything she wanted.

"I mean, it's cool, but your man's really got the *Juice*," Nyree replied with a shrug, making them holler.

"A'ight, a'ight. I give you that." Neeko laughed.

Juice was even more intrigued about her now. "Like that, huh?"

"Straight like that."

While they became acquainted, Loriana's focus was on Projex. He was back standing by the yellow Tahoe with a different girl in his face. One Loriana was certain had been staring at her and Nyree while they were fixing their plates. Watching him laugh with another woman annoyed her in a way Loriana wasn't used to. Her skin grew warm thinking of all the things Projex could've been doing when he wasn't with her. *Why is he smiling all in her face?* she questioned, ready to see what the hell was so comical. She loved a good joke, too.

When they hugged a bit too long for her liking, she said fuck it. Having had enough of her back-and-forth contemplation, Loriana mustered up the courage to walk over to them.

"I'll be right back," she quickly told Mhyale since Nyree was wrapped up in a conversation with Juice.

Her flip-flops smacked the warm pavement as she made her way across the street. Her lithe but curvaceous body drew the attention from men posted up on their cars. Loriana paid them no mind. That was until one of them boldly grabbed her hand that swung with each stride.

"Gotdamn, baby. Let me holla at you for a minute."

She pulled her arm away from him. "I'm fine."

"Hell yeah, you are."

He creepily eyed her frame, putting himself more into her space. She immediately got a whiff of the cheap whiskey on his breath, and her stomach churned. He smelled like he'd drunk the entire bottle before polishing it off with a pack of Newport shorts.

"Let me get your number and take you out sometime," he said, trying to hold her hand.

"No. I'm okay. I'm in a relationship," she let him know, thinking that'd stop his advances. Something in men hearing that a woman had a man always prompted them to ask if she could have friends. Loriana wasn't aware of this.

"I am too, baby. You can't have friends or something?"

She gave a tight smile, walking away from him. "Something like that."

Across the street, there was no longer a smile on Projex's face. Pushing himself away from the hood of the truck, he marched in her direction. Loriana was off-limits. He knew some niggas didn't know that, but he was about to make that shit clearer than the lenses in her glasses. The guy let her walk off while still talking his shit.

"You bitches be acting like y'all so faithful," he said disrespectfully. "Probably don't even got a man."

Loriana's body jerked around to face him. "What? Don't disrespect me."

He shooed her away. "Gon' head, baby. I'm good on you."

"Aye, nigga," Projex voice thundered, walking up beside her. "What the fuck you just say to her?"

Loriana tried grabbing his hand, but he moved her to the side. She knew this wasn't going to end well and wanted to deescalate the situation. The crowd's eyes were already on the drama unfolding.

"He was just asking for my number."

Projex quickly looked at her and gritted his teeth. "Don't lie. Yo, Ceez. What you say to my girl?"

"Nothing, man. I was trying to get shorty's number. I ain't know she was yours."

"Yeah, but what the fuck you just say to her, though? What he call you?" Projex looked at Loriana again. Her eyes were pleading for him to let it go, but she knew better.

Loriana swallowed hard. "A bitch, but—"

BAM! BAM! BAM!

Projex blacked out, knocking Ceez into the group of people behind him. Even though they'd both been drinking, Projex had the upper hand. Ceez was no match to Projex when it came to disrespecting. Blows to his face dropped Ceez to the ground, where Projex proceeded to whoop his ass. Having already been annoyed at Loriana for her attitude, he was taking his anger out on the man.

"Yo, P. Come on, cuz. Get off that nigga," Kordell insisted.

Paralyzed, Loriana stood with reverence flowing through her veins. Strangely, whenever he turned his gangster up around her, not letting any man come at her crazy, she was turned on. She didn't understand it, especially with a man now lying bloodily on the concrete.

Projex didn't stop until he was ready to. If a nigga touched him, he was pulling his gun out. Heavily, his chest heaved as he stood over Ceez with a menacing glare and wrath in his eyes.

"Damn, Ceez. Did you even pinch the nigga?" Neeko asked jokingly, making people shake their heads and hold back laughter.

Ceez spit out a wad of blood. "Fuck you."

"What's going on?" Mhyale huffed as she and Nyree rushed over to Loriana.

"He called me out of my name, and that's what happened."

Nyree looked over at him and winced. His face was bruised badly, with both eyes already swelling. "Dang."

When Projex stormed by her, Loriana about lost her shit. Not wanting to cause another scene, she didn't know what to do other than mosey behind him to the truck he was standing at.

"Now, why you go and beat that man like that?" Yari asked with a chuckle.

"These niggas gon' learn to stop disrespectin' me. On God. Hand me some napkins."

Behind him, Loriana sucked her teeth. "Really? You're going to seriously walk by me after what just went down?"

He wiped the blood off his knuckles. "L-Boogie. I ain't in the mood right now."

"What?" Her heart beat wildly in her chest. "You

were just in the mood to fight, but now you don't want to talk?"

"Nah. I don't. I thought you told me not to say anything else to you?"

She scoffed. "You know what? Okay. Fine. I should've given him my number. At least he wanted to show your girlfriend some attention."

She tried walking away, but Projex snatched her back to him. "Don't make me beat that niggas ass again. Fuck you thought you were going?"

His mean expression didn't scare her. "I'm about to go give him my number since you want to act funny. You might as well be single, then."

"Now, you talking stupid."

She tried jerking away from him. "Now, I'm stupid? Let me go."

When Yari chuckled at their antics, Loriana's eyes shot laser beams her way. "And who the fuck are you?"

"Whoa, little mama. No need for the hostility. I'm Yari."

"Okay," Loriana replied in a sarcastic tone. "Who are you to *him*? Another nobody like the first girl?"

Projex couldn't help but chuckle. "You crazy, man. Chill out. This my best friend."

Loriana had never heard of her, but she wouldn't

count her title in his life out yet. She too had a male best friend once before, so she got it.

"What girl she talking about?" Yari asked, having an idea, but you never knew with Projex. All these hoes were nobodies to him.

"Brittany's ass."

"And you've yet to tell me who she is," Loriana reminded him.

"Whew, honey. Y'all got too much going on for me. Projex, I'll see you later. My ride here to get me."

When she went to hug him again, Loriana didn't bother to move out of the way. While she was making a fuss about him letting her go, she wasn't moving out of his face. She made Projex give Yari a side hug while shaking his head.

"Who picking you up? I know them?"

"Yeah. You know Sky from the club?"

He nodded. "Yeah. Be safe."

"You too. You got a wild one on your hands," Yari laughed, switching over to the pearl-colored Benz that just pulled up in front of them.

From the driver's seat, Sky waved at Projex who didn't acknowledge her greeting. Loriana took in Yari's outfit and wondered how she was comfortable in the cut-off booty shorts that seemed to be stuck in her ass. She didn't think it was that hot out here but to each his own.

"You got an entire fan club, I see," Loriana told him.

"I could say the same thing. Got me out here fighting niggas behind you."

"No one told you to do that."

He looked down at her, loving the way she always looked at him when she was upset. Loriana unnerved him. His hard exterior always softened in her presence with ease.

"And nobody gon' ever have to tell me to check a nigga behind disrespecting you. I don't know what you not understanding by that." He tapped her temple and loosened the hold he had on her. "Get in."

"Whose truck is this?"

"Bruh. Can you just do as I ask you? Please?" he urged, getting annoyed all over again.

Loriana crossed her arms over her chest. "No. I've been asking you questions all day, and you seem to have amnesia. I told you everything doesn't go your way. I don't know what you not understanding," she said, mocking him.

Projex didn't want to, but he smirked. "You really get on my nerves, man. Fuck. You wanna argue with me? Huh? Why you wanna do that? Have all these mothafuckas in our business again. Got yo' friend and cousin mugging me like they ready to beat my ass."

Her cheeks lifted. "Because you pissing me off."

"That liquor got you loose at the lips," he said, nixing her chin. "Don't make me throw you in here. I'm trying to be a gentleman and ask nicely, but I see you don't want that Projex. You want a nigga to snatch your lil' ass up out here."

Her eyes twinkled with lust, and she felt her pussy get wet. "I don't. I'll get in by myself."

Projex stepped to the side and smacked her booty as she climbed in. "You better have."

"Whatever. Mhy! Nyree!" she shouted, getting their attention. They came over to the passenger side as he started the truck.

"I can't deal with you two crazy mothafuckas. So, you leaving with him?" Mhyale asked, already knowing the answer.

"Yeah. Ny, tell Ms. Nakita I caught a ride home with Mhyale."

"Okay. I'ma leave too then. You got this man beating all on people."

Loriana looked his way as he rolled a blunt up in his lap. She licked her lips, ready to taste his.

"I didn't do anything. Did you get Juice's number?"

Nyree smirked. "Nope. Not yet. I don't want to seem too thirsty."

"But you are, though," Loriana said so plainly, they couldn't help but laugh.

"Girl, whatever. I ain't giving y'all no five dollars either. That nigga pushed up on me, so the bet still counts as a win."

"Child, boo. If you scared to get his number, just let us know," Mhyale said.

"Aye, man. Is y'all done gossiping?" Projex asked.

"Boy!" Nyree and Mhyale shouted while Loriana chuckled.

"I'll see y'all later," Loriana told them. "Wait. Ny, you want us to drive you to your car?"

"Yeah, that's cool."

She hopped in the back while Mhyale gave her cousin a hug, told her she loved her and to be safe. When they dropped Nyree off at her mama's car, Loriana saw Projex keep flexing his hand. It was swollen and stiff from the fight.

"You want me to drive?" she offered, and he nodded his head.

Hopping out of the driver's seat, he walked around to her side while she climbed over into his vacant spot. She felt so small sitting behind the wheel but loved it. While she adjusted the seat and mirrors, Projex sparked his blunt and leaned his seat back.

"Where are we going?"

"To hell if we don't pray."

She gasped, making him chuckle. "Don't say that."

"My grandma used to say that shit to us when we were younger. It's a joke, ma."

"I don't play like that. You'll be in hell by yourself."

"I pray. You pray for me too, so that's double protection."

A smile graced her face. "Triple. God got you, too. Probably more because I know your grandma and mama stay talking to Him about you."

"See. Now you doing too much," he spoke calmly.

"What! I'm just saying what I know is true. That's why you need to relax sometimes. Everything doesn't have to end violently. There are other ways to handle things."

"When it comes to you, no there's not."

"I'm not just talking about me, in life period. Situations can be talked out. Fighting, shooting, killing, and all of that just brings you unwanted enemies and demons."

While it was hard for Loriana to sleep at night, whenever Projex stayed over it helped some. The first night he spent the night, she was woken up out of her sleep by him. His body kept jumping as if he were having a nightmare. All she could do was cuddle closer and hug him tighter. Projex was facing some things only himself and the Lord could hash out, and she knew it.

She continued her speech. "Not just that, but broken families. Black men going to jail or being buried because they can't end things civilly. Everyone always wants to be the tougher person. They kill one of yours, you kill one of theirs, and it goes back and forth until what? Everyone dies or goes to jail, then what? All these broken families, kids without parents, and a community full of anger and hatred. It's a cycle we have to break. The system wasn't designed for us to make it, and we make it so easy for them to take advantage of us. I hate it."

Stumped but even more amazed at how she just schooled him, Projex's chest tightened. Hearing her speak on his and plenty of other men's lifestyles so passionately had him wondering if she could handle him completely. The glimpse he'd given her in the last four months was nothing compared to what was ahead. He hit his blunt, needing the heaviness surrounding them to ease up.

"I hear you, ma. It is a vicious cycle, but that's all niggas know sometimes."

She sucked her teeth. "No, it's not. So, you're telling me instead of punching ole boy, you couldn't have just talked to him about calling me out of my name?"

"Fuck no. That's different. You acting like the nigga took your seat, and I punched him for not moving. Nah, wait. That ain't a good example. Cause I would've punched his ass then too."

Loriana laughed. Projex was seriously too much. "I'm glad you take up for me."

"Always. You be making me act out of character. That shit crazy."

"That's on you. Why do you be acting like guys can't speak to me? Acting all mean and stuff when you don't get your way."

He pulled from his blunt and released the smoke slowly. "You really don't know why?"

"No. Tell me, so I can have a better understanding."

"Cause I love your ass. Why you think?"

Loriana's breath got caught in her chest. Tears of happiness pricked her eyes. "What?"

"You heard what I said, ma."

A rush of butterflies creeping from their cocoons and flapping their wings swarmed her belly. Leaning his way, Loriana whispered, "Say it again."

She needed to hear the words repeated. Projex didn't mind repeating himself for her. When the three words were spoken truly from the heart and not in a mundane manner, they were easier to accept as real. So many women had told him they loved him; they held no validity after a while. He'd spoken them to Loriana with his heart because she'd captured it without permission. That's why he moved how he did when it came to her. No one else had ever brought this side of him out and for this long.

"I." *Kiss*. "Love." *Kiss*. "You." *Kiss*.

Each word was spoken with a kiss to her lips because he knew she liked that corny shit. Loriana's bottom lip poked out at how open he was with her.

"Loving me makes you act crazy?"

"Yeah. Can you believe that?" he asked sarcastically, making her grin.

She smacked his arm. "Yes. I understand now. If you really love me, tell me who that girl is you claimed to be a nobody."

Projex shook his head, knowing she wasn't going to let up if he didn't tell her. "My ex."

"Hmm. Now was that so hard to let me know? You make things difficult for no reason."

"Wasn't no need to be worrying about her," he said with a shrug.

"Yeah, okay. Now, where are we going?"

Projex relit his blunt. "My grandma's. You remember how to get there?"

"Kind of. Help me if I get confused."

"I got you."

He meant that in more ways than one. When they finally pulled out of the park, Projex took in his city. He wasn't even tripping that Loriana hadn't told him she loved him back. He knew she would when she was ready to express her feelings. That was one thing she never held back from him, and it was the same reason why he'd said those three words. It was easy to tell her.

———

At his grandma's, they routinely entered the back door like they'd done before and made their way downstairs. Loriana yawned loudly, slipping her sandals off and scratching her scalp.

"I forgot to get me a to-go plate," she said,

walking over to the bed. Projex went to pee, and after washing his hands, he came to the door.

"Come get in the shower with me."

She turned around. "What? What if your grandma comes home?"

"Ma, you act like she don't know what we be doing down here. Come on."

Projex began to slip his tank top over his head and shorts from his ass as he turned around. Loriana's feet stayed planted until he called her name again. Scurrying, she met him in the bathroom.

"I don't want my hair to get wet," she told him while he adjusted the water.

"You want a shower cap?"

"Uh, yes. Does your granny have one?"

"Prolly. Go look upstairs."

Her eyes widened. "No. Go get one for me. I'm not going up there and going through her things."

Projex chuckled. "Scary ass. I'll be right back."

He jogged up the steps, searched a few drawers in his grandma's bathroom, and came right back down once he found one. Loriana was sitting on the toilet, anxiously waiting for his return. She'd never thought of showering with him, let alone any boy before. The act was so intimate.

"You still got this dress on, playing. I'ma get in

here without you," he told her, handing her the floral print shower cap.

Standing up, Loriana pulled her dress over her head. Longingly, she stared at Projex, wondering what was on his mind. Even though they'd had sex, Loriana was still somewhat shy about being naked in front of him. Projex didn't care as he slipped his briefs off and kicked them to the side. Her eyes roamed his tattooed body, loving every single detail of it. She learned what most of his tattoo's meant, when he got them, and why. Her favorite would always be the bold SAG tat etched across his lower stomach. It lead her eyes right to his third leg that was swinging, making her mouth water.

"You need help undressing?" he asked, and she nodded.

She shivered at his hands brushed across her frame. Attentively, in no rush for her to be naked, Projex kissed her soft skin. First, her neck, where she squirmed but tilted, giving him more access. The second kiss was on her chest as he unclasped her bra with one hand. That was a skill she didn't know he possessed. Thirdly, it was supposed to be her stomach, but his lips were wrapped around her nipple.

"Mmm," she moaned softly. His hands were now tugging her no-show panties down.

When he did make it to her stomach, Projex planted kisses over it before lowering his head to her already wet center. Making her lift her leg onto the toilet seat, he pulled her fat lips apart, rubbed the hood of her clitoris before pulling it back, and flickered his tongue over it. Loriana's stomach caved.

Projex loved eating her pussy. If he could, he'd never skip foreplay because he always wanted her in his mouth. While some men liked to get straight to the point, Projex relished in taking his time with Loriana. She was a quick learner, got super soaker wet, and was getting freakier each time they fucked. When she rolled her hips into his face, he spanked her ass before lifting up. Sloppily, they shared a kiss.

"Bend over," he commanded.

Legs shaking, she went to bend over the toilet seat, but he guided her to the sink. "Nah. Right here. Yeah. Arch your back just like that."

Loriana was in a lust-induced state. Staring at their reflections in the mirror, she bit her bottom lip as he slid inside her. Her mouth fell open at his intrusion, and his eyes closed. Slowly, he stroked her tight walls, reintroducing himself.

"Uhhh, baby," she whined, gripping the counter.

"Throw that ass back like I taught you."

She was trying to but couldn't keep up. Seeing her

struggle some, Projex slowed his movements and let her take over. Pushing him back some, Loriana put a deeper arch in her back and rode his dick all the way to the tip and down. Rotating her hips, she looked at him through the mirror and grinned. He was focused, watching her cream his dick. When she unintentionally contracted her muscles, his eyes shot to hers.

"Yeah?" he questioned with warning in his tone.

Loriana couldn't reply before he was slamming into her roughly. The kind of rough she was growing to enjoy. Projex was going deep, making her shout his name.

"Bryshon! Wait, wait!" she huffed, lying flat across the counter.

Projex lifted her right leg up and gripped her hair. "Yo pussy so fucking good. You know that?" He breathed against her ear, now rubbing her clit from beneath.

"Yes! Ooooh!"

He pulled her head back so she could see them in the mirror. "I can't hear you."

"Yes! Yes! Oh, shit." Her eyes fluttered.

Bending toward her, Projex sloppily tongue kissed her lips while long stroking her. The bathroom was so fogged up, Loriana could hardly breathe, let alone see. Gripping her waist, he hit curves in the pussy that had Loriana gasping for air. She felt like he was touching her soul, poking at it, telling her that he was all hers and no one else's. Fuck what the critics said.

"Oooh. You feel so good," she moaned, making him hold her tighter. He loved how she sounded when she moaned. He loved everything about her.

Projex gripped her neck softly and kissed her cheek. "You look so pretty taking this dick."

"Oh my gooosh," she groaned, face twisted in the most pleasurable scowl he'd seen. She didn't understand how such nasty words turned her on and made her wetter.

Projex was swimming. The more he stroked, the more aroused she became. When she started bouncing back on him, he almost nutted but shook off the urge. He wanted his baby to get hers first.

"That's it," he encouraged, holding tight of her waist with both hands now.

"Ooou. Right there. Yes! Right there. Don't stop… don't stop. Oooh, fuck! I love you! Oh my gooosh. Babe! I love you!" She was losing it; screaming, crying, shouting, cumming, and expressing her love for him.

His strokes increased. "What you say? You love me, huh?"

"Yes! Oh my… I love you so much, Bryshon! You

gon' make me cum," she whined, feeling the urge to pee, but she knew it wasn't that. He taught her what her body was doing.

Rubbing her own clit, Loriana felt the first trickle of her essence squirt out of her before Projex pulled out some, and she busted like a broken pipe. Watching her combust, Projex did the same, coating her vibrating ass cheeks with a nut he was sure would've gotten her pregnant had she not been on birth control.

Her body shuddered as he massaged her shoulders and back. Kissing her damp neck, he said, "I knew you loved a nigga. You ready to shower now?"

Twenty minutes later, they were under the covers. Loriana was lying damn near over his entire body half-awake while Projex caressed her velvety smooth skin. He had a lot on his mind and just wanted to talk. Had his grandma not tripped about him smoking in her house, he would've sparked one up.

"L-Boogie," he called out.

"Hmm?"

"You sleep?"

"No. What's wrong?" she askcd, voice barely there.

"You ever been out of state?"

She sat up some and looked at him. "You trying to

go on the run? I know I just told you I loved you but not on no Bonnie and Clyde type of love. That's dangerous."

He stared at her for a brief second before laughing. She was so serious; he couldn't do anything else. When she smiled, his heart leaped.

"I missed that."

"What?" she questioned.

"Your smile. Glad I'm the one putting it on your face."

She snuggled closer to him as if there was any more room to. "Me too. Why'd you ask that, though?"

"Was gone take you on a trip before my court date, but I gotta check and see if I can leave the state first."

"Where would we go?"

"Somewhere with a beach and some palm trees. You ever been to Florida?"

Her head shook no. "Nope. I bet it's so nice out there."

She imagined how the sand would feel in between her toes and wiggled them. Neither of them knew that was the destination Linette had planned on taking her.

"Hell yeah. We gon' have to fly out there one day. Get away from the city and just enjoy the world."

Loriana hated to ruin the mood, but she had to know. "What's going to happen if you go to prison?"

His eyes closed, not wanting to imagine that but needing to. "You better come visit me and answer my calls." He chuckled, trying to lighten up the darkness now hovering over them.

"I wish heaven had phone lines."

Damn. He thought, knowing where her mind had ventured to. Projex agreed with her, though. He'd call Chevy and let him know he could rest now. Their silence lulled Projex into sleep until Loriana called his name.

"Yeah?"

"Whatever happens, just know I love you. I wasn't saying it because your dick was in me," she spoke honestly, in that proper tone that hooked him in the first place.

"You sure?" He chuckled, massaging her scalp.

"I've never been surer in my life. You have to be patient with me, though. I'm new to all of this, and I get afraid sometimes, you know? Just the thought of you leaving me makes me ill, but I have to be real with myself."

He knew exactly what she meant and didn't coddle her feelings. Not even when he felt his chest become wet from her tears. Projex simply held her tighter. From the moment they met, he was drawn to her, pulling her into his world with her curious antics and needy ways. He wanted her there. Needed her by his side, and when she needed him most, he was right there. Never too far away because the thought of not being able to feel her touch, smell her scent, or hear her voice made his head hurt. Projex was addicted and wasn't ready to incur the adverse effects without her.

The truth was, he was new to all of this too and was tossing his heart to her in hopes that she didn't fumble it. They were young, though—the kind of young where hearts were unintentionally broken, so lessons could be learned. Projex was who he was. He couldn't help the circumstances he'd placed them in but knew deep down, they were ones that'd make Loriana resent ever falling in love with him. The beginning stages of any relationship required patience, and Projex hoped she would have enough to deal with him if things hit the fan.

Chapter Eight

Needing a day to herself and some fresh air, Loriana decided to go to the mall. Spending money on clothes and shoes had been her form of therapy lately. It seemed like every other day; a box was getting delivered to the house with her name on it. Coping the only way she knew how for now, Loriana tossed another pair of lounge shorts over her arm. Summer was in full effect, and she needed to re-up on certain things. Specifically, shorts, tank tops, dresses, and sandals, just to name a few things. Anything else that caught her eye was added as well.

"Ooh. This is cute," she said, holding up a white crop top that laced up in the front.

Moving through the sale rack in *H&M*, Loriana looked down at the pile in her arm, then up toward the front of the store. The line was sort of long for a Sunday, but she should've expected that. It was a few days before the Fourth of July, and people were rushing to get outfits. While some parties were thrown over the weekend, many people were still hosting events on the day of in a few days. When she and another customer reached for the same item, she pulled her hand back and looked up.

"Oh. My fault, go ahead," she said.

"Loriana? Hey, girl. I thought that was you."

She looked at the girl's face and gave her a smile. "Hey, Candace. How are you?"

"I'm good, girl. Just trying to get me an outfit together. How's your summer been going since we graduated?"

Candace, a high school classmate of hers, hadn't noticed that Loriana hadn't even attended the graduation. Loriana didn't expect her to know that she was having one of the most life-altering times of her life, so she gave a blasé answer. Her summer was shitty outside of her newfound love life.

"It's going good."

"That's what's up. I don't know if you saw my message on Facebook, but when I heard your mom passed, I reached out. Was just sending you my thoughts, prayers, and virtual hugs," she spoke sincerely.

She swallowed hard. "Thank you. I had a bunch of messages, so I probably missed it."

"That's okay. You're still in my prayers."

Loriana nodded, and another classmate of theirs named, Trell, walked up. Flamboyantly, he switched over to them, making a smile easily appear on Loriana's face. His tight tank top showed off his abs with a pierced belly, while low-rise capri jeans covered his long legs. A big black purse sat in the crook of his arm.

"Hey, Loriana, honey. What y'all over here talking about?"

She grinned. "Hey, Trell."

"Nothing. Just catching up. You good?" Candace asked.

Trell's lips tooted out. "Mhm. My shit didn't have any buzzers."

Trell was a known booster and thief. You couldn't take long to blink around him, or something would end up missing. It didn't matter where he was or who he was with; if he could stuff it in his purse, it was his for the taking.

"Right. Loriana, you got plans for the fourth?"

She shook her head no. "No. Not that I know of."

"Cool. You should come to this kickback with us. One of my homeboy's god mom is letting him throw a party at her crib."

"And that bitch is nice. I'm talking about sitting on acres of land with a pool and a tennis court in the back and all," Trell added.

She gave a nervous chuckle. "Um, I don't know. I'll have to see."

"Okay. That's fine. Just wanted to get you out of the house and show you how we turn up. We don't have to be strangers just because school is out. We're cool people."

Trell waved her off. "I'm the cool one, hoe. Lo, put your number in my phone so I can hit you up. Knowing Candace, she gon' forget." He'd given her his own little nickname.

"No, I won't!"

Ignoring her, Trell handed Loriana his phone. She typed her number in and saved it under Loriana, but Trell changed it to Lo. Right there, he sent her a text, letting her know it was him.

"You better not ignore me when I call or text you either," he said in a playful manner but was serious.

"As long as you don't Facetime me unannounced."

Candace groaned. "Well, hell. You might as well block him now."

The trio shared a laugh.

"Girl, boo. We gon' become real good friends. Ain't that right, Lo?"

She smiled, loving his energy. "Right. Where is the kickback at?"

"In Overland Park."

"Dang. All the way out there?" Loriana complained.

Trell smacked his lips while adjusting his purse. "Now, you know it takes thirty minutes to get anywhere in Kansas City. That is not that far. You out here in Lee's Summit."

"I like the outlet more, and it is when you really just started driving," she fussed.

Greg had taken her out to the car lots one evening and let her pick out a ride of her own. It wasn't a new booty, but it got her from point a to point b. Loriana liked her 2014 Toyota Camry and was planning on giving it a name soon.

"We can pick you up," Candace offered. "I mean, that's if you decide to go. You got a swimsuit?"

Loriana shook her head no. "Not one that fits. I need to buy a new one."

"I got you," Trell said. "Those titties are sitting up, honey."

Loriana laughed. She was rocking a strapless orange romper with a pair of white sandals. Her outfit was simple and something she'd just thrown on.

"Um, thanks?" She laughed. "I'll text you on Tuesday and let you know if I'll make it or not."

"Give me your number too, just in case," Candace told her.

"You about to checkout?" Trell asked.

Loriana nodded. Moving closer to the middle of them, Trell grabbed the clothes in her arms, thankful for them being small enough, and stuffed them in his purse. Loriana's heart was about to jump out of her chest. When he walked away toward the entrance, Candace followed behind him. Stunned for a second, Loriana caught on and tried not to look suspicious as she speed-walked behind them to Candace's car up the hill.

"You look spooked as hell." Trell laughed while unpacking his purse and putting her things in an empty *H&M* bag. Where he magically pulled that from? Loriana had no clue.

"I wasn't expecting you to do that," Loriana told him.

"Of course, you weren't. You still need a swimsuit, right? JC Penny's had some real nice ones the other day. Let's go in there. They be short-staffed on Sundays."

Candace shook her head while Loriana fidgeted in her stance. She had never stolen anything besides some candy from the corner store. Trell peeped the hesitation on her face.

"I'll go in by myself. It's better that way, anyway. Don't need you getting caught up in my bullshit," he snickered. "Now, what size you wear?"

"A medium. Don't get anything too revealing."

Trell waved her off. "Girl, bye. I'ma get whatever I can get, and we'll go from there. Go get an ICEE from the cookie shop and chill out while I work my magic."

He walked away before Loriana could give a rebuttal. "How do you put up with him?"

"I don't. Trust me, we argue like siblings. Speaking of an ICEE, I want one now. You got some-where to be?"

Loriana shook her head no. "Nope. I guess I can hang with you guys for a little while."

"Cool," Candace said as they made their way across the parking lot.

Loriana hadn't been searching for any new friends and wouldn't give them that title yet, but it felt good to be around new energy. Especially since Nyree was out of town with her family for the holiday weekend. Hanging with Mhyale was cool, but she had her own thing going on. What Loriana did know was that she'd already made up in her mind that she was attending the kickback. The only burning question in her brain was if she was going to invite Projex or not.

"You weren't lying," Loriana whispered in awe as they pulled into or around the driveway.

It was more like a parking lot how big it was. The extravagant 7,964 square foot million-dollar home took them all of thirty-two minutes to arrive to from Loriana and Mhyale's place. In the backseat, her eyes were bugged as she took in the scenery. Even though it was late in the evening, light fixtures outside of the home had it extremely lit up. The fireworks going off in the distance and behind the house helped as well. Loriana cared nothing about showcasing the wonderment on her face.

Though in a nice neighborhood, the closest house was so far away, you wouldn't even be able to tell what your neighbor looked like. Loriana couldn't help but wonder what the person who owned the home needed all this space for. But more so, what they did for a living.

"I hope everyone hasn't gotten too drunk yet. I need to catch up!" Trell exclaimed, sipping from a straw.

He offered Loriana some of whatever he was drinking, but she declined, opting to wait until they got there.

"Right. Now, Lo. Just a few rules when we get in here. Have fun, and don't sip anything you didn't see anyone pour straight from the bottle, okay?"

She nodded. "That's it?"

"Yep. Other than that, let's get turned the fuck up!"

Loriana smiled and slid out of the back seat. Thanks to Trell, she had a plethora of swimsuits to choose from now. Today, she chose to wear a cobalt blue two-piece. Jean shorts covered her bottoms that she had unzipped and unbuttoned, while her breasts sat on display in a sheer short-sleeved top that Trell tied into a knot at the front.

The trio stepped inside the house, and Loriana's eyes roamed. It was humungous. The type of home you only saw on HGTV when those people hit the lottery type of huge. The foyer alone could be used to park a car inside. Candace and Trell hugged a bunch of people and introduced Loriana to each of them. She simply smiled or waved, feeling like everyone was staring because she was the newbie. That was only her nerves, though.

"You okay?" Candace asked, wanting to make sure all of this wasn't too much.

Loriana nodded her head. "Yeah. This place is… man. Talk about goals."

"Who you telling? I be trying to become a squatter every time we come out here. They'd never find my ass." They all laughed. With it housing eight bedrooms, seven bathrooms, and so many other rooms, Trell was probably right. "Let's go to the kitchen and take some shots," he suggested.

Loriana's white sandals flopped along the wooden floors as they made their way to the kitchen. They were greeted by a cacophony of voices hollering, rapping loudly to music, and yelling out aye. Before she knew what was happening, Trell was bent over in front of her, twerking.

"Ayyye!" Candace yelled, hyping him up.

Girl, I wanna see you twerk
I'll throw a lil' money if you twerk
I don't really think you can twerk

(Twerk twerk), twerk
If you broke, go to work
Make that big booty twerk
Make that big booty twerk
(Twerk twerk)
Can I touch that booty?
That booty, that big ol' booty

Skillfully, Trell popped his ass and dropped it low. He wasn't the only one, though. Almost every girl, scantily dressed and all, was bent over shaking ass. *Booty* by Blac Youngsta seemed to be one of the songs of the summer already, and it had just been released the month prior.

"Show em' yo' mama made a hoe!" Candace rapped, smacking him on the butt.

When Loriana did a slight twerk, Trell screamed. "Yas, Lo! You better get that shit."

She cracked up laughing and waved him off, not wanting the attention on her. When they did finally make it to the marble island that could comfortably sit nine, bottles were everywhere. Food was laid out on the counters in burners, and there was a sheet cake sitting off to the side.

"Why do they have a cake?" Loriana semi-yelled in Candace's ear.

"You know black people buy a cake for any occasion."

Loriana chuckled because that was true in some cases. She remembered one of her uncles buying one for a football game party and wondered why back then.

"Light or dark?" Trell questioned.

He was holding a bottle of Patron in one hand and Fireball in the other.

"Dark!" Candace answered.

"What does Fireball taste like?" Loriana asked.

"Like Big Red gum. It's cinnamon flavored and easier to take shots with," Trell explained, grabbing a few plastic shot cups.

Loriana shrugged. When the first shot was poured up, they toasted to having a good night and tapped their cups on the counter before tossing them back. Loriana's face immediately scrunched up as she pressed a hand firmly against her chest.

"Ugh! That mess burns."

"It's not nasty though, is it?" Trell questioned, daring her to say it was.

Her head shook no. "No. It just burns like hell going down."

"Good. Let's take another one."

When they were on shot number three, and Loriana's skin was warm, her eyes closed for a brief second as the alcohol invaded her system. When she opened them, Candace was hugging some guy.

"Well, look who it is," Trell said in a playful manner. "The man of the hour himself."

"What's up, Trell."

"Shamari, this is Lo. Lo, Mari."

Loriana waved as his head tilted upward. "I hope me being here is fine."

"Yeah. You see all these mufuckas in here?" Shamari laughed.

"It is packed, and we haven't even been outside yet," Trell said.

"Right. We had to get some liquor in our system first. What time is the firework show starting?"

Shamari shrugged. "I don't know. Whenever bro tells them people to do it. He around here somewhere. Y'all was drinking this bullshit?" he asked, holding the Fireball bottle up.

"Yep. Take one with us. Lo, you want another one?"

She rubbed her rumbling stomach. "Um, no. I'ma chill for a minute. Those three got me hot already."

Candace smiled. "Okay, girl. Whenever you ready

to drink some more, let me know. We got all night to sober up."

That's what she had planned, at least. A number of odd hours later, Loriana was six shots in. The bartender outside made her a drink after a quick dive in the pool, and now she was back inside the kitchen, trying to prepare her some food. As she went to scoop some of the pasta salad onto her plate, her weak hands failed her, causing her to drop it all over the floor.

"Aw, man," she whined, putting her plate down. When she bent over, she half expected for someone to walk up behind her.

"Damn. What a sight," the voice murmured behind her.

She stood too quickly, woozy from the liquor. Whoever he was caught her arm as she leaned against the counter.

"Uh, thanks." She giggled.

"No problem. Looks like you made a mess."

Loriana looked down at the floor. "Yeah. I'ma clean it up, though."

"I got it. Finish making your plate."

She stammered for a bit. "Okay. Thank you…" She paused, waiting for him to give her a name.

"I'm Damien."

"I'm Lo." She grinned, admiring his bulky arms

and thick beard, before turning to continue fixing her plate while he cleaned up her mess.

When she was finished, she told him thank you again and headed back outside. The firework show had started on the tennis court, and drunken bodies were scattered about the massive backyard. Loriana's eyes went from her plate of food to the sky until it was empty. She let out a satisfied sigh and licked her lips as her eyes searched for Candace. She was by the rocks when she went inside.

"Or was she on the patio?" Loriana mumbled to herself.

Having no energy to get up and look for her right that second, Loriana relaxed on the chaise chair she was lucky enough to snag before anyone else could. A waitress came by with bottles of water, and Loriana hurriedly grabbed one. She knew she was drunk. The laziness in her eyes, weakened limbs, and numb lips told her so. Mhyale had always told her to drink water and eat bread if she needed to sober up some.

The second she finished her bottle of water, her bladder screamed at her. "Dang it. I gotta pee," she whined, pushing herself up to stand.

"Lo! Where you going, love? Come get in the pool!" Trell hollered for her. He was hugged up on some guy with a blonde fade.

"To the bathroom! I'll be right back."

Rushing inside the house, she momentarily forgot where she was. Searching for a bathroom in this place wasn't going to be easy. The first door she came across, someone was having sex in, and she hurriedly shut it.

"Sorry!" she yelled out, scurrying away.

The second door she opened was a whole laundry room the size of a bedroom.

Frustrated, she went to find someone who could help her before she lost her morals and peed inside one of their fancy ass plants outside on the porch. When she went to walk into the kitchen, Damien was walking out.

"Lo, you good? Where you in a rush to?" he asked.

"Uh, no. Do you know where a bathroom is around here? I have to pee so bad," she whined, bouncing on her feet.

"Yeah, upstairs. The ones down here are occupied."

"Obviously." She laughed, thinking back to the first door she opened. "Lead the way, please."

"Ladies, first," Damien insisted.

When they walked out of the kitchen, he directed her to the steps. There were a lot of them, and he was thankful. The view of her from the back had him licking his lips and squeezing his dick in the shorts he was wearing. Her shorts had been misplaced long ago, and she didn't care to look for them. Her body was on fire. The sheer damp top did cover her up some, though. When they made it to the top of the steps, Loriana immediately spotted the toilet at the end of the hallway and rushed to it.

Even drunk, she knew not to sit on the toilet. On wobbling legs, she squatted and sighed. After peeing for what seemed like forever, Loriana washed her hands and splashed some water onto her face. Snatching the decorative white towel from the towel bar, she wet it before squeezing it out and patting her neck. Her body felt too warm, and she wanted to cool off. A knock at the closed door startled her, and she quickly threw the towel under the sink.

"Coming!" she shouted, pulling the door open seconds later.

Damien stood right at the door, making her jump back some. "You good?" he questioned.

"Uh, yeah. Thanks again."

"It's nothing. We should get to know one another a little more."

He stepped closer, and Loriana's heart began to beat differently. An uneasy smile formed on her face.

"U-Uh. Sure. We can talk downstairs. I need some more food."

"Nah. I wanna talk in here," he spoke sternly, in a voice that made Loriana's skin crawl. A voice that he hadn't been using with her until now.

When he pushed her back roughly into the bathroom, all drunkenness fled from her body. She tried screaming, but the clasp of his hand around her neck cut off her breathing that quickly. Her back slammed against the edge of the counter as Damien pushed the door shut. A fear like no other paralyzed her as he used one cruddy hand to roughly caress her body and the other to shut her up. She wanted to scream, but her body had become petrified stone. Damien had his body pressed up against hers as her nails dug into his arms, and her eyes stung with tears.

"P-Please," she wheezed, barely above a whisper.

Her arms flapped along the countertop, knocking the items in her reach down. When he tried turning her around to face the counter, Loriana used all the strength she could muster up and kneed him in his groin. The action crippled Damien, but not before a punch to Loriana's jaw resounded throughout the bathroom.

"Bitch," he hissed as she tried her best to scurry around him and to the door. He gripped her hair that was down and yanked back so hard, she felt some rip from her scalp. "You gon' pay for that," he spat in her ear.

BOOM, BOOM, BOOM!

Boisterous bangs of fists came to the door, and Loriana sucked in air to scream.

"Help! Help me!"

The door flew open immediately, and the guy on the other side's face made her even more alarmed. *No, no. He came to help him rape me.* She thought, trying to run away. This time she found it much easier. The hold Damien had on her hair was gone. Loriana fell into the chest of the man at the door, and he protectively caught her around the waist. Her chest heaved as a blanket of relief covered her fear.

"What the fuck are you up here doing?" the man asked.

His voice was hard and his gaze angry as he stared with burning eyes at Damien. He sniffled, adjusting his wrinkled t-shirt Loriana had clawed at.

"Nothing, man. We were having an argument."

"That ain't sound like no argument to me," he let him know.

Had Loriana not been pressed up against his chest, with her arms wrapped around him, he would've snatched his gun from his waist and really started an argument.

"Aye, love. Do you know him?" the man asked Loriana, who hurriedly shook her head no.

The trembling of her body let him know she was terrified of what had just taken place. They stood there eye-to-eye before the guy stepped to the side. Damien's jaw flexed, and he flicked his nose before stepping out of the bathroom and walking by them. The guy's eyes stayed trained on him until he hit the top steps. Digging in his pocket, he pulled out his phone and called someone.

"Handle the nigga with the black du-rag on. Yeah. It don't matter. Get it done."

He hung up the phone. Exhaling, he peeled Loriana away from his chest and cringed on the inside at her swollen cheek.

"You gone need to put some ice on that."

Her lips trembled, and she nodded as tears formed in her eyes. She could hardly mumble, "Okay."

Loriana watched him intently as he sat on the black ottoman across from her. He'd gone to get her a pack of ice for her cheek and was right back at her side. The power in his seated position made it hard for her to look away. Openly, she admired how he sat with his back straight, shoulders squared, and brooding dark brown eyes gaping at her. They were staring into her soul, waiting for Loriana to make a peep about what had gone down.

The illumination from the lamp lights bounced off his unblemished dark chocolate skin. Loriana was a bit envious of his perfect complexion. There wasn't a pimple in sight. A crisp line was followed by the deepest set of black waves she'd seen in a while. The lower half of his face was covered in a neatly trimmed beard that came an inch or so off his face. When he licked his lips, Loriana cleared her throat and frowned to herself. She was annoyed at her attraction to him, considering what just happened.

"Um. Thank you, again."

"You're welcome. Who you here with?"

Finally, he talks, she thought. All it took was for her to speak to get him to say something. That's what *he* was waiting on.

"Candace and Trell."

He shook his head, knowing exactly who they were.

"I'ma go get them for you, so y'all can leave."

He stood up— towering at six-foot-two, making

Loriana feel small in the cushioned chair she was sitting in.

"Wait. Do you live here?"

He shook his head no. "No. I'm monitoring the party and glad I was on my job."

Her head bowed some, feeling ashamed of herself.

"Don't do that. What happened wasn't your fault."

"I got too drunk. I should've never trusted a stranger to look out for me."

His brow dipped. "You trusting me." It was more of a statement than a question.

Her face contorted in shock to the challenge in his voice before it simmered seeing the empathy in his eyes. Loriana didn't know why, but her gut was telling her he was safe. He hadn't done anything so far and knew he wouldn't. The call he made hadn't gone unheard by her either. Her shoulder shrugged as she brought the ice pack to her lap.

"I guess so. What's your name?"

"Symir."

"You kinda look like a guy I met earlier. Sha-something."

He smirked, and her heart leaped. "Shamari. My brother."

"Oh. Is he the youngest?"

His face went back neutral. "You think you good to go back downstairs?"

"I'm ready to go home."

Her voice cracked a bit. Tonight had been a lot of things. Fun, but fearful more than anything. Loriana's foggy brain kept replaying the night and where she'd went wrong. She didn't know if it were a lack of poor judgment or the irresponsibility of having too much to drink. Either way, it hadn't ended disastrously but bad enough to make her want to stay in the house for a while.

With a gentleness in his approach, Symir helped her up from the seat. Loriana blinked her eyes behind her lenses and looked up at him.

"Can we keep this between us?" she asked, pleading with rattled nerves for him to say yes.

Symir's head bobbed forward, and she exhaled.

When they made it downstairs, the kickback was still in full effect but less loud. Party stragglers laid around on furniture, while others sang and ate from half-filled plates, trying to curb their drunken appetites. Trell came in from the pool area, rapping Cardi B loudly.

"I be in and out them stores so much, I know they tired of me!" His head bobbed, and hands moved animatedly as he put a spin on the lyrics. "Lo, Lo! Your stomach must've upset you."

She gave him a weak smile. "Yeah. Where's Candace?"

"Chile. Who knows. Her little boyfriend showed up, and she been M.I.A."

Hearing the word boyfriend made Loriana's stomach swirl. *I have one of those,* she thought before moving about the kitchen in almost a frantic manner.

"Have you seen my purse?" she asked Trell.

"You left it in the car when we went out there earlier, remember?"

The reminder made her calm down some, but not enough. She'd left it in there for this reason alone; she didn't want to lose it or have it get stolen. "Let's find Candace, so we can leave."

"None of y'all are in the position to drive home. The police probably out right now waiting to catch somebody," Symir told them.

That was true, considering it was a holiday. Loriana huffed. If neither of them could drive, she was about to call Mhyale and have her come get them.

"Hey, friends!" Candace squealed, walking from some part of the house. A lazy, goofy grin was on her face. The guy who Loriana saw her talking to earlier was following closely behind her.

"Lo is ready to go home, so pipe down. Big bossy here, says none of us can drive, so I guess we'll call an Uber or something."

"That's too much money. We live on opposite sides of the city almost," Candace complained.

Symir dragged a hand over his head. "How about this… I'll drive y'all home in my car, and Wayne can drive your car back."

Candace looked up at Wayne and smiled. "If you're cool with that."

"Yeah. Where your keys?"

"You're gonna drive us all the way to the city and make a turnaround trip?" Loriana questioned, thinking of how much time that would take.

Symir's heart twisted at the uncertainty on her face and in her voice. As if he wasn't a man of his word or had some type of interior motive. That wasn't Symir; he didn't move with malicious intent. Especially not with women.

"Yeah. It ain't nothing," he replied.

"Who's going to watch after the house?"

Her question came from a place of protectiveness. Loriana didn't want what happened and what could've happened to her to be done to anyone else.

Symir understood her concerns right away. Pulling his phone out, he sent a text to someone. Within minutes, four thickset men were in the kitchen with them. Symir gave them a few orders to clear everyone out of the house because the party was over.

Loriana looked at him with eyes full of curiosity. *Who is he?* she thought.

Within twenty minutes, the house had cleared out for the most part. The only people left behind were the ones who were staying the night. Shamari walked around with his shirt off, smacking on a bag of chips, while Trell helped himself to another drink that he did not need. Symir was off in the corner, giving the men instructions on what to do while he was gone, while Candace and Wayne headed for the door. Absent-mindedly, Loriana followed them. Her jean shorts, wet from the pool, were wrung out and in her hand.

Symir glanced her way. His eyes took in her uncovered legs, and his jaw clenched. "Yo, Mari. Grab Lo a pair of shorts to put on."

"A'ight, bro." Shamari smacked, jogging down a set of steps Loriana hadn't paid much attention to.

When he came back up, he handed them over to her. Though he was tall, Shamari wasn't big, so his shorts fit perfectly around her waist and hung low to her calves. Loriana looked up at Symir.

"Thank you."

His head bobbed, and they headed out the door.

"You riding with them?" Symir asked Loriana as she headed toward Candace's car.

"I was going to. Should I ride with you?"

He lifted his shoulder in a half shrug. Though he wanted her too, Symir was giving her the option. "If you want to. It don't matter."

"That means yes, girl," Trell added. "And I'm riding with y'all. You not about to be taking my Lo home by yourself."

His protectiveness amused Loriana but not in a humorous way. She couldn't help but wonder where that energy was when Damien had her cornered in the bathroom.

"Good," Candace said, giving Loriana a quick hug. "I'm tryna be nasty."

"Oop," Trell chirped before letting out a loud belch. "Well, excuse me."

Loriana's nose crinkled. "That came from deep within."

"Hell yeah. All this liquor just sitting on my stomach. Ooh. I can't wait to get dropped off at my boo's crib," he said as they walked over to Symir's ride.

The all-black Porsche Macan was one Loriana had never seen before. Not the inside of anyway.

Climbing in the passenger seat, she closed the door and relaxed against the leather. The liquor was still heavily in her system, and she couldn't wait to sleep it off. Inhaling deeply, her eyes searched for whatever had his car smelling so good. A black pine tree hung from the rearview mirror with the words Black Ice on it.

"It smells good in here," she told him.

"Thank you," he replied, running the windshield wipers. Dust from the fireworks had covered their cars, and Symir was definitely hitting the car wash up tomorrow.

"These seats real comfortable," Trell admired, rubbing his hand across them.

Loriana sat still in the front seat, subtly moving her jaw. It was still tender touch, but the swelling had reduced some. She shook her head, not believing she'd gotten punched and almost raped. If she hadn't thought about therapy before now, it was definitely an avenue she needed to look into. So much had spiraled out of control in her life in such a short timeframe; it was only a matter of time before Loriana exploded.

Wayne started Candace's car and pulled up on the side of them. Candace rolled her window down. "I live closer, so you can follow him," she told Symir, who nodded.

When Symir pulled out of the driveway, Loriana searched inside her purse for her phone. Her eyes bugged out of her head when she saw the tons of missed calls, texts, and Facetime calls from Projex. There were a few from Mhyale as well. When she finally noticed the time, almost one in the morning, her chest caved. With sweaty palms, she hovered over the options to text or call Projex back. Replying to a text he sent a little over thirty minutes ago, telling her he hoped she was safe, had her tapping the phone icon.

"Why you ain't been answering your phone?!" his voice boomed, making her flinch.

Symir glanced her way at the sound of Projex's voice yelling at her.

She rushed to lower the volume on the side of her phone. Meekly, she said, "It was in the car. I'm just now leaving."

"Leaving from where? I don't even know where you at, ma. I been blowing yo' phone up, thinking something happened to you. Had me calling yo' cousin and shit."

She cringed. "I'm sorry. I was at this Fourth of July party with some friends. I'm on my way home now."

"Bruh. It's one in the morning, and you sound like

you been drinking. Who bringing you home? I'll meet y'all."

She panicked. "No, no. That's okay. I was a little bit. I'm kind of sober now, though."

"So, that's what we doing now?" he asked in a disappointing tone. "When we start lying to each other? Nah. Better yet, when do you not tell me where you going?"

Loriana's eyes closed, and she squeezed them tight. "It was just with some friends from high school. I didn't think it was a big deal."

"Not to you. You forgot you got a nigga that give a fuck about you? Huh? Man," he groaned, shaking his head and climbing from his bed. Projex left the studio early when she didn't answer her phone or texts. He'd been waiting for her to hit him back.

"I'ma wait on you at yo' place. Let me find out you been on some sneaky shit, ma."

She gulped. "I haven't."

"Yeah, a'ight. Who party was it?"

"Un, un. You gotta get off the phone doing all that explaining. We trying to listen to music," Trell said.

Mortified, Loriana's head whipped around to the backseat. Her eyes burned into his with warning. Trell tossed his arms in the air.

"Man, who the fuck is that? Tell em' I said to get out yo' mothafuckin' conversation," Projex spat.

"They aren't. I'll be home in like thirty minutes. We're dropping people off."

He sucked his teeth. "You still ain't answer my question. Whose party was it?"

"My friend's friend. Can we just talk when I get there?"

Projex released a pissed off chuckle. "Yeah. We fasho doing that when you get here. Be ready to talk my ear off. You good, though? You sure you don't need me to meet y'all?"

His now soothing tone softened her up. It always did. How he went from upset to concerned that fast was one of the many reasons she loved him. Projex wasn't hollering out of anger, but more so an unsettling mood. It was too much going on for her to just go missing for hours like she'd done.

"No. That's okay. I'll call Mhy and tell her to let you in."

"A'ight. Aye, L-Boogie," he called out.

"Huh?"

"I love you, a'ight. Don't have a nigga stressed like that again."

She simpered, tense jaw lifting into a smile. "I won't. I love you, too."

"You better."

When they hung up, the car was uncomfortably quiet. Symir tried his best not to listen in on her conversation, but it was hard not to. The sense of still wanting to protect her hadn't left him. Removing her sandals from her feet, Loriana folded one leg underneath her.

"Can we play some music?" she asked.

Symir took his eyes off the highway and briefly glanced her way. "Yeah. What you wanna listen to?"

"Some Nicki Minaj," Trell said from the backseat. He was a Barb for sure.

"Ugh, no. We not trying to hear her. Sit back and be the backseat rider," Loriana told him playfully.

His body fell back into the seat. "Yes, ma'am. Check me then."

"You got an R&B playlist?"

Symir nodded. Tapping the music app on his iPhone, he pressed shuffle on his go-to R&B playlist and turned the volume up. *Forever My Lady* by Jodeci blasted smoothly through the speakers, setting the mood in the car immediately. The tunes and smooth motion of the car ride eventually lulled Trell to sleep. Loriana snickered some when she heard him start snoring.

"I guess that liquor caught up to him," she said, trying to engage in conversation.

"Yeah. What about you? How you feeling?"

Loriana wasn't sure. His question was kind of loaded, and she didn't want to spill her guts out, so she kept it simple.

"I'm okay."

Her dry reply told him all he needed to know. Symir didn't bother to respond. Deep in her own thoughts, Loriana couldn't help but wonder how tonight would've gone had Damien achieved his goal. Chills covered her frame as the scene played on a loop in her head. She shook it from side to side, trying to rid the images. Loriana squeezed her eyes tight, thinking of how she would've had to explain to her mom what had gone down.

Pain funneled into her heart, realizing Linette wasn't even here to tell her. Heaving, Loriana tried keeping her tears at bay. It was no use, though, especially when the lyrics to *My Life* by Mary J. Blige met her now unclogged ears.

And you'll be at peace with yourself
You won't really need no one else
Except for the man up above

Because He'll give you love
If you looked in my life
And see what I've seen...

Loriana's tears of shame turned into ones of pain. They crippled her inebriated frame as they slid down her face. Her shoulders jumped as silent whimpers escaped her. Symir's eyes looked from her and back to the road a few times when he realized she was crying. He turned the music down some.

"Lo, what you crying for?"

Seeing women cry in his presence caused discomfort to swarm his chest. It always had since a youngin'. She tried making out a sentence, but the words came out in a jumbled manner. So, Symir drove quietly while she sat crouched in his seat with her head in her lap and the weight of the world clinging to her skin like a second layer. Her unexpected emotions caught him off guard, but from the sounds of it, she needed to release them.

When she was done, her breathing coming to a shaky but stabler pace, Loriana exhaled. "I'm sorry for just crying like that. I miss my mom."

"You don't have to apologize. I get it."

She wiped her face and looked at him. "Do you, though? Everyone says they can only imagine what I'm going through, and they're right. But they shouldn't. Who would want to imagine living without their mother forever?"

A vice grip seemed to lock around his heart, restricting Symir's breathing for a few seconds. He choked on a cough before grabbing the bottle of water from its cup holder and drinking from it.

"I'm sorry for your loss." It was now his turn to apologize, and he felt dumb for using the mediocre reply with her.

"I am, too," Loriana mumbled. "I'm so sick of being strong. I'm strong for myself and everyone around me. I just want to shut the world out. There's no peace here without her."

Her words sounded all too familiar. They reminded Symir of a time when he couldn't escape his thoughts longs enough to enjoy the day. Nothing back then made them enjoyable. He was just living them, barely breathing. He learned to keep pressing through. That's the only reason he was here right now, able to coax Loriana down from the ladder of grief she was ready to leap from.

"You know," he began, "you don't always have to

be strong. One of these days, when you think there's no hope left, God gon' come through and provide a crack in the wall. It might be small, but it's all you need. If being strong ain't you, don't be. Just be, Lo. Whoever she is that day."

She licked her trembling bottom lip. His words soothed her aching heart in the gentlest of ways. Loriana wanted to be herself, but she couldn't find the old her. She may have still been young in age, but grieving had aged her so quickly. It hardened her once soft personality, making her have a completely different outlook on life. Her eyes now saw the world for what it really was; a place that would suck the life out of you before it breathed it into you. That's if you let it.

When they made it to Candace's place, Wayne stayed behind and told Symir to come back and pick him up. Loriana's place was about ten minutes away and before Trell's, so she tried waking him up to tell him bye once they were close.

"I'm up, dang," he grumbled, wiping at his eyes.

Turning around in her seat, Loriana could've crawled under a rock when she saw Projex's car parked in the driveway behind Mhyale's. She texted him and let him know she'd call when she made it home, but Projex wasn't going for that. He wanted to be there when she arrived to see who she was with. When he climbed out of the car, seeing headlights, she said a quick prayer, asking the Lord to not let Projex flip out.

Symir pulled up to the curb and tossed the gear in park. "This you?"

"Yeah. Thanks so much. I really appreciate the ride and everything else."

"You're welcome."

In the driveway, Projex was trying his best to see who was in the driver's seat, but the tint was too dark. Boldly, he walked down to meet her and get a look inside the nice ass ride. If they were a friend of Loriana's, he wanted to meet them. Loriana rushed to climb out, forgetting all about the basketball shorts she had on.

"Aye." Projex chuckled, feeling himself get pissed off. "You really trying me right now, ma. Who shorts you got on? Aye. Roll this mothafucka down." His knuckle rapped on the driver's window.

Loriana grabbed his arm. "All that is not called for."

"Yeah?" Symir said coolly.

"Who are you dropping my girl off at one in the morning?"

Symir could've said some slick shit, but that

wasn't what he was on right now. He wouldn't disrespect Loriana, but Projex was out of his body for questioning him.

"The chaperone."

"Nigga, do I look dumb to you?" Projex spat. "Somebody better start talking 'round this bitch 'fore I spazz out."

Trell climbed from the backseat. "This is my cousin. He was just dropping Lo off. Sheesh. No need to start thuggin' on us."

Projex looked at Loriana. "This that nigga's cousin?"

Her head bobbed. "Yes. I don't know him like that."

"You don't know him, but you let him bring you to the place you lay yo' head at?" Shit wasn't adding up to him.

"Well, what was I supposed to do? I didn't drive."

"You heard me ask you twice if you wanted me to meet you. But a'ight. Play dumb all you want."

Unlike Projex, Loriana didn't see anything wrong with Symir dropping her off at home, and she wouldn't have. Projex's paranoia and the life he lived was embedded in him, and that was just one rule amongst many that he lived by. Not just his lifestyle but the way he was raised as well. Joseline didn't play that having everybody and their mama coming to their home.

Yet here Loriana was lying again, and Projex didn't know whether or not to believe her. For all he knew, they could've come up with the lie in the car. He glared her way for a few more seconds before backing up from Symir's car. His window was rising, having no more words for the youngsta' calling himself trying to check shit. The only person who owed him some answers was Loriana.

"Lo, can I spend the night? I don't even feel like going to his house anymore."

Projex's necked snapped his way. "Fuck nah! You better get yo' ass back in the backseat with yo' peoples."

Loriana sighed, shaking her head. "This is not your house. Stop all that. Yeah, Trell. That's fine. I'll see if my cousin has something you can change into."

He sashayed by them and up the driveway. "Thanks, boo."

Projex followed behind him and shook his head. Loriana eyed Symir's truck as he took off down the street and a strange feeling bubbled inside her. She didn't know if it was relief of nothing popping off or what, but she noticed a difference in her body immediately. All night, it'd been going through changes.

Later on, in the early parts of the morning, Loriana lay awake while wrapped in Projex's arms. His face was buried in her neck while her bare back pressed into his chest. They didn't have sex tonight. Instead, Projex listened while she talked about the night she had. Loriana told him everything except the bathroom incident and how protectively, without thought, Symir was. She kept that to herself, battling in her own mind as to why she'd suddenly become so dependent on the strength of others.

I'm not some weak girl, she thought to herself. Angry with herself.

She wasn't. Loriana was defining what strength meant, but she so badly wanted to give up. Her smiles were a façade, wearing them like a mask and snatching it off once no one was around. Conversations, if not interested, were forced. Any daily tasks, such as simply getting up to brush her teeth, required a pep talk. One that consisted of deep breaths, some tears and gentle reminder's that her life mattered. That God was bigger than her grief.

I'm going to be okay today. That was her mantra.

God, please keep me covered. That was her prayer.

I need all of the strength to survive. That was her plea.

Sighing, she snuggled closer to Projex as he held her tighter in his sleep. Her eyes closed again, hoping sleep came sometime soon. All Loriana needed was a sliver of faith, and God would provide the rest. As He always did.

Chapter Nine

"How long you think she's going to have this song on repeat?" Nyree whispered to Loriana.

There was no use in whispering. Mhyale was in her room blasting *I Don't Wanna* by Aaliyah at the highest volume possible. She didn't even know they'd made it home and didn't care either. She was deep in her feelings.

"Until she's tired of it, I'm sure," Loriana replied, untying the knot in her bag of Chinese food they'd picked up on the way home.

"I should go knock on the door and see if she's okay."

Loriana shook her head no. "No. She'll come out when she's ready."

If there was one thing she knew for sure about her cousin, she did not like to be bothered when she was irritated or in her feelings. When she was ready to talk, Loriana was sure she'd come on out of her room for some fresh air. The song started over, and they had no choice but to listen to it for a third time now.

"Did they put some duck sauce in yours?" Nyree asked, leaning over to look in her bag.

"Yeah. You can have it. I like hot sauce on mine."

The duo had just come from picking up a few things for Nyree's dorm room. She'd be leaving for school in about a month or so. Nyree wanted to spend as much time with Loriana as she could... or as much time as she would allow her to.

"We gotta find something to do tonight," Nyree said, crunching on her crab rangoon.

"Trell asked me to go out with them, but I may just chill with Projex."

Nyree side-eyed her. "Mm. You and these new friends. I don't think I like that."

"You acting like you've never met them before."

"So, what. You're *my* friend," she enunciated, trying to get her point across.

Nyree didn't like sharing Loriana. Especially because she knew how good of a person she was. The fake friendship Akira tricked her into believing was real made Nyree leery of newcomers. She didn't care if she knew them from school or not. Loriana was more than her friend; she was her sister, and she'd knock a bitch upside their head for playing with her.

"Ny. You are going to be making new friends away at school. So, I don't know why you're tripping."

"Not because I want to."

"You should, though. We can't be each other's only friends for the rest of our lives."

Nyree gave her a blank stare. "Says who?"

Laughing, Loriana shook her head. "You're funny, but I know you're serious. That's what makes it even funnier."

"I am serious, but whatever. You already got a whole ass boyfriend on me." That time, she grinned. She loved Projex for her girl. Him, she could tolerate.

"So do you. I mean, you used to."

They snickered, knowing she'd just broken up with Coop a few days prior. Nyree liked him, but that was it. She didn't get all fuzzy inside when she saw him or even want to reply to his texts some days. Coop thought something may have been wrong with him, but this was definitely one of those it's me, not you situations. In Nyree's case, she didn't want to prolong their breakup any longer. She knew doing it right before she left for school would be worse, so she went ahead and got it over with.

"Right. I'm just trying to have fun my last month before I leave."

"Have you talked to Juice?" Loriana asked.

Nyree blushed. "Yep. We're texting now. He keeps trying to pull up on me, but I don't know."

"Well, he can't pull up over here."

"Why not?"

Loriana didn't really feel like going into detail about Projex checking her the other night, but she knew Nyree would keep asking why.

"One of the guys from the party I went to with Candace and Trell dropped me off, and Projex was here waiting for me. He was mad that I let some random guy know where we stay at."

Nyree's eyes stretched wide. "He saw you get out of his car?"

"Mhm." Loriana nodded her head. "Came up to the car and everything. Trell had to hurry up and tell him it was his cousin."

"For what? Like that meant anything."

Loriana shrugged and broke eye contact. Telling her what happened sounded good in her head, but now saying it aloud, she knew she'd spoken too much. It wasn't that she didn't want to tell Nyree about Symir, but just the thought of him reminded her of that night. She was trying to forget about it... and him.

"Ah, hell," Nyree groaned, having already caught on. "You were feeling him?"

"Not really. He just looked out for me that night because I got way too drunk, and he had good taste in music."

Nyree ate a spoonful of her shrimp fried rice. "But was he cute, though? That's what really matters. Forget all that other irrelevant shit."

"Yeah. He was. Like, hella fine."

She did a little dance in her seat, making Loriana laugh. "Okay then. Let me find out you trying to be single like me for the summer."

"Now, you know that's not what I'm doing. I actually like the person I'm in a relationship with."

Playfully, Nyree rolled her eyes. "Trust me, I know."

They both laughed, but it was quickly cut short by Mhyale's yelling. The music was now off, and her voice boomed from behind her closed bedroom door. That lasted for all of one minute, and then her door was open.

"I don't care! I really do not care, Naaz. No! I'm

not opening this door. Fuck you!" Mhyale screamed, causing shock to register on Loriana's face.

She thought they were on good terms but clearly had been wrong. Silently, Nyree and Loriana watched her pace with anger around the living room. She peeked out of the blinds with the phone pressed to her ear. She was dressed in some pink cotton lounge shorts, a sports bra, and mix-match socks. Her hair was down from the braids she was wearing and was now framing her head in a crinkly manner.

"You might as well go back home. I'm so serious. You ain't coming up in here."

On the other end of the phone, Naaz just breathed into the receiver. He was calm, and that was pissing her off even more.

"Can you stop yelling?" he asked.

"No!" she screamed and hung up in his face.

Naaz shook his head, cut his car off, and hopped out. He didn't know why Mhyale wanted to be difficult with him today, but he wasn't in the mood. She'd been texting him crazy text messages all day, in her feelings about them, and she'd clearly gotten what she wanted, his attention. So, yes. She was most certainly about to open the door, so he could see her face-to-face.

"Um, Mhy. He's knocking on the door," Loriana told her.

"I can hear! I'm not letting his bitch ass in here."

Loriana stared at her cousin, trying to see if she'd been drinking or something. She'd never seen her like this, especially while dealing with a man. It was rare and had her on alert.

Naaz's knocks persisted. He was going to annoy the fuck out of all of them if she didn't let him in, and he didn't care. Mhyale wasn't about to play this game with him, not today or after.

"He's not gonna go away," Loriana told her.

"I'll call Memphis. Bet his ass leave from over here then."

"Just let him in. I'm sure what he did can't be that bad."

Mhyale's neck snapped her cousin's way. "Whose side are you on?"

"Yours!" she replied quickly. That shouldn't have even been a question. "But y'all clearly have something to talk about. It looks like you've been crying."

Mhyale patted underneath her eyes that were still damp from shedding tears. She was so annoyed with herself for still crying behind Naaz; it wasn't funny. He was the only man who could bring these types of emotions out of her.

"I don't wanna see his face," Mhyale muffled.

"Mhy-Mhy," Naaz's called out. His commanding voice traveled through the door.

Mhyale's lids closed as she inhaled a deep breath. Her resolve crumbled when he called her that. He knew it too. She stepped closer to the door. Her footsteps were almost heavier than her heart.

"Just go away," she spoke back.

"Nah. Ain't no more of that, remember?"

More tears came. She hated him for making her go through the motions all over again. Her hand trembled as she reached for the knob.

"We promised to communicate with one another. I'm not doing this through a door."

She drew her hand back. "*You* made a lot of promises. Remember that?"

Naaz exhaled hard. "I do. I'm talking about right now, Mhy-Mhy. Fuck the past. I mean, damn. Not fuck it, but…"

He was flustered and, in his feelings, too. Saying the wrong things definitely at the wrong time.

"See! You don't even care," Mhyale cried out, banging her fist on the door.

Loriana looked over at Nyree, who was blinking away the moisture in her eyes. She was already

PMS'ing, and this scene wasn't making it any better for her.

"I do. I swear on everything I love. I care. Just let me in, and I can show you."

Her hand went for the knob again.

"Please, baby. I hate when you cry. You know that."

"Oh, my gosh," Loriana whispered, placing a hand over her chest. This was too much for her. Naaz was ready to beg; he didn't give a fuck anymore.

The door was unlocked, the knob turned, and their feelings merged. The pain she was going through was bothering Naaz, and it was written all over his face. Before he could say another word, Mhyale swung on him, hitting him in the chest. Pounding against it, she let out her frustrations on him. Pain filled her chest at the sight of him.

"**F**uck you, Naaziq."

"You don't mean that," Naaz said, bearhugging her.

He pulled her into his chest and held her tight. Mhyale twisted, trying to break free from his hold on her. Being in his embrace made her feel weak. A feeling Mhyale despised. It was only because she'd been here before. She'd cried these tears over the same issues before, only now Naaz was present to witness them.

"Let me go," Mhyale hissed, writhing against him.

"Never."

His answer was spoken with finality. Naaz was never letting her go. He didn't care how much of a protest she put up. What they had was past real, had been placed on pause, and it was time to start the track again. Loriana and Nyree looked on as Naaz walked them to the back of the house and into her room. When they heard the door close, they released their breaths. It was like watching a scene from a movie play out in front of them, and they were both anxious to see what happened next.

"Whew," Nyree breathed, standing up from the couch, "that was intense."

"Right," Loriana mumbled.

Her brain was still trying to come up with reasons that scene played out and unfolded in front of them like it had. She made a mental reminder to ask Mhyale what was really going on later on when her phone rang. Projex's name on her screen always put a smile on her face.

"Hello," she answered.

"What up, ma."

"Nothing. How'd the interview go?"

Across town, Projex had just left an interview Laurent did with a radio show host that had their own app. They played nothing but underground, unreleased music, and lots of local artists who hadn't been discovered yet. Laurent brought Projex along simply because that was his nigga, and he wanted him to get some publicity too.

"That mothafucka was cool. I'd been hearing about them but never had a chance to reach out. They gave me a shoutout and everything." The happiness in his voice made her happy.

"That's so good, baby. I'm happy for you. You're going to have a lot of people in your inbox now, watch."

Projex chuckled. "Yeah, we'll see. And thank you. It feels weird cause shit been looking up for me these last few weeks, and I guess I'm just waiting on something bad to pop off. Is that bad?"

He was in his head again. It was normal for him and now for Loriana to hear. She'd always have to talk him off the edge of overthinking and downplaying like he wasn't deserving of the blessings coming his way. Projex didn't see them as blessings, though. As much bad as he'd done in the world, he knew nothing good would come his way and not for this long.

"It is bad, and you already know what I'm going to say," she scolded.

"Yeah, I do. You deserve everything good in your life, so act like it," he said, mimicking her tone of voice when she got serious with him.

Loriana cracked a smile. "Exactly. You do, so stop being in your head and enjoy the moment. It's all about timing, and maybe this is your time."

"You right. Shit, maybe it is. What you on, though?"

"At home chilling with Nyree. You coming to see me?"

"Don't I always? You need to pull up on me, so I can bust that pussy down at my crib."

Loriana gasped, then chuckled. "Projex. Do not talk like that. I'm not having sex in your mama's house."

"But you'll bounce all over this mothafucka at my granny's? What's the difference?"

"You literally have like your own little apartment downstairs, and she's hardly home. That's what. Plus, you had that girl, and who knows how many others in that bed."

He smirked. It was just like Loriana to say that.

"A'ight. So, now you wanna act brand new like I ain't eat your pussy in it."

"You caught me slipping!" She laughed.

She stopped by to visit one day, and while Joseline ran to the store, Projex pulled her to his room. She refused to let him slide his dick up in her, knowing how loud she got, but she didn't stop him from licking on her.

"Yeah, yeah. I hear you, ma. You ate yet?"

"Mhm. I just got finished eating some Chinese food."

His stomach growled. "Damn. That sound fire. You ate it all?"

"No. I ordered extra for later, but you can have it."

"Bet. I'ma stop and get me some Backwoods, then be over there. Yo' cousin there?"

"Yeah. She in her room with Naaz."

"A'ight. Tell Nyree she can gon' head home. You mine for the rest of the day."

With his court date approaching in ten days, Projex wanted to spend all his time with her. The unknown of what his verdict would be that day wasn't as heavy on his mind, but he knew it would be as the days dwindled down. In Loriana's presence, his mind wasn't on that. Nothing negative surfaced when she was around. The energy she brought him was godsent, and he wanted to cherish it as long as he could.

"I like the sound of that." She giggled. "Make it to me safely."

"Always."

When they hung up, Loriana smacked her lips. Forgetting she picked Nyree up, she stood from the couch just as Nyree moseyed back into the living room.

"Projex on his way over."

"Oh nah. I'm not about to be the third wheel."

"Whaaat? You can stay. We're just going to chill."

Nyree tooted her glossed lips outward. "Yeah, in here until he wants to toss dick down your throat."

"Nyree!"

"Loriana!" she mocked as they both laughed.

"Why do you have to be so vulgar?"

"Girl, bye. You know you be going ham. Just tell me this, and I won't ask nothing else about it ever again."

"It?" Loriana's brows raised. "I'm not telling you about his dick."

"Is it long?"

Her face reddened, and she nodded.

"Like the last hour of work long?"

Loriana hollered. "Eh, more like the last five minutes of church."

Nyree's head flew back as she cackled loudly. The last five minutes of church always turned into twenty, so she knew exactly what Loriana meant.

"That's why you're in love," Nyree told her.

She shrugged. "Nah. It's more than sex with us, but it is good."

"I'm happy for you, friend. At least you're getting some. I'm not giving this up to anyone else anytime soon."

"You regret losing it to Coop?"

Nyree shook her head no. "No. I'm not beating myself up over it, but I guess I want to feel like you do about it. I want it to be more than just sex. I want to actually have a connection with the next person I share my body with."

Loriana nodded, understanding completely. "And that's your decision. It's still a prize, so don't let anyone win it. Make em' work for it, girl."

Nyree playfully rolled her eyes and smirked. "I will. Dang, he got here fast," she said, hearing knocks at the door.

With a pep in her step, Loriana went to open it. Projex was on the phone, but that didn't stop him from kissing her lips and squeezing her tight as her arms wrapped around his neck.

"What's up, ma," he spoke, ready to finish up his conversation with his grandpa.

"What you say?" Joe asked.

"I was talking to Loriana. I just got over here."

Joe grinned on the other end. "Tell her I said hi. We're gonna have to meet one day. You talk about her a lot, and I like that."

Projex grinned and relayed the message. All of his family—the people she met—loved her. Loriana's aura wasn't just good, she was a good person, and they could feel that.

"Yeah, we gon' have to make that happen. You said you'll be down here the night before my trial?"

"Yeah. The day before. Probably a few days before, actually."

"Grandma know that?" Projex asked, being nosy.

"There you go in our business. You need to get you some of your own."

Projex laughed, knowing his grandma probably already knew he'd be in town. "Y'all ain't slick, man. But a'ight. I guess, I'll see you in a few days."

"Don't get into any bullshit between now and then. Go somewhere and get your mind right."

"I will," Projex let him know, already planning to be ducked off in the studio.

"Good. I love you, son. Talk with ya' later on."

"Love you too."

He slid his phone in his pocket and sat down. Loriana had stepped into the kitchen to warm his food up.

"What's up, Projex," Nyree spoke, looking up from her phone.

"What's good?"

"Who you be getting yo' weed from?"

His brow raised. "Why?"

"Damn, nigga. Cause I wanna buy some."

Projex would've thought by now that Loriana would've told Nyree he sold drugs. Specifically, weed. He wasn't complaining that she hadn't but was surprised, honestly. That was just confirmation that she didn't tell her friends every move he made, and she never would. His business was his, and their business was theirs.

"My fault. I got you, though. Let me eat right quick."

Loriana brought his food back just in time. His stomach was touching his back, and the blunts he and Laurent blew down had him high as ever.

"Thank you, ma," he said, widening his legs and getting comfortable.

"You're welcome. I put hot sauce on there, but not a lot."

Projex was already eating a mouthful of bourbon chicken. He knew how she ate her food, so, he was cool with eating some things after her.

"Projex, you know Juice, right?" Nyree asked.

His head bobbed as he chewed. "Yeah, why? You asking too many questions, cuz."

"Oh, my gosh," Nyree laughed. "I asked you two questions. Dramatic ass."

"I know that nigga. You on that?"

She smirked, knowing his ass would peep game without her saying anything. "Maybe."

"That's what's up. Don't ask me shit about that nigga personal life cause I'ont know."

Nyree sucked her teeth. "I wasn't even about to do all that. I was just trying to make sure that it was cool for him to pick me up from here."

"You asking me like this my shit," he said, making Loriana give him a puzzled expression.

"Says the man who was big tripping over Symir dropping me off."

Projex stopped chewing. "I thought you said you

ain't know the nigga like that? Now, you calling cuz by his name?"

Oh shit. Loriana gulped, missing her slip up. "Well, I did have to get his name. Stop being weird."

"I ain't being weird, I'm just watching you. Making sure I don't have to check a nigga behind what's mine. You already know how I'm coming behind you, so act silly if you want to. I'll pull my mothafuckin' clown suit out for both of us. Have a whole circus in this bitch. Keep on."

Nyree laughed under her breath while Loriana sucked her teeth hard and rolled her eyes.

"I'm not even about to go there with you on that. I don't know why you think I would cheat on you."

"Nah. I know you wouldn't do no crazy shit like that, but I know how niggas move. Especially when they see a female who ain't out here. Niggas is vultures, but they don't know me. You do, though."

She did, and that was the exact reason why she would never play on his top like that. Projex was different. The type of different you didn't want to test. She loved him too much to do so, anyway. Leaning his way, she pecked his soft, greasy lips and stayed in his face while he ate.

"I do, so stop tripping on me 'fore I put you on punishment."

Projex smirked. His hand slid between her legs and palmed her entire pussy. "That ain't no threat to me. You know I'ont follow rules no way."

Lustfully, she stared down at him before shimmying away. She wasn't about to have him feeling all on her in front of Nyree. Projex didn't give a fuck.

"You should start." She chuckled, grabbing her phone from the table. "I'll be right back. I gotta go pee."

"Don't go in there playing with yourself either," Projex called after her. "Leave that to me."

"Y'all are so nasty." Nyree faked gagged.

Loriana laughed as she closed the bathroom door behind her. Her smile was stuck on her face as she released her bladder. His simple touch had her excited, and she couldn't wait to lay up for the day. While she washed her hands, her phone pinged with a text from Candace. Loriana's hands stopped moving, and her body heated at the text.

Candace: Hey! Shamari's brother wanted to know if he could have your number.

. . .

I *spoke him up*, she thought. After finishing up washing her hands, she dried them and picked up her phone. Hesitancy filled her as she struggled to reply. It was really a simple yes or no, but Loriana didn't think so. She wanted to ask her why he wanted her number, but deep down, she knew exactly why. Loriana was sure Symir knew she had a boyfriend, so what was the reason? Instead of replying, feeling guilty for even considering carrying on a conversation involving him, she exited out of her messages and locked her phone.

"He's outside," Nyree said soon as she stepped back into the living room.

"Okay. I'll walk you out."

Soon as the door closed behind them, Loriana whispered in a rush, "Why did Symir ask Candace to ask me if he could have my number?"

"What! Shut up."

"I'm serious. She just texted me when I was in the bathroom."

"What'd you say?"

"I didn't reply. I'm not about to cheat on Projex."

Nyree smiled. "You shouldn't. I'm not going to be a bad influence and tell you to get his number 'cause that'd be wrong. I will say save the exchange for a rainy day. You never know when you might just need a friend to talk to."

Loriana pondered over her words. It made sense, but she didn't see herself needing a male friend to talk to when she had Projex. It was a nice thought, though.

"So, where are you taking my friend?" Loriana asked Juice as she leaned inside the passenger window.

Juice's eyes were trained on Nyree and the sundress she had on. He licked his lips and looked up at Loriana.

"Shopping."

"Shopping?!"

Nyree laughed, and Juice shook his head. "Right. She didn't wanna go out to eat, talking 'bout she needs some more stuff for school."

"And you're buying it? Never mind. I guess that's a yes since y'all going shopping."

The trio chuckled. Nyree loved a nice meal, but she had priorities. Plus, she'd just eaten. She was about to make Juice spend some bread on her. She told him so casually to get the rest of her things for school, and he didn't go back and forth about it. He simply told her he was on his way, and here he was. That was the type of energy she loved.

"Yep. Want me to bring you something back?"

"Back? You stuck with me for the day, baby. You might as well gon' head and cut that phone off. We on my time now," Juice told her.

Nyree's thong instantly got wet while Loriana grinned wide.

"Well, okay then. You heard the man. Be safe and text me later. I love you."

"I love you too, friend."

Loriana walked back into the house, and Projex was coming out of the kitchen with a cup of juice in his hand. Comfortably, he'd made himself at home since she moved in. Loriana took in his appearance as if it were her first time seeing him. He rocked a half-white, half-black Midstate shirt, black jeans, and a pair of Workout Plus Altered Reeboks. She loved how he dressed. It was so simple but very well put together.

He downed the rest of his juice and licked his lips. "Yo' favorite color orange, right?"

"Yes. How'd you know?"

"I be paying attention."

He smirked and went to sit back on the couch. He patted his thigh and told her to come sit down on his lap. Obediently, Loriana's feet moved, and she strad-dled him. Running her hands over his hair that was back in its signature twists, she smiled as he palmed her booty.

"This mothafucka getting fat, ain't it?"

She giggled. "No. You always say that."

"It is. You ain't have this much before. What you been feeding it?"

"Your tongue."

His head fell back against the couch as he laughed. "I should push yo' ass off of me. Got me messed up."

"Did I lie?"

His head lifted, and he made both cheeks jiggle in his palms. "Nah. You ain't lie. Get yo' mind out the gutter right quick, though."

Loriana straightened her posture, not missing the feel of his dick hardening underneath her. She didn't know how she was supposed to focus on whatever he was about to talk about, but she'd try.

"Okay," she told him, trying not to touch on his face.

"You listening? Stop looking like you wanna kiss all on me." He laughed, making her steal a quick kiss anyway.

"Okay. Now, I'm listening."

"A'ight. So, look. I'ma give you some money. I

don't want you to touch it. Just hold it for me. Can you do that?"

Her head bobbed up and down. "Yes. What is the mon—"

Projex placed a finger to her lips. "No questions. Just hold it for me, a'ight?"

She nodded her head again, struggling not to ask him any questions. He always gave her money, that was nothing new. What he never did was tell her what to do with it.

"Okay," she spoke softly. "Anything else?"

"Yeah. Come up out of these leggings," he said, trying to tug them down.

Loriana's hand came to his wrist. "Not in here. Mhy has Naaz over."

"They probably in her room doing the same thing. What, you scared?"

She blushed bashfully and nodded. "Yeah. I don't wanna get caught doing that. If no one was here, I wouldn't care."

"It's all good, ma. Let's go to the room right quick. I wanna take you with me to the studio later on."

She hopped up from his lap so quick, Projex couldn't help but laugh. In the room, instead of them having sex right away, they ended up turning a movie on and falling asleep. Some hours later, Projex heard her door being opened, forgetting they didn't lock it, and his hand went to his gun on the dresser before realizing it was Mhyale checking in on them.

"She sleep?" she asked quietly.

Projex nodded his head, and she closed the door. He didn't know what time it was, but he felt sleepier than usual. That didn't matter to Loriana, though. She wasn't asleep, and her hand that made its way inside his briefs was proof of that. Facing him, she stroked his dick and licked her lips. Projex had his eyes open, watching her every move. How she'd came into a woman and explored her sexual urges always humored him.

When her eyes opened, she grinned lustfully and said, "Hi."

"Hi," he replied, voice deep and making her quiver. Kissing her lips, they shared a tongue kiss before Projex was slipping her panties off.

Turning her on her side, he pushed his briefs down, lifted her leg, and rubbed his dick along her lips. How she was this wet, and he hadn't touched her blew his mind. His thumb toyed her clitoris, and her eyes rolled to the back of her head. When his tongue danced along her neck, her favorite spot, she moaned softly, and he slid inside her.

"You bet not hold back either," he spoke against her ear.

"Mmm... okay."

Projex's strokes were slow and purposeful from this position. His hand clasped around her neck while the sound of him stirring her juices echoed throughout the room. His breathing was hard, and he hadn't moved his lips from her ear.

"This pussy so fucking good. You gon' make me nut all in you."

Her muscles clenched as she fucked him back harder. His hand slid down to her breasts and rolled her nipple between his fingers. Loriana moaned out in pleasure; it was feeling so good.

"Oooh, you feel so good," she moaned, needing to let him know.

When he dug deep, hitting her spot, Loriana placed a hand on his leg. He just knew she wasn't trying to run. Projex didn't play that. She groaned when he slid out of her but moaned loudly once he had her on her back and legs pressed into the bed.

"You runnin', ma?" he asked, long stroking her while staring into her eyes.

Her head thrashed against the pillow. The light from the TV gave him the perfect view of her wetting his dick up. Projex pulled all the way out to the tip before diving back in. Loriana's back arched as she pulled him closer. Chest to chest, she spread her legs more, giving herself all of him.

"I love you," she spoke against his lips.

He pounded into her, feeling his heartbeat increase. "I love you more." He meant it.

Loriana shook her head, not believing him, but it was the truth. He knew from day one she was going to be his. Her wetness splashed against his abdomen as he let out satisfied grunts. Her eyes watered as he gripped her waist.

"Damn, ma," he moaned, feeling his stomach cave.

Loriana's pussy was too good, too wet, and had him too gone. Her left foot came up to his chest, causing him to maneuver them some. Grabbing her foot, Projex freakily sucked on her toes as he beat her pussy up. The combination had Loriana blasting off into a different stratosphere.

"Yeees. Right there," she cried out.

He brought the freak out of her, making her roll her hips and caress her own nipples. Projex was in heaven looking at her body underneath his. Her untainted body that she willingly shared with him. Her heart, though... he loved that most. His head spun, thinking about her leaving him. Projex pounded into her.

"You mine?" he asked through clenched teeth.

Loriana nodded, feeling her pussy spasm.

"Tell me."

"I'm yours," she breathed heavily. "All of me."

She was looking him dead in the eyes, snatching his mothafuckin soul from his body while she did it. He belonged to her too, nobody else. When he went deeper, her mouth fell open, and she screamed his name.

"Bryshooooon!"

Her body tensed, toes popped, and pussy wet him up like he'd set off the fire alarm. He might as well have. Loriana's body was on fire for him. Her soul had been set ablaze, burning down every doubt and fear coming their way. Projex's face fell to hers as their tongues danced. He kissed her with need as her arms wrapped around him. Projex's release sucked the last bit of oxygen he had left in him. Loud huffs escaped him as his face lay in the crook of her warm neck. Lovingly, Loriana rubbed his back. His heart swelled at the endearing act.

"Damn, ma. I wish you weren't on birth control."

Her hand stopped, and she whispered, "Why?"

"I can see you carrying my child. Like, I be having dreams about it."

"We have time for all of that. Gotta reach our goals first."

Projex kissed her neck, appreciating how she always got him back focused. "You right. When we accomplish them, know it's a wrap. How many years you think we got?"

She chuckled, highly amused that they were having this conversation with his dick still planted and twitching inside of her.

"Let's not put a date on it. If it happens, it happens. You better take care of us too."

"Always. I'ma always be there for mine."

Loriana believed him. She trusted him. Not too many had come along and made it easy, but Projex had. She wasn't sure if it was just sex talk or what, but his actions always matched the words he spoke. Loriana hoped she'd never have to call his bluff because she needed him to be there for her. Not just now, but for those days when it wasn't all good. And it wasn't always all good... that she knew for sure.

Chapter Ten

After two hours of deliberation, the jury had finally reached a verdict in the second-degree murder indictment against Projex. Standing tall to his feet, with broad shoulders squared ahead, he smoothed down the front of his suit jacket. The dark grey slim-fit, tailored suit looked impeccably good on him. His hair was neatly braided to the back, and he rocked no jewelry. He adjusted his sleeves while crossing his hands in front of him.

Everyone had been anxiously waiting on this day yet dreading it as well. The courtroom was semi-full of his people, including a few people from the victim, Malcolm's, family as well. Loriana's eyes were trained on the judge while Joi and Joseline held hands tightly. Grandpa Joe sat beside them, holding his breath. Projex wanted Kordell and Laurent there but didn't want to bring any unwanted attention their way. Ross, Projex's lawyer, gave him a solid pat on the back.

Ross had reassured him that he'd be walking away today a free man, and Projex was waiting on it. Loriana's leg bounced as an entire minute of pure silence smothered the room. The judge, an older white man in his sixties, focused his attention on the lead juror. The prosecutor had a smug look on his face, and it'd been there the entire day.

"Have you reached a verdict?" the judge asked.

"We have, Your Honor."

Projex held his breath.

"For the charge of second-degree murder, we, the jury, find the defendant, Bryshon Emery, guilty."

Shock flew through Loriana's body as her eyes darted to Projex. His heart had sunk to his stomach right along with his family's. A look of dread crossed Ross' face, but there was nothing he could do. Not right now, at least. Projex was holding his emotions together as best as he could, but they almost got the best of him when he saw his mama crying.

"We gon' be good," Projex told her as she hugged him tightly.

Loriana sat shell-shocked as panic filled her chest. "He promised not to leave me," she mumbled.

Tears dripped onto her black dress, and she didn't bother to wipe them. Not one, but two people she loved were taken from her in less than six months' time. She was sick to her stomach. Projex urged for her to come to him after hugging Joi.

"Baby, come here. Give me a kiss and hug right quick."

Her chest heaved as she shook her head no from side to side. She couldn't move.

"Mama, help her up," Projex urged as the guards prepared to cuff him.

Joseline shook her head in disbelief. Cheers of joy and praises to the Man above from Malcolm's family was tearing her up inside. Projex told her he was innocent, and she was riding with her son regardless of what the juror's decision was.

"Loriana, please go hug him."

She let Joseline help her to her feet, where her heart was. She was stepping all over it, not giving a fuck because clearly, she didn't need it anymore. He leaned her way, inhaling her scent and kissing her lips as they cuffed him. Loriana's arms went around his neck, and she held him tightly.

"I love you, ma," was all he could say without getting choked up.

Loriana didn't have to say it back. Projex felt it. It was radiating from her quivered body as she tried her best to be strong for him. A warm kiss was placed to the side of her face before he was pulled back.

"I love you too," her voice cracked.

Projex wanted to tell her he'd be home soon and to hold shit down, but the look in her eyes let him know she didn't want to hear any more promises. The ones he couldn't keep were out of his control and eating him alive. He should've known what the outcome would be when they brought a witness to the stand. Deep down, he knew he was fucked, but there had to be another way to get out of this. Loriana was hoping for it too.

"You gon' answer my calls, L-Boogie?" Projex asked, trying to cheer her up.

She nodded her head, hating what their relation-ship would now be reduced to. Loriana didn't have the slightest clue of how this would work. All she knew was that as Projex walked out of the courtroom, he took the last bit of hope and understanding she had with him. Her heart... it'd been gone long before now. She was just sharing the remnants of it with him in hopes he'd make her whole again. A hollow space now occupied where it used to be.

Being the girlfriend of an inmate was stressful. Projex had been locked up for two weeks, and Loriana felt like she needed to take a class to keep up with how to communicate with him. Learning how to put money on her phone was just the first step. Peaches, being the auntie she was, schooled her on what she could and couldn't say over the phone. Hardly did they ever talk about his case, but that's all Loriana wanted to discuss.

During their first call, she cried hard before the operator scared the shit out of her. Being put on a time constraint was torture. She had so much she wanted to get off her chest—one of two things being when he was coming home.

"We won't know that for a while, huh?" she asked him.

Projex sighed. He wouldn't know until the judge gave him his sentencing. "Nah. Not for a lil' minute. Don't worry 'bout that, though. What you eat today?"

"A bowl of cereal this morning," she mumbled.

"Ma, it's almost seven. You need to eat something."

"I'm not hungry and stop telling me what to do!" she snapped, then immediately felt bad. "I'm sorry. It's just... we normally would eat together."

Projex shook his head, hating how fucked up he'd made things between them, but there was nothing he could do from behind bars. Asking her to eat was one thing; being sure she did it was another.

"I know, ma. That don't mean starve yourself, though. You wildin'," he said, making her laugh. It was just like him to brighten her mood all while talking shit.

"I'm not starving myself. I just haven't had an appetite."

Grief would do that to you. One day she had no taste for anything at all, and the next, she'd eat everything in sight. It didn't help that she was on her cycle either. Those depressing ass four days of back and butt cramps, a bloated stomach, breakouts, and binging on snacks was hell. Loriana was really going through it.

"Still try to eat, though. What you do today?"

She felt like this was the perfect time to bring up what she'd been seeing on social media. Loriana was never that girl to go snooping for information to piss her off, but here lately, it'd been falling into her lap.

"I went and got my hair done," she told him.

Projex smiled. "Yeah? I bet you look hella fine. Moo did it?"

"Mhm. She gave me some curls even though I just wanted it straight."

"She gon' always do what she wants." He chuckled.

"Right. It's okay, though. While she was curling it, I was on Facebook. You know, just scrolling trying to catch up on there. I'm never on there."

Projex blinked his eyes a few times, trying to see where she was going with their conversation. "Right. You ain't ever on there."

"Exactly, but I think I should start getting on more. You seem to have a lot of girls waiting for you to get out."

He sucked his teeth. "Man, don't start with that shit."

"No. I think I want to."

"So, you wanna argue? You wanna argue right now over the phone? I can just hang up, for real."

Her jaw tightened. "And watch you be single. I told you about that hanging up in my face stuff a long time ago. I don't care that you're in jail."

"I'm in prison."

It was her turn to suck her teeth. "Whatever. You're still locked up."

"And I ain't tryna talk about what you done seen on social media from some attention-seeking ass bitches."

"The money I put on this phone to talk to you is mine, so we gon' talk about whatever I want," she sassed, making him chuckled in disbelief.

While Loriana hadn't been privy to the South Ave living since moving there, a lot of Projex's old ways had surfaced. She was scrolling Facebook, something she never did but was bored, and came across a post from Projex's ex-girlfriend, Brittany.

She'd posted a picture, multiple ones actually, of her and Projex. A long, drawn-out status about their history and how she was missing him on some extra bullshit had Loriana seething mad. Brittany's wasn't the only post though. Several girls from around the way had tagged him in posts, saying free him. Loriana wanted to know what for? It wasn't like they were going to be his girlfriend or something, but clearly, they knew something she didn't.

"You gon' let that social media shit stress you out."

She rolled her eyes. "No. You and these hoes are."

"I don't give a fuck about none of them hoes, ma. That's what they do when any nigga they used to fuck with go to jail. It's all for clout. You think I'm calling them up and asking what they ate for lunch and shit?"

"I don't know what you're doing."

Her tone let him know she wasn't dropping this.

"I'm on here talking to you. Them hoes can starve and eat dick, for real."

She choked on a laugh. He was upset now because they made his girl mad.

"I guess. They made it seem like y'all were talking or something. I don't like that."

"I don't either, but now you know how messy some females can be. I been laid up with you for months. Ain't no way I had time to fuck around on you. Stop tripping over that and tell me you sorry."

Her laugh sputtered. "Tell you I'm sorry? For what?"

"Cause. You just sat up here and talked bad to me about something I don't have nothing to do with. I want an apology."

"Are you serious?"

"Yep. You better tell me before our call hangs up. You heard the lady."

They both laughed, even though Loriana had just been mad at him.

"I'm sorry, baby. Not for me being mad, but for them girls ever having a chance with you."

Projex laughed loud. "Aye, yo. I love you, girl. Goofy ass."

Her heart melted. "I love you too. Call me later?"

"Always. Go eat!"

He shouted just before the call hung up. Sighing, Loriana sat with a smile on her face at the edge of her bed. She knew Projex was right, but it still bothered her that they felt the need to post him as if he belonged to them. Not ever being the one to go tit-for-tat, but feeling like she had to let these girls know, Loriana opened up her Facebook app. She had a lot on her mind and decided to share with the world and the group of girls watching her page.

"If you couldn't post him when he was out, don't post him now," she said aloud while typing the words.

Loriana Simms
5 mins · 🌐

If you couldn't post him when he was out, don't post him now. #FreeMine

Like · Comment · Share

👍 20 like this.

↪ 2

Write a comment...

Before sharing it, she thought about adding a picture of them but figured her words were enough. When she saw Mhyale and Nyree share it, adding their own two cents as well, Loriana laughed. Of course, her road dogs were going to have her back and check shit behind her always. Within five minutes, it'd gotten twenty likes which was a lot for someone who didn't post at all. Loriana exited out of the app, not caring to clock what traffic the status was getting. She said what she said.

"Now, let me go eat like my man said." She chuckled, standing from the bed.

———

"Somebody go tell Chris to check those hot dogs on the grill!" Nakita yelled from the entryway of the kitchen toward the backdoor.

Music blasted in the home of Nyree's Uncle Chris for her go-away party. Having applied for a freshman learning program that let you arrive a day before everyone else got on campus, Nyree was leaving this Thursday. In four days, she'd be out of Kansas City and almost three hours away at school.

"He said they're done," Nyree told her, walking into the kitchen with a plastic cup in her hand.

Loriana was right behind her. Nakita looked their way.

"What y'all got in them cups? Peaches better not have y'all drinking. Y'all asses ain't grown."

Loriana and Nyree snickered. They weren't grown, but it was a celebration. To disguise the Seagram's wine cooler Peaches gave them, she had them pour it into cups. It was the only one they were getting, so they were trying to cherish it and sip slow.

"It's just juice, mama."

"Mhm. Why y'all in here bothering me?"

Loriana fanned her face. "It's hot out there. We're waiting until some more people get here to go back out."

"Well, come make yaself useful and cut up these tomatoes and cucumbers for the salad."

"On that note," Nyree said, standing from the barstool at the island. "We gon' go back outside."

Loriana shook her head. "*You* can go back outside. I'll help you, Ms. Nakita."

"Thank you, baby. She gon' miss my homecooked meals when her behind eating a pack of noodles for a week straight."

Nyree laughed. "Noodles be fire. Especially the chicken kind. I am going to miss it, though."

As always, their mother-daughter interaction

made Loriana's chest ache for her mother. She was no longer crying at the drop of a hat, but moments like this did get to her. They always would. That's one of the reasons she didn't mind helping Ms. Nakita in the kitchen.

"Am I cutting these in half?" Loriana asked while rinsing off the Cherubs grape tomatoes in the sink.

"Yep. Just straight down the middle and put them in that glass container right there. When you're done with those, slice those cucumbers. We gon' put em' to the side 'cause everyone doesn't like them in their salad."

Loriana nodded and began her duties.

"You came by yourself today?" Nakita asked.

"Yes. Mhy had to do two people's hair."

"On a Sunday? I ain't mad at it. She better get her money. I'm so happy you girls got some hustle to y'all. So many young girls just be out here lost and chasing behind these nappy-headed boys."

Loriana snickered. Having that hustler mentality was embedded in them. Coming from the hood, Nakita knew nothing but how to get money. She was raised on survival first and love second. Same with Peaches and Linette. Even if they were struggling, their kids never knew it. If they did know it, it was never felt.

At one point in time, Peaches had a full-time job, an overnight job, and was making plays for a local drug dealer. She called it her side hustle, telling Mhyale and Memphis when they got older that they should have one too. Not an illegal one, but something they enjoyed doing. For Mhyale, it was hair.

"You still tutoring?" Nakita asked.

Loriana shook her head no. "No. Not right now. I was thinking about doing it for the kids in summer school, but I'm not sure yet."

"Nothing wrong with that. I'm sure them kids need all the help they can get," she said, lowkey talking shit but being serious as well.

"I was gonna apply for some jobs until I enroll in school. You know, just to occupy my time."

"It's a lot of places hiring too. I'ma ask my home-girl that works at Penn Valley if they have some tutoring positions or something. That way, you'll have some money saved up when you go to school."

Those were Loriana's exact plans if she stuck to them. With her newfound shopping habits, it'd been hard for her to save like she told herself she would. Getting a job wasn't strictly for the money. She wanted to get out of the house. With Projex locked up, Nyree getting ready to go to school, and Mhyale having her own life, she felt stir-crazy sitting in the house by herself.

"That's what I was thinking too," she replied.

"You still dating that boy? What's his name?"

She blushed. "Projex, and yes. We're still together."

"You ready to hold him down while he in there?"

It wasn't a secret that Projex was in prison. The entire hood felt his presence being missed. Nakita wasn't their age, but her ear stayed to the streets thanks to her boo.

"I guess so," was Loriana's reply.

Nakita looked up at her from the banana pudding she was layering. "That didn't sound too confident to me."

"I am. I mean, my mind hasn't really thought about how long he'd be in there, so I just take it day by day."

"You ready to wait years for him? A murder charge isn't a slap on the wrist."

Nakita had to ask her these questions because she knew for a fact, Loriana's vulnerable state of mind felt like she had to hold Projex down. It was what most all young girls thought when their man got booked. In Loriana's case, she wasn't sure what to expect but didn't know anything else. Those phone calls, jail visits, lonely nights, missed holidays, and his absence hadn't really hit her yet. It would soon, though.

"Honestly, I don't know. I know I don't want to just leave him hanging. He needs someone in his corner right now."

"And who's in yours? I'm not saying he's not, but from the inside, he can only do so much. Trust me, I know from experience how draining it can be. You're young. You have your entire life ahead of you and spending it being worried about him isn't healthy."

Loriana's nostrils flared. She loved Nakita, but she didn't like how she was talking.

"Him being locked up isn't taking anything away from my life. I can still do what I have planned and hold him down. It's really not that hard."

Nakita chuckled. "Baby, okay. My mama always told me the best lesson in life is when you learn it on your own. You'll just have to wait and see. Nothing wrong with wanting to be his support system, but make sure he's yours as well. I done seen plenty of women get caught up behind niggas in jail, putting their lives on pause for them, then not having nothing to show for holding him down. Move smart with your head, and not make decisions with your heart. It might cost you."

While Loriana may have thought Projex being locked up wasn't taking anything away from her, it was. His protection was one of a few things. She didn't realize it until he was gone that the safety net he'd magically cover her with was no longer there. Yes, he had his mama, Joi, and Kordell check in on her, but it wasn't him. The stability he provided wasn't solid anymore.

Loriana yearned for it. In the wee hours of the night, when her nightmares became too much, Projex's arms around her weren't there anymore. He couldn't physically wipe her tears and tell her, *It's going to be a'ight, ma.* Her being able to pick up the phone and tell him she just needed to vent wasn't an option. His freedom had been snatched, and she felt like hers had too. Being responsible for caring for not only her heart but her mental as well could only be done part-time now.

Later on in the evening, the mid-size home was packed with family and friends, all for Nyree. The gift table that she didn't want to have was full of bags and boxes. Nakita didn't care that she was staying in a dorm. If people wanted to donate and put less of a dent in her pocket, she was letting them.

"When we cutting this cake?" Nyree's grandpa, Slim, asked.

"You know you can't have any of that, Paw-Paw," Nyree whispered to him.

He kissed her cheek. "Sshh. It's our secret. You're grandma already took my damn 'nana pudding."

"I put you some up in the fridge downstairs."

"That's my girl. Here before I forget," he said, digging in his pocket. "We put a little something in your card, but here's some more. I'm proud of you."

Nyree kissed his cheek as he slid a folded one-hundred-dollar bill into her hand. What was funny was that her grandmother had done the same thing when they walked in. They stayed handing her money on the sly as if it were a secret from one another.

"Thank you. Now, go sit down. I'll save you a piece when it's cut."

Slim did as he was told while Nyree pulled her phone from the pocket of her jean romper. A mega-watt smile covered her face at the text Juice sent her. They'd been talking heavily since he picked her up that day from Loriana's, and Nyree couldn't mask the infatuation she had for him. Whether something more became of them or not, she was having fun. The kind of fun she thought she'd have while dating Coop. Juice was older, more experienced, and letting her enjoy him while she could. He knew once she got down there to school, he'd be a distant memory.

"You must be talking to Juice," Loriana said, walking up on her.

"Yep. I asked him to pull up over here, but he was like, *You know Raytown police be hot. Just come see me later. I got something for you,*" she mocked, sounding like a girly version of him.

Loriana laughed. "Now, why would you tell him to come over here? You want him to meet all of your family?"

"I don't care. It's not like he's my boyfriend. He's just a friend," she told her with a shrug.

"Yeah, a much older friend."

Nyree rolled her eyes. "He's not even that old."

"If you say so. Your uncle Chris walking over here."

Dressed like the cool uncle he was, Chris had on a Nike outfit he'd changed into after grilling for the day, with a pair of all-white forces on. He shared the same toffee-colored complexion as Nyree, sported a short cut with just enough length to see his curly texture, and a full beard with grey hairs she was sure was because of her. He'd been more than a father to Nyree than his brother, Nyree's dad had. Chris had been letting Nyree run his life from the second she was born, and nothing was going to change about that.

"You ready for your gift from me?" he asked with a smile.

"I'm always ready for a gift from you."

"A'ight. Let me get everybody to come out front."

Her mouth dropped open. "You didn't. You got me a car!?" she screamed before taking off inside the house.

Chris just shook his head. "Aye. Everybody come out front right quick," he told the crowd.

Everyone made their way to the front of the house and down the driveway. Nyree searched the cul-de-sac area for any unfamiliar cars but didn't spot one out of the blue.

"I don't know what you looking around for." Chris laughed.

Nakita sighed. "Girl, he done spoiled this child of mine rotten. Can't even lie, right."

"Shit. He can spoil me too," Peaches said, full of liquor. "He still an officer?"

"Mhm."

"He can handcuff me all he wants," she said, tossing her hands behind her back and bending over. Her ass shook in the white linen shorts she was wearing.

Nakita laughed while Loriana groaned.

"Auntie, please. He's like family."

"Girl, he ain't no blood of mine. Better gon' on somewhere. Mmm. Look at that strong back. Make me wanna climb his ass."

Loriana cringed and moved away from them. She couldn't handle her auntie when she was drunk, but that seemed to be her only vice. Peaches meant no harm, but Loriana didn't want to hear all that. Walking into the street, she stood next to Nyree, who had an anxious expression on her face.

"Scoot out the street, so this car can get by," Chris said, as a black jeep came down the street.

When it pulled around the circle and stopped in front of Nyree, the fresh braids in her head swung wildly as she jumped up and down. Her excitement made Loriana smile, but the person who climbed from the driver's seat made her lash strips she wore, fly up.

What is he doing here? she thought as Symir handed the keys over to Nyree and slapped hands with Chris. His wide smile made her insides quiver. She stared wordlessly at him, already feeling over-whelmed by his masculine energy. His smooth dark skin glowed underneath the rays of the sun, seemingly brightening her already good day even more.

While Nyree fanned out over her 2016 Jeep Rene-gade, Symir's peepers fell on Loriana. She gave a shy wave as he smirked. Loriana never did give the okay for Candace to give him her number, and he was about to figure out why. He told Chris he saw somebody he knew—wanted to get to know—and made his way to her. Symir had no intentions of staying, but her presence put a halt to his plans.

"I'd ask what you were doing here, but it's pretty clear," Loriana told him with a chuckle.

Symir half-grinned. "Yeah. Just being the drop-off. She your family?"

"Best friend but might as well be family. How do you know Chris?"

"Friend of the family."

His reply didn't explain much, and now she really wanted to know who and what Symir did for a living. His mysterious aura made Loriana want to take out a pen and jot down notes on him. Eyeing the beauty in front of him, Symir let it be known he liked what he was admiring. In an off-the-shoulder, ruffled yellow top that stopped right above her belly button, white distressed boyfriend jeans, and fake Birkenstock slides, he loved her chill yet cute get-up.

Loriana felt naked under his intense gaze. "What?"

"You look nice. Yellow looks good on you."

"Thank you. Do you sell cars or something?"

Symir nodded. "Yeah. You need one?"

"Really? And, no. I have one, but that's such a cool job to have."

"It's a'ight," he replied just as his ride pulled up to get him. "I was just coming over to speak. Didn't think I'd see you again."

"But you were asking around about me."

What came out as a question was more of a statement. Symir smirked.

"Nah. I didn't ask about you; I just asked for your number. Which, I see you decided not to share. I can respect it. You're in a relationship and all."

"I am. Why, though?"

"Why not?"

She didn't have to ask the full question; Symir knew exactly what she meant. He wanted her number for more reasons than one.

"I don't like when people do that," she told him.

"Duly noted. I'll remember that for the next question you ask me."

Loriana smirked, knowing there was another one coming. She could do this all day.

"Were you trying to check on me?"

Symir nodded and licked his lips. "Yeah. Somewhere in my mind, I convinced myself that if I had my own way of reaching out to you, I wouldn't worry as much."

Her stomach was being weird again. "You don't have to worry about me. I'm a big girl."

"Being a big girl has nothing to do with being cared for."

Who is this man? her mind wondered, not transmitting a quick enough answer to stop her next question.

"Who are you?"

Symir laughed. His bright smile making her lose all sense. "Right now... I'm whoever you need me to be."

"Friends," she blurted out, not knowing where that answer came from. "I mean, we can be friends. No harm in that, right?"

"Ask yourself that, Lo. You're the one in a relationship."

"It's not. I can have friends."

Symir chuckled lightly. "A'ight then, friend, put my number in your phone."

"Why can't you put mine in yours?"

"Because I'm leaving the start of this friendship up to you. Whenever you hit my line, I'll know you serious."

She sighed, hating the pressure, but loving it all at once. Loriana didn't really know what she was doing as she typed in his number and saved it, but it felt okay. She didn't feel bad for getting a guy's number when they would be nothing more than friends. That's if she built up the courage to reach out to him.

"Okay. I got your number saved now," she told him.

"Bet. Don't be afraid to use it. I think we have a lot in common."

Her lips poked out as if he were fibbing. "A lot like what?"

"More than you know." Symir gave her a wink and backed away while facing her. "I'll see you around, Lo."

Her eyes stayed trained on him until the Porsche truck he dropped her off in that night was out of her sight. His energy hung in the air like a potent odor, forcing her to look again at his name in her contacts. Editing his name, she added a question mark because really... who the hell was he, and what would be his purpose in her life? At the moment, Loriana wished she could see the future. She was praying it brought about something worth wishing on.

Later that night, after she left Nyree's party, Loriana drove home while talking to Mhyale. She was staying the night at Naaz's crib but promised to be back in the morning.

"One day, you're going to tell me what the deal is

with you two. The real deal, not the watered-down version," Loriana told her.

Mhyale laughed. "One day. Go straight home and text me when you get there. Want me to stay on the phone with you?"

"No. I want to listen to my music. I'll text you as soon as I get in."

"Okay, love you."

"I love you, too."

When they hung up, Loriana pressed play on her music. *Complicated* by Nivea was her jam and instantly made her think of Projex. She loved hip-hop, but on late nights, R&B was her preferred genre to cruise to. Coming to a red light, she snapped her fingers and sang loudly.

"Well, love works like magic, and it's so true my mind can't grasp it... I'm so glad that you made me your wifey."

As the lyrics resonated with her entire soul, she frowned at how long the light was and thought back to Projex telling her that he never stopped at red lights this late. Not because he was on some daredevil shit, but because that's how people got caught lacking. *Whatever that means* is what she thought that night. It was only going on eleven, which wasn't that late to her. When the light turned green, she sighed and pulled off.

Coming up on a gas station near the house, she decided to stop and run in to get her some snacks. They planned on going grocery shopping in the morning, but Loriana was out of all her late-night grubs. When sleep didn't come easy, which was most nights, she'd watch movies and pig out. Locking her doors, she waltzed inside, making the jingle go off above her head.

Picking up a pack of peanut M&M's, a bag of hot fries, some Oreos, gummy worms, and a strawberry lemonade Calypso, Loriana looked down at her items.

"I think that's all I need," she mumbled, walking to the counter.

"You have the munchies?" the guy asked and chuckled.

"Nope. Just snacking."

He nodded and continued to ring her up. Once she paid and grabbed her bag, she walked out of the store. Before she could place her bag in the passenger seat, someone came up behind her, shoved a gun deep into her side, and demanded they give her what was in her purse.

"Run me all that cash, bitch," the robber hissed.

"P-Please don't shoot me."

He yanked on the purse. "Shut the fuck up and empty this bitch out."

Trembling, Loriana fumbled to grab all the loose money she had inside her purse. She wasn't trying to die over a couple hundred dollars. He could take the entire purse if it meant she'd get to keep her life. When she handed him the money, she hated that the mask pulled over his face hid his identity. His voice, though... she'd always remember it.

"Tell your man he not the only shooter out here," the man whispered before pulling the trigger.

"Aaarggghh!" Loriana's gut-wrenching scream echoed as she fell into the seat.

As much as she prayed for her life to end so she could be with her mother, Loriana never thought she'd go out this way. She hadn't lived by the gun, so why was she dying by it? One thing was for sure, though... words were powerful.

Chapter Eleven

Sweat dripped from Projex's face as he pushed himself up, then downward for another push-up. He stopped counting a long time ago and couldn't feel the concrete floor underneath him, just adrenaline. His hands were numb, muscles burning, and mind somewhat clear. He'd been working out in his cell for the last hour, trying to rid himself of the stress he was plagued with. Thinking of the reason, the person rather, who had him ready to flip out, made his nostrils flare in annoyance and confusion.

For the last week, he'd been calling Loriana's phone only for her to not answer. When he talked to his mama, Joseline told him she hadn't answered her calls either. Neither of them knew why she'd been distant, and it was tearing Projex up because he hadn't heard her voice. At first, he thought something may have been wrong, then realized she just stopped picking up. Projex didn't get what happened for her to act like this with him. On his Aaliyah shit, he thought of sending her ass a letter letting her know she had him fucked up, but he hadn't gotten around to it yet.

Projex expected a few people to go MIA during his stint, but not her. Not his L-Boogie. It'd only been a little over a month, and she'd given up on him already. Prison wasn't for him. He'd already made a promise to himself that if he got out of this jam, he wasn't coming back. He didn't understand how prisoners enjoyed being in here. Following the rules of other fake tough-ass niggas all day had him on pins and needles. He wasn't trying to bring himself any more unnecessary charges, but he could see himself catching another case real soon.

Pumping out ten more pushups, he hopped up with his chest heaving and body stiff. The days in his six by eight cell dragged, while his nights haunted him. It didn't help that his cellmate talked in his sleep either. The nigga never shut the fuck up, so Projex was up half the time thinking. Plotting on his next move. Projex hadn't gotten to the point where he was reading books yet to pass the time, but he was writing songs. There was nothing but time, and he was using it to his advantage.

"Emery!" one of the guards yelled out, stopping in front of his cell. "You got a visitor."

Not expecting anyone, Projex wondered if it was his mama doing a pop-up visit. He'd spoken to her on Friday, two days ago, and she hadn't mentioned anything about coming to see him. Dabbing his face and body with some tissue, he got dressed. Being the type of man who didn't play about his hygiene, Projex hated what being locked up had reduced his privileges to. He'd thugged it out with his mama and Joi on more than a few occasions with boiling water on the stove to get clean, but it'd been years since they experienced that. Adjusting to his new normal while locked up was a process for sure.

With his wrists cuffed, another reminder that his freedom was no longer his, they headed toward the visitation area. When he felt the guard tug him, Projex jerked his body.

"I know where we going, cuz. Quit tryna drag me 'round this bitch," Projex spat.

He may have been locked up, but his manhood was still intact. One too many mothafuckas had tried him already, and Projex wasn't no hoe, so of course, he fought back. It seemed like everyone was in there trying to prove something when he gave not one fuck about any of them, what hood they claimed, or none of that. Projex kept to himself and only spoke when spoken to if that. Niggas had nothing to do but run their mouths in jail, and Projex wasn't trying to hear any of them.

"Yeah, yeah. Keep it moving," the guard told him.

The chatter of inmates greeting their friends or loved ones caused a small relief in Projex's chest. In here was their only sense of freedom from those metal bars. He didn't like his family coming up here to see him, preferring to talk over the phone, so they wouldn't see the disappointment in his eyes. Projex didn't regret any of his past dealings and planned to do his time, however long it'd be, like a soldier.

His long legs covered in the uniformed pants, matching every other inmate in the room, moved at a snail's pace. The last person he was expecting to see was Loriana waiting at the metal table to see him. Though happy as hell to see her, Projex didn't let that be known as he walked over to the table. Loriana's face was unreadable, and he didn't like that. *She look pretty as hell,* he thought, smirking a bit. Her beauty lit up the entire room and him.

"You ain't gone stand up and give me a hug?" he

asked her with his heart ready to jump out of his chest. He missed her ass something terrible.

Nerves still rattled, Loriana stood up and walked around to him. The brief two-second hug and quick kiss to his lips wasn't enough, but they made it enough. Anything longer than that, and Loriana was sure she'd get escorted out. She wanted to crawl under his skin and stay there. Before her arrival, she'd studied the jail's visitation rules as if she were preparing for an exam. This was all so foreign to her, and she didn't want to mess up her first visit.

Dressed in what she figured was the dress code since she got in, Loriana wore blue jeans, a white V-neck, and a pair of classic Adidas. Her hair was pulled into a slick bun, with perfectly swirled baby hairs. Her chain was left at home, purse in the trunk of her car, and emotions all over the place. On the drive up, she didn't know what to expect. The entire procedure of just getting inside had overwhelmed her to the point where she wanted to turn back around. She couldn't though, not after coming this far and seeing the light in Projex's eyes.

"Hi," she mumbled, unable to hold her smile back.

Even with his hair untamed, he was still fine to her. Loriana studied his face unhurriedly, feature by feature. She noted how thick his mustache had grown in. His chin hairs seemed to be the same. She missed him so much and was trying not to cry and ruin the mood, but the waterworks were inevitable.

"Don't cry, ma. You look too pretty for all that."

"I can't help it. I miss you so much."

Projex's chest ached at the whine in her voice. She needed him. "I miss you more, on God. I ain't know you was coming to see me. You ain't been answering your phone. What's up? I do something wrong?"

Loriana's head shook as her chin met her chest, and her palm rubbed at her wet eyes. His confused tone hurt her more. "No. I've just been having a rough week. I didn't want to make you worry about me."

"I'ma always worry, especially when you don't answer. That shit had me sick," he finally admitted to himself and her aloud. "I was calling my granny trying to see if she could hawk you down and shit. She asked could she have your number, too."

That put a smile on her face. "Yes. You know that's my girl."

"Shit, I can't tell. What's been up, though. Tell me something good."

She was stuck. There really wasn't anything good

to reveal. That's not what she'd come for anyway. Loriana hadn't answered his calls all week because she didn't know how to tell him that because whatever he had done out in these streets, someone had robbed her and sent a warning shot. The shooter had sent a message, and she was here to deliver it.

Her shoulder lifted, trying to find the words to say. "I don't know. It feels good outside."

"Yeah? The sun prolly shining bright and shit. You been out kicking it?"

Her head shook from side to side. "No. Not really. I've been in the house. Nyree is at school, so I don't have anyone to hang with like that."

"You ain't cool with ol' girl you went to that party with?" Projex asked, not remembering her name but recalling Loriana talk about her.

"Oh, yeah. Candace. We're still cool, but everybody just doing their own thing with school right now."

"You still enrolling for the spring semester, right?"

She nodded. "Yes. As of now."

"Nah. You are. We ain't backing out of that."

We. Everything she did, Projex supported, letting her know she wasn't doing it alone. She loved that about him. She also hated that he was locked up.

Loriana sighed. "I know. My mind is just all over the place right now, but enough about me. What've you been doing?"

Projex chuckled. There wasn't much to do when you were confined to your cell for most of your day.

"Not a damn thing. I been writing. Laurent told me you been asking questions about my pay cut from his songs."

Knowing he had someone besides a few of his niggas, and family looking out for him made him feel good. When Projex asked Loriana to hold some money for him, it came in a safety deposit box that he tucked away in her bedroom closet. Being nosy one day, he discovered there was an empty crawl space in it. He put some of the composition notebooks he wrote in, in there as well.

"Yes. I wanted to make sure he wasn't trying to get over on you. I mean, I don't think he would, but you're in here."

"He wouldn't. That's my man uh' hunnid grand. Did Kordell get that money to you?"

She nodded. When she did finally emerge from the confinements of her home, Loriana ran into him at the grocery store, and he gave her some money. Of course, he asked where she had been at, a message he was sure to get back to his cousin when he called. Projex hadn't called, though. He chucked it up, at that moment, as Loriana needing some space.

"Yeah. You don't have to keep giving me money. I'm not doing anything with it."

"Not yet. You never know when you might need it."

"I won't. Give it to your mama and Joi."

He smiled at her. "Baby, chill. I know you feel like you know everything but let me do me. My mama nem' straight."

Projex made sure of that. When her eyes watered again, he frowned.

"What's wrong?"

"I-I just. I don't know. This is all so much."

A slight panic filled his belly. "What is? What you talking about?"

Sniffling, she looked him in his eyes. Those chestnut-colored eyes bore into her soul and fed it nonverbal promises. They glimmered with uncertainty, not ready for what she had to tell him.

"I have something to tell you, but please don't get mad."

His jaw flexed. "Nah. I'ma get mad, so tell me." Projex wasn't about to lie. Whatever she had to say was going to piss him off, otherwise, she wouldn't have warned him. A thought flickered in his mind, and he smiled a bit.

"Wait. You pregnant?" he whispered, showing nothing but teeth.

Loriana's pupils dilated. "What? No, no. I'm on birth control, remember?"

"Damn. That's right. A nigga can dream, though." He chuckled then got right back serious. "Talk to me, baby. What you think I'ma be mad about?"

She gulped, feeling like she now had to vomit. "Um. The other night when I was coming home, um. Somebody, this guy, he robbed me at the gas station."

His eyes were now icy, matching the ice now flowing through his veins, and hands balled into fists atop the table. The vein sprouting from his forehead made Loriana nervous because she wasn't done yet. She licked her lips and continued.

"He told me to tell you that you aren't the only shooter out here and sent a warning shot at me."

There was a spark of some indefinable emotion in his eyes. His voice though...it was hard and disturbing. "He shot at you?"

"I don't know. I think it was in the air or something because I wasn't hit."

Loriana would never forget that night. The shooter wasn't sent to harm her but to shake her up a bit, and he'd definitely done the job. She stayed crouched in the seat of her car until the store clerk came running out to check on her. All Loriana could do was cry. Too shaken up to drive, she called Mhyale to come and get her. Naaz broke every speed limit to get to her and was there in less than fifteen minutes.

With a gun pressed into her side and fear crippling her body, Loriana just knew he was about to take her life. She couldn't seem to catch a break, and it was depleting her. So many tragic events had occurred in her life in such a short period of time, she started questioning if the prayers she sent up weren't being received. Still having not recovered from her almost being raped, Loriana's mind was fucked up behind her being robbed and shot at. The energy and effort she tried to keep pushing through just wasn't there anymore. No matter how hard she tried shaking back, she just couldn't.

Right now, she wanted to let everything go. At least try to. She'd never forget her past; the trauma was too real for her to do that. Loriana wanted to escape it, though. At every turn in her life, she was running full speed away from it, but somehow, it kept chasing her. It caught her off guard each time, forcing the healing process to restart. Loriana had started over so many times, she never knew where to begin next.

"Did you see his face?" Projex wanted to know.

He didn't care that he was locked up. There was a crew of SAG niggas on the outside that would put in work for him if requested. Whoever had touched her was going to feel him regardless. Projex hated that niggas was trying to test him behind her because he was choosing violence every single time. The nigga would've been better off robbing the store instead of her.

"No. It doesn't matter anyway. There's nothing you can do from in here."

Her words made his chest spasm. The way she said them burned his ears.

"What you mean?" he spoke lowly, trying to control his budding anger. "Ain't shit stopping 'cause I'm locked up."

"But it is!"

Loriana spoke a bit too loudly, and a few heads turned their way. She didn't care. Projex may have thought he could be Superman from behind bars, but he couldn't. It just wasn't realistic, and she didn't want him to be, though he was trying.

"You can't protect me from in here," she mumbled sadly, breaking his fucking heart. "I know you think you can, but you can't."

"I can if you let me, ma. You know that."

Her head shook. She didn't know anything anymore. Not even who she was. Loriana knew what she wanted, though.

"No. I don't want you to. You have enough on your plate and me adding to it makes no sense. This all makes no sense."

She felt guilty. Her burdens were weighing her down, and she'd place some of the weight on him to handle but couldn't anymore. It was unfair in her eyes. Projex's body became backed up with disdain. She was talking crazy, but he could read between the lines.

"So, we don't make sense? That's what you really trying to say?"

A tear slid down her cheek, and he knew her answer before her lips moved.

"Yes. I'm... we're not in a position to be strong for each other right now. Like, I literally can't, Bryshon. I feel like I'm dying a slow death every day. So much has happened, and I can't mentally understand why. It's disturbing me and my sanity."

As gangster as he was, the defeat in his baby's voice and look of weary on her face, made him want to shed tears. Angry ones. When he was younger with a much worse temper than now, he'd cry when he was pissed off. It was out of frustration as a teen, trying to learn how to place his emotions. He felt thirteen all over again, but he wasn't a quitter. It was life; shit happened. You bounced back and kept it moving. He wanted her to know that resilience still lay somewhere within her.

"It's all gon' get better, though. We can learn to be strong for each other. You ain't gotta push me away to do that."

Loriana nodded her head. "I do. Your expectations of me are so high, and that's not healthy. I can't even be there for myself right now. I'm okay with disappointing myself, but I don't want to be the one to blame when it comes to you. I love you *too* much."

"But not enough, huh?" His voice was no longer confident.

Projex was struggling to keep his composure and not break down. Not only did his life make her a target for his enemies, but his decisions were causing her to resent him. She didn't say that, but Projex knew it. He could feel it. The way she said she loved him was still warm but had a bite to it. Loving him too much was a sacrifice. Before, it was easy. She felt protected in his arms and at peace with his energy. The feeling was so underrated; Loriana didn't just want it from anyone.

Her trauma was forcing her to close off her heart.

When it was time to heal, it'd teach her to open it again but with boundaries. Right now, she had none. She was completely open in every aspect to him. It was dangerous, and before it got out of control, to the point of no return, she had to pump the breaks.

"Don't say it like that," Loriana pleaded, hating how he was now looking at her. As if she'd just spit in his face.

"Nah. I gotta keep it one hunnid with myself. Shit, I guess, sometimes love ain't enough. I ain't gon' ever tell you how to feel, so it is what it is."

Loriana fought hard against the tears she refused to let fall. Projex wasn't about to beg her more than he already had. What he wanted to do was hold her and let her know everything was going to be a'ight, but those were promises of the past. Her world outside, once leaving this cold place, was different now.

"What does that mean?" Loriana asked. His reply was too vague for her to comprehend.

"If it's that easy to give up on us, then fuck it. Maybe this shit was fake."

Loriana felt like she was about to throw up. "No. Don't say that. It's real. It's too real if you want me to be honest."

"Yeah, too real for *you* to handle, and I ain't never

been the type of nigga to force my hand with you, so I won't now. You young, I get it. Ain't no need to hold me down and waste your life on a nigga in prison. What would be the fun in that?"

Projex watched with an emotionless expression as Loriana cowered back with evident shock in her eyes. That quickly, she tucked her feelings away from him. He was being the sarcastic asshole she knew he could be. He wasn't supposed to be this way with her, but she couldn't blame him.

Projex chuckled when she didn't say anything. "On the real, you coulda' answered the phone and told me this. You bold as fuck coming up here to break my heart in my face."

Loving him had clearly turned her into a savage. This was a straight chess move in his eyes. A move Projex never saw coming, like Loriana was an opp and had been plotting to attack.

"I'm not trying to, I swear. Telling you in person just made more sense."

"Nah. None of this shit makes sense, remember? You sitting here, me listening. After all the shit we been through, man. This how you do me?"

He was about to lose it. His voice cracked, and his jaw was clenched so tightly, he could've broken a tooth. His heart was aching like a mothafucka. Being in love was sick. He got it, though. Loriana wasn't built for his lifestyle. She wasn't raised to move on and act like she didn't get robbed and shot at. She was raised on love and learned that if you loved something, letting it go was best. If it came back, it was meant to be. Right now, they just weren't meant to be, so she was letting go.

"Just because we aren't together doesn't mean we can't still be friends," she said pathetically.

"Man, you better get the fuck on."

Her eyes widened at his reply. "What? Don't talk to me like that."

"Nah. 'Cause you got me fucked up. Don't bring your ass back up here. You ain't gon' be able to get in."

When he stood from the table, Loriana stood up too.

"So, that's it? You just gon' walk out? You don't love me enough to be friends?"

"Nah. Go love yourself, ma. Looks like I wasn't doing a good enough job."

He'd never tell her to try and find another nigga to love her like he did because there weren't any. Projex was it for her, and he knew it... but life. Life was a mothafucka with karma in its back pocket. *Maybe, this is my karma,* he thought, walking back to his cell with his heart left splattered across the table. Loriana could clean the mess she made up on her own. He was done.

"I don't see why I have to ride with you," Loriana groaned to Mhyale while buckling her seatbelt.

"Because I need help making a decision, and I want you to get out of the house. All you do is sit in your room, looking at that damn phone. If he called, you probably wouldn't even answer."

Loriana rolled her eyes. She'd spent the last month moping around the house, hoping Projex called. Even though she ended things, she still considered him her friend. She couldn't believe he actually hadn't called and took her off his visitation list. Crushed by their last visit, Loriana reached out to Joseline, who let her know Projex just needed time, but she knew her son. He was stubborn, and once hurt, there was no getting back in good with him unless he let you. She'd seen it happen firsthand with his dad.

"Yes, I would. I just don't get why he doesn't still want to be friends. That's way less pressure."

Mhyale chuckled. "Loriana. No man, especially a

real man who loves the fuck out of you, just gonna wanna be your friend. I mean, he may settle for that for the time being, but deep down, he wants you as his. Now, if he's okay with that, that means he doesn't want anything more, and being friends is as far as he thinks y'all will get. You and Projex are beyond that, baby."

Loriana groaned. "I thought we were. I'm sad he doesn't want to talk to me. Joi be letting me listen in on their phone conversations, sometimes. He doesn't even mention me anymore."

Her bottom lip poked out, thinking of him completely forgetting about her. The first time she and Joi were on the phone and Projex called, Joi merged the calls and told her to mute herself. Projex asked Joi had she spoken to her and if she was talking to someone new. That was the second week after her visit. Now, he didn't bring her up at all. Thinking of her pissed him off, so asking about her only made it worse. He still cared, though, that was for sure.

"You gotta stop doing that. You're just hurting yourself more. I thought we were trying to heal?" Mhyale asked, exiting the highway.

"I know you're not talking. You and Naaz be at it every other week. Well, you be hollering at him. Now, look at us. On our way to get you a new car because you're spoiled rotten. You should've had him take you."

Mhyale smirked. "I sure am, and he knows it. He gets me, and instead of me having to ask for something, he just provides. I be hollering cause I'm crazy. He loves me, though."

She wasn't telling not one lie. Mhyale had been whining about wanting a new car because her Mustang was too small now. She sent subtle hints to Naaz for the past week and a half, and he showed up to her doorstep yesterday with cash, told her to go buy a new one, and to wait on her pink slip in the mail. Naaz knew Mhyale's love language very well. She had two of them, and he catered to them both equally.

"I can tell. Are you going to spend all of that money on a car or save some?"

"I don't know yet. That's why I brought you with me," Mhyale told her as they pulled into the lot of Royal Motors.

"Well, I'm not going to tell you to spend it all. Nothing is wrong with this car."

"It's not. I just want a new one. As women, we deserve to have whatever our hearts desire, especially if we worked for it."

Loriana gave her a blank stare. "But you didn't."

"Dealing with Naaz is a full-time job. I earned

every single dime of this cash. Now, come on and let me show you how to do this."

Shaking her head, Loriana unbuckled her seatbelt and followed her cousin to the entrance of the building. The parking lot was as big as a baseball field and covered with almost every car you could imagine. Complimentary snacks and drinks were offered when they walked in, and the smooth jazz music playing over the speakers gave the place a nice ambiance.

"Do Black people own this?" Loriana asked, looking around. There was nothing but Black faces, and she loved it.

"Yes. Someone Naaz referred me to."

"Good afternoon. Welcome to Royal Motors. What brings you in today?" a woman with a black skirt, tucked in white button-down, and black heels on, greeted them. An iPad was in her hand, and a smile present on her face.

"I'm looking to buy a new car," Mhyale replied.

"Any specific name or price? We have a nice selection of used cars that won't break your pockets and have you riding in style still."

"No. Nothing used. If it is, nothing over ten thousand miles on it."

The lady, whose nametag read, Ciara, smiled.

"My kind of shopper. Follow me this way, and I can get some more information from you. I'm Ciara."

"I'm Mhyale, and this is my cousin, Loriana."

"I thought that was you," a male's voice Loriana knew all too well spoke from behind her.

Pivoting, she couldn't stop the smile that lifted her cheekbones. Symir stuffed one hand in his pocket and took in Loriana's beauty. She was dressed casually as always in a flowy sundress that had her back out. Her hair was wild from a twist-out she'd done a few days ago, and her skin was glowing. It didn't look like she was going through a breakup at all in his eyes.

"And this is the owner himself, Mr. Royal," Ciara introduced him, but Loriana didn't need one.

"The owner? How old are you?" Mhyale asked, not caring how her question came out.

Symir chuckled, and Loriana swallowed hard.

"Yes, one of the owners. I'm old enough to help you purchase one of these cars today."

"Hmph. That's good enough for me. Y'all better hook me up today, too. My man, Naaz, said he knows the owner, and I'm guessing it's you."

"It is. You and Lo getting a ride?"

Mhyale's brow dipped as she faced Loriana. "Lo? Y'all know each other?"

"We've met a few times," Loriana answered.

"And you know what they say about third times a charm," Symir told her with a smirk.

Looking back and forth between them, Mhyale was wondering how she didn't know who Symir was before now. *This sneaky little heffa,* Mhyale thought. Loriana wasn't sneaky. She just kept her business to herself and moved how she wanted to. Too many critics with opinions on her life wasn't her thing anymore. She didn't care who they were. Plus, there wasn't much to tell about Symir... yet. The number he'd given her still hadn't been used.

"It brings fortune."

"Indeed. You mind if I steal her for a few?" Symir asked Mhyale, who grinned.

"Nope. Go ahead. Me and Ms. Ciara here about to go handle business."

"I thought you wanted my help?" Loriana asked, fake hurt that she just tossed her to the side because Symir asked.

Mhyale waved her off. "I'm a big girl. Go see what the boss wants."

Ciara and Symir snickered at that. Loriana just shook her head as she watched her cousin walk off. Now back facing him, Symir's intoxicating cologne warped around her. It smelled expensive, matching the navy tailor-fit Tom Ford suit he was wearing.

Honestly, had Loriana not just found out that he did indeed sell cars, Symir could've passed for a model. He had a face that was so symmetrically flawless, had the perfect height, body, and charm that drew you in.

"So, you do sell cars," Loriana said, breaking the ice.

"Yeah. I didn't lie to you."

She nodded her head. "I didn't think you did."

"You want something to drink?"

"No, I'm okay. Thank you, though. What did you need to steal me for?"

Symir looked at her as if she didn't know. Honestly, Loriana didn't. Her mind was so over the place these days, she thought she'd done something wrong instead of remembering that she'd never used his number. Symir wasn't worried about that.

"How you been? Ya' mental straight?"

Whoa. Her heart fluttered. No one had asked her that. Not anyone she didn't have a personal connection to. She hardly knew Symir.

"My mental? It's good today. Yours?"

"It's better. Had a crazy morning, and then I saw you walking in here and had to come show my face."

She smiled. "So, I helped turn your day around?"

"Flipped it right side up."

They shared a laugh.

"So corny. Really, how old are you? You never told me."

"You never asked. I'm twenty-three."

Loriana stood there, amazed until she found her voice. "Shut up! You're only twenty-three and own this? That is such an accomplishment. Wow. Congratulations to you."

Her true surprise and happiness made him feel a way. "Thank you. I appreciate that."

"You'll have to tell me how you got started. I'm much too nosy not to hear about this." She chuckled.

"My number hasn't changed."

She nodded and smirked at his reminder. "Of course, it hasn't. I can still use it as a friend, right?"

"Use it however you please."

"Noted. I feel like we should introduce ourselves again. You know, the proper way. I'm starting to think running into you isn't by accident anymore."

"I never thought it was," he told her and stuck his hand out for her to shake. "Symir Royal. It's nice to properly meet you."

She grinned and placed her hand in his. A calmness immediately covered her.

"Loriana Simms. It's nice to properly meet you as well."

Chapter Twelve

3 Years Later, August 2020

Laurent's head bobbed as the track he'd just laid down blasted throughout the luxurious studio. In his hand was a cup of tea his boo told him to sip on instead of the alcohol decorating the room. He drank it slowly, loving the warming sensation and relief it gave him. The lemon-ginger-honey concoction was his antidote.

With his third album doing crazy numbers since it dropped in February, Laurent wasn't letting up. There were no days he could take off, and he preferred it that way. It'd been a long time coming, and he was taking advantage of every moment. He was at the top of his game, high off life, and loving the direction his career was going. Right beside him was Loriana, who'd become his right-hand woman in a sense. She played a vital role in his glow-up.

"What you think?" Laurent asked without looking down at her.

Loriana stopped writing in her notebook and glanced upward. She'd been so engrossed in the review she was preparing to type up, but her ears were still listening. The creative hat she seemed to always be wearing was never taken off.

"It's missing something. Or it has a little too much of something else," she paused and let the song take over her mind.

Laurent was the type of artist that you just vibed with no matter what. From his singing, rapping, and laid-back personality, it was hard not to love him. He could hold the type of melody over a track that made you restart the song because it was just that good. He'd perfected it over the years, including his rapping. With ease, his once small performances at clubs became sold-out tour dates he was on. Laurent had real-life fans; people who played his shit on a daily and had helped turn his life around. It was amazing to see how far he'd come, but Loriana was still going to keep it real with him.

"You need a woman on this one."

Laurent's mouth twisted some to the side. "Singer or rapper?"

"Singer. Misa would be perfect, honestly. Want me to shoot her assistant an email?"

He smirked. "Nah. I'll have my assistant do it. You think you her, but you not."

"Whatever. I can make things happen, too."

"And you do. Always. I appreciate you. What you working on?"

Sighing, Loriana stretched her legs out from underneath her. She'd come to the studio to get some work done, finding it the best place to get in her mode, but only when Laurent was here with his producer and a few people. She couldn't stand the studio sessions where she could hardly think or see due to the potent weed being smoked.

With two and a half semesters of school left, Loriana was getting ready to buckle down. Work didn't even really seem like work because she loved her job. As one of the newbie writers for Aspire, a Black-owned music magazine and webzine company, Loriana felt right at home. She'd always had a niche for music and credited her first love for his attributes to furthering a career in it.

She received the position by the grace of God and her diligent work ethic. One of her college professors last semester was blown away by a twelve-page paper she'd masterfully written on the evolution of Hip-Hop and R&B. It was their final for the class, and she passed with flying colors and a recommendation that had her planted in the career she didn't even know she wanted.

It'd been nine months since she was hired, and her name was buzzing. No one seemed to give thorough reviews, written blog posts, or do interviews like she could. Loriana was a gem in the industry but lowkey with it. She loved working with those artists who were slept on, overlooked, and had mad talent. Her boss gave her a platform, and she was standing tall on it while pulling others up with her.

"A review for Dre. You remember him from back in the day?"

Laurent scratched at his beard. "Dre from The Dubs?"

"Mhm. He submitted his album to us, and of course, I took it to review. It's kind of good."

"But what?" Laurent wanted to know.

"But nothing. I like it. I don't love it, though."

"Not everyone will. Text me the name of it, and I'll listen."

She smirked. "And then what? You gon' reach out to him?"

"Yep. Might slide on a feature if the shit nice."

"That's why you'll always get blessed, Laurent. Your heart is pure."

"Yours too, big head girl."

Loriana hugged around his waist in a brotherly manner, then shooed him away. She had to turn her review in by five, and it was close to four in the evening already. When her phone vibrated against the table, she frowned.

"I thought I put this on do not disturb," she mumbled before picking it up and stepping into the hallway where it was quiet. "Hello."

"Hey, sis. You busy?" Joi asked.

"A little bit. What's up."

"Don't tell me you forgot about our dinner date."

Loriana palmed her forehead. She most definitely had. Her schedule was almost never open due to work and school, but she did try to find time for her friends and family. She'd learned one thing about herself over the years that she planned to stick to, and that was to keep busy. Having an idle mind caused her to be stagnant. She'd simply have too much time on her hands just thinking and not fulfilling her purpose now that she'd found it.

"I did. I'm almost done, though. What time should we meet?"

"Six or seven is cool. Can you pick me up from the house?"

Her lips pursed outward. "Why can't you drive? Where are we going anyway?"

"I don't feel like it," Joi whined like that baby girl she was. "And I have a taste for Jack Stacks. Mmm. I can taste the cheesy corn now."

"Of course, you don't feel like it. I'll be there when I leave the studio."

"Oooh. You in there with Laurent? Tell him I said hi."

Loriana playfully rolled her eyes and pulled the door open. "Yes, and I will. Bye, girl."

"See you later!"

She shook her head with a smirk. Joi was a mess, but she loved her like the little sister she didn't have. It wasn't often that they got to spend time. That was Loriana's decision. Too many memories, though good, came with Joi's presence. So, once or twice a month, they'd meet up and catch up. Some days it was at a restaurant, while other days were at Joseline's house. They'd moved from South Ave a few years ago and now lived in a nice townhome about twenty minutes from Loriana.

Sitting back down at the table, Loriana got straight to work and sent her review over to the editor right before five. Packing up her things, she looked up when the door opened. She smiled genuinely at the woman walking through the door.

"Hey, Loriana. I didn't know you were here. I would've brought you something to eat," Maliya said as they hugged.

"Hey. That's okay. I'm getting ready to head out to eat anyway."

"With who?" Laurent questioned as he walked over, kissing Maliya on her cheek and grabbing the Chipotle bag from her hand. "Thanks, my love."

"None of your business," Loriana told him, tossing the strap of her pink metallic Glam-Aholic tote on her shoulder.

"I knew I should've bought the pink one," Maliya said.

"Which one did you get?"

"The matte black collection."

"I love that one too. I'ma probably buy it during the next restock."

As a Black woman business owner herself, Maliya loved to support others. She loved everything about Mia Ray, especially her hustle and transparency. Owning multiple businesses and having a plethora of titles wasn't an easy job, but she made that shit look easy.

"I like how y'all showing love and all, but Loriana ain't answer my question," Laurent said, interrupting their moment.

"I did," she laughed, "it's none of your business. Just because you're a little older than me doesn't mean you run anything."

Laurent smirked. "It must be with a nigga. If you got a man, why you hiding em'?"

"If I had a man, hiding him wouldn't be the issue. Thankfully, I'm single."

"Aw, okay. Good."

"You're so annoying. You just wanted me to say I had a man so you could run and tell your boy." She still didn't like to say his name aloud.

When Laurent didn't say anything and continued to eat his chicken bowl, Loriana mushed him upside the head.

"Gon'. He laughed as Maliya shook her head.

"I'm leaving now. Don't forget to have your assistant or manager reach out to Misa's. It'll be a good look."

"I won't. Be safe and hit my phone when you make it in."

"Will do. See you later, Maliya."

Maliya waved. "Later."

On the elevator ride down to her car, Loriana couldn't help but think about what Laurent would've said had she told him she had a man. She was single but dating, so there wasn't much to tell. Laurent wasn't a gossiper, but he and Projex were brothers. Even if done unintentionally, she was sure her name had come up in plenty of their conversations and visits.

Hopping in her 2018 Lexus RX, an upgrade from her first car, Loriana placed her bag in the backseat and her purse in the passenger seat. She thought about going home to change, but her growling stomach made the decision for her.

Now living on her own in a two-bedroom apartment, Loriana loved her space. At twenty-one and on her shit, she cherished how far she'd come. The place where she laid her head was her safe haven. Pulling herself out of depression had been rough. There'd been many of dark days where she didn't think she'd make it, but she knew He wouldn't fail her.

Praying had got her through it all.

Believing in Him had made her much stronger.

Her faith had been restored and life anew.

She thanked her mother too because Linette was for sure her guardian angel.

Thirty minutes later, thanks to traffic and a wreck, Loriana was pulling up to Joseline's townhome in Lee's Summit. The property was newly built and close to her job. Dialing Joi up, she picked up on the second ring.

"You outside?"

"Yes. You said between six and seven. It's six-thirty."

"You're so punctual," she said, making them laugh. "My mama said you not gon' come in and speak?"

"I wasn't planning on it, no."

"Oh. Okay. Well, here I come."

Loriana hung up and sighed. She knew Joseline would be texting her phone soon. Their relationship was weird, but not in a bad way. Loriana loved her like her own mother, but she wasn't. She was Projex's, and that connection to him had made her not want to be too attached. It was inevitable, though. Joseline had already claimed Loriana as her daughter-in-law and was standing ten toes down on that.

When Joi came out of the house, skipping down the steps, Loriana couldn't do anything but shake her head. Her phone was pressed to her ear and mouth going. Whoever she was talking to was going to have to call her back.

"Hey!" she spoke cheerfully, closing her door. Loriana mumbled a hi. "Yeah. I'm about to go get something to eat," she said, then pulled the phone from her ear. Muting it, she said, "This Projex. He just called me. Can I put him on speaker?"

"I don't care."

She did, but she didn't. Hearing his voice was either going to make her annoyed or put her in her feelings. Today, it was the latter of the two.

"From where? Every time I talk to yo' ass, you eating?" His voice greeted her ears like silk. It was so much deeper than the last time she'd heard it, and it'd been a while.

"I be hungry and at Jack Stacks."

"Damn. That sound fire. I can't wait to come home and bash some food."

"I can't wait until you come home. I miss you, bro."

Loriana's stomach quivered. *I miss him too.*

"I miss you too, man. It ain't gon' be long, though. Just wait. I got a court date coming up soon and praying for the best."

"As you should. Free my nigga, man." Joi laughed, making Loriana chuckle.

"Straight up. I'ma hit you later on, though. I gotta call this girl and see if she came through for me on these clothes."

"What girl? I know you ain't got no girlfriend."

"There you go in my business." He chuckled.

Loriana's face was so frowned up, her forehead was wrinkled. They were carrying on as if she wasn't sitting there.

"Whatever. You better not. You know where home is."

"Shit, where that's at?" He laughed, twisting her gut even more.

"With L-Boogie. Don't play."

On the other end of the phone, Projex was grinning. "Yeah, I hear you. You talked to her lately?"

"Mhm. Earlier. She was in the studio working."

"That's what's up. I'm proud of her man, for real. She still pretty?"

Loriana wanted to scream out, *Hell yeah, nigga. I'm fine now, and you'd know that if you didn't take me off your visitation list,* but she kept quiet and blushed.

"So pretty. Y'all would have some cute kids," she said, catching Loriana off guard.

"She's talking crazy," Loriana uttered, and Projex said the same thing. Weirdly, they were still connected.

"You talkin' crazy. Bet nobody be having nothing, I know that."

Loriana's lips pursed, and brows lifted.

"Yeah, yeah. You ain't running nothing. Call me later, though. I love you."

"I love you too. Tell mama to check her account in a couple days. It should be something in there."

Joi told him okay and hung up. Releasing a deep breath, she looked over at Loriana.

"Sorry about that. I know you weren't trying to hear him talk about you."

"It's fine. So, when are you going to tell him?"

Joi shrugged her shoulders and placed a hand over her baby bump. It was small but very noticeable on her slim frame.

"I wasn't until the baby was here. He's going to flip the hell out."

Loriana nodded. "He is, but there's nothing he can do about it now."

"You're right. I just don't want to disappoint him," she said sadly. She'd already taken her mama and daddy through it. Joseline still wasn't used to her being pregnant.

"The only person you should be worried about disappointing is your child. No one else matters anymore. Projex will get over it just like everyone else has."

"Can you be there when I tell him?"

Loriana's head snapped her way. "Be where? At the visit? Hell no. No, ma'am. I love you, but that's not my place."

"Lori," Joi whined. "He won't come down as hard on me if you're there."

"Girl," Loriana laughed, "your brother does not care for me like that."

She didn't know if she was trying to convince Joi or herself more. From the elation in his voice when he said how proud of her he was to the letters he'd sent her, Projex definitely cared. Like Joseline said, he just needed some time.

"He does too. He loves you, and I love you. You're my baby's auntie."

Loriana groaned. "I'll think about it. I'm not making any promises. Now, come on so we can eat. I need a drink now."

Joi snickered and unfastened her seatbelt. "Yay. Thank you. You're the best."

"Mhm. I know."

Later that night, after dropping Joi off at home,

Loriana was laid up in bed listening to music. *Ride With Me* by Rachel Black & SonofSoul had been on repeat ever since she came across the artist's page on Instagram. Loriana loved when she found new music to listen to, especially if it was good. She literally played the song out and at its highest volume. The lyrics reminded her of her and Projex's relationship so much.

When her phone rang, stopping the song, she yawned and answered, already knowing who it was.

"I'm at the door," he said, and she hung up.

Climbing from her queen-sized bed, she slipped on her leopard print house shoes and walked to the door. Even though he said he was outside, she still looked through the peephole. Seeing his handsome yet tired face, she unlocked it and let him in.

"Long day?" Loriana asked as he locked the door.

Symir's head bobbed forward. "Yeah. How was dinner?"

"Regular. I should've gone to get some tacos from the city."

Symir chuckled. Her love for tacos amused him, having not a clue who'd put her on them.

"You and them tacos. I'm tired as hell." He yawned, pulling his suit jacket off.

On her tippy toes, she wrapped her arms around

his broad shoulders, loving how he easily engulfed her.

"Too tired to give me some?"

Symir smirked and kissed her lips. "Never too tired for that."

Loriana lowered herself and went to walk off, but he grabbed her hand. "What?"

"Where you going?"

"To the bedroom."

With authority, he shook his head no and said, "Nah. Come fuck me on this couch."

Her pussy purred at his demand, and he didn't have to tell her twice. Loriana hardly ever wore clothes to sleep, so it was nothing for her pussy to be in his face merely seconds later. All Symir wanted was a little taste. Suckling on her clit, he spanked her ass. While her hands held his head in place, Symir dug in his wallet for a condom. He sat it beside him and got back to the task at hand.

"Ooooh, fuck," Loriana moaned as her eyes rolled. "Don't stop."

The flickering of his tongue had her breathless. Symir didn't stop until she was clinging to his shoulders, begging to ride him. Doing the honors, she sheathed his hard dick that curved slightly to the left.

Squatting, she looked him in his lust hazed eyes and toyed at her opening.

"You have me so wet," she moaned, sliding down slowly.

Her mouth dropped open, and his eyes fluttered. She felt heavenly. The only place Symir loved to be after a long workday. Laying her head on his shoulder, Loriana road him slowly and kissed on his neck.

"This dick is so goood," she whined as he smacked her ass.

"Show me."

Symir wasn't as vocal during sex, but that was okay. He didn't lack anytime he put it down, and that's what mattered. His sex game was superb in a quiet manner and it had her losing her mind. He hit angles in the pussy that had Loriana screaming. While she rode him faster, Symir sucked and licked on her nipples.

"I'm about to cum," she warned him, breathing hard.

"Do it," he encouraged her before sliding his tongue in her mouth.

Symir held her tightly around the waist and pounded into her as she creamed on his dick. Her body stiffened, and her toes popped. Lazily, Loriana laid chest to chest with him and rode him slowly. With each swerve of her hips, Symir grew closer to his release. She was so warm and tight; his head was swimming.

"Your pussy feels so good, Lo."

He knew she loved to hear that. She got wetter from his voice alone; the words intensified her dripping essence. A burst of energy took over her when Symir spun her around to ride him the other way. With her feet planted on the side of his thighs, she bounced up and down like she was on a pogo stick. When he toyed with her clit, her knees gave out, but he caught her around the waist.

"Nah. Keep going. You got it."

He always rooted for her to take the dick like a G. Loriana never backed down. When he tweaked her nipples, her hands squeezed his hairy thighs. Symir dragged his tongue up her back and placed feather-light kisses on her neck. One hand wrapped around it while the other stayed between her legs.

"Syyy," she cried out, climaxing again. "Damn, baby!"

"I know," he whispered in her ear, still giving her nothing but dick.

When she contracted her muscles, he gripped her waist tightly and came hard. Thank goodness for condoms. Breathing hard, his arm wrapped around her waist protectively. Loriana leaned her head back once her legs were lowered and kissed his cheek.

"Mmm. I'ma sleep good tonight. Thank you, baby."

Symir chuckled. "You're so appreciative. That's why I love you."

Her eyes flew open, and her heart slammed against her ribcage. He'd never told her that before. She felt it, but for him to say it had her freaking out. Not because she didn't believe him, but because she loved him too. Loriana didn't want to be the first to say it, though.

Symir rubbed her body and massaged her boobs. "What you looking all spooked for?"

"Y-You said you love me."

"I know what I said, Lo."

She moved his hands and straddled his lap. "You mean it? Don't say something you don't mean because I love you too. Just don't hurt me, okay?"

He nodded and pecked her lips. "You worry too much. I'd never do anything to mishandle your heart. You know me better than that."

She did. They'd grown extremely close over the years, never placing a title on what they were doing, but that didn't matter. Loriana was okay with that, and he was too. They knew what it was between them.

Nothing but love, power moves, and a solid friend-ship that was built off him being the man he is. Symir was a protector and provider. The one thing Loriana seemed to always search for.

Their relationship didn't become sexual until about a year ago. Before then, Symir had stuck to his word and was simply her friend. He still was, but now with benefits.

Loriana wanted to tell him that she'd heard those words before, but she'd stopped dwelling on the past long ago. It didn't do anything but hold her back.

"I do," she said and smiled. "I'ma really get on your nerves now."

"Aw shit. Here we go." He chuckled. "What time you work in the morning? I'ma go get your truck detailed. It looked dirty."

"I have a late day tomorrow."

"Coo'. We can do breakfast then."

"Um. I kind of wanted to sleep in."

He knew she was lying but didn't call her bluff. Symir's head tilted upward, and he tapped her butt. "A'ight. You can do that while I get your truck right. Lift up."

She stood from his lap on wobbly legs. "Where you going?"

"To shower and lay down."

"Oh," she chirped. "Okay. I'll be in there. Let me clean up."

Symir wasn't the confrontational type. Loriana did move sneakily, but he chalked it up as her not wanting people in her business. He was the same, yet less apparent about it. Going out to eat with him was fine sometimes, but she didn't necessarily want to. Not now, at least. To some extent, her loyalty was still with Projex.

The crazy thing was, she really loved them both... for the same reasons. One just couldn't do for her like the other could. Loriana wasn't settling; that wasn't the case at all. She told herself she moved on and with someone who genuinely cared for her, and that was real. She just had to believe in her mind that her present and future would be nothing like her past. Reliving those moments would take her out of the game completely this time around.

***

"Damn, girl. What you been eating?" Nyree laughed, smacking Loriana on the butt as she came from the kitchen.

Loriana swatted her hand. "Move! You and Mhy get on my nerves with that."

"I'm just saying. You finally got some ass to go with them hips, and it looks good, friend. Let me find out Symir been tossing dick to you."

When she didn't laugh or say anything, Nyree yanked her around. "He has, hasn't he?"

Mhyale laughed. "Yep. Look at her face. She can't hide that blush if she wanted to."

"And you been holding out? That's fake."

"Oh, stop. It hasn't been going on for that long."

Nyree tossed her hands in the air. "Long enough. I guess it takes for me to do a pop-up visit, for me to get the tea. Niggas ain't real."

Still away at school, Nyree decided to come home since her last class was canceled and she didn't have any on Fridays. It worked out perfectly because this was her weekend off too. They were all chilling at Loriana's, catching up and making plans for the weekend.

"You're not going to let this go," Loriana groaned.

"Nope. Cause I told you about me and Juice when we fucked."

"You gave it up in the first night!"

"So, what! I still told you!"

They stared each other down before busting out laughing.

"Friendly pussy self," Loriana tittered.

"Girl, fuck you. You and I both know I was going to give him some, so let's not play. He still be on my line and making trips to see me too."

"Y'all are too much," Mhy chimed in. "I remember those days."

"Giiiirl," Loriana and Nyree dragged out.

"What? I do."

Loriana waved her off. "You acting like *those days* were that long ago. Let me not remind you of Jasheer."

Mhyale gave them a tight-lipped smile.

"Exactly. Quit playing, hoe. We learned from you," Nyree told her as she and Loriana high-fived.

"Sure did."

Going into the kitchen, Loriana searched inside her junk drawer for her candle lighter. Whenever Symir came over, he always cleaned up her place and moved things around. She appreciated him for that but liked to keep things where she knew they'd be. Coming across an envelope, her heart skipped a beat.

Of all the letters Projex sent her, which weren't many because he was stubborn, this one was her favorite. It was his first one, and she couldn't get over how neat his handwriting was. She'd seen it plenty in his notebooks, but these words were written specifically for her. Unfolding the paper, she smiled, feeling warm all over but also hating Projex's circumstances. This would be the only way he'd be able to communicate with her for a while… if they spoke again.

To: L — Boogie

It feels crazy even writing you. I know we ain't spoke in a while but, I miss you. We ended shit rocky, but know it's all love still, ma. You gon' always be my baby. I heard you in school. I'm proud of you. I told you you'd bounceback. What you tell me that time? God don't play bout you. He don't.

Keep going and making yo mama proud. Next time I call, answer. You don't gotta ignore me no more. Since we friends and shit now. I love you, ma. I'll be home soon.

I more thing, you bet not be givin' my pussy away. That's mine. 🖤
                    From my hood with love,
                              Projex

As she got to the end of the letter, Nyree's loud gasp had her head shooting up in her direction.

"What's wrong?"

"Bitch," she whispered, then yelled. "Bitch! Did you know he was getting out today?"

"Who?"

Nyree hopped up from the couch. "Who else! Projex. Your man is home, girl!"

Loriana sucked in a sharp breath. *What? How? When?* Those were all questions she had. The main one, though, was how in the world did he beat a murder case? He was just locked up two weeks ago.

Projex had gotten caught up in a jam but was out now. Out and ready to claim what rightfully belonged to him, his L-Boogie.

Chapter Thirteen

Projex felt weird being a free man.

It'd only been a couple of days, but he was still adjusting, which was normal. Hadn't much changed on the outside, but he felt like a new man. Being locked up gave him time to get his mind right, but he'd still take it there if need be.

Projex felt balanced.

Renewed in a sense.

He'd come home to love. The real kind and not any of that fake shit. It felt good. He felt good. As soon as he walked out of those metal gates, he promised to never go back. On Chevy, he vowed that there would never be a judge or jury to snatch his freedom away again.

"You had enough to eat?" Joseline asked, washing her hands at the sink.

She hadn't stopped cooking since he touched down. All his favorites had been prepared and laid out before him like a king. Leaning back in his chair, Projex rubbed his belly and yawned.

"Yeah, for now. I'ma come back and get some of that 7-Up cake."

"That's mine," Joi let him know.

"Dang. I can't have one piece? You done got stingy."

Emotional thanks to her baby, Joi hopped up from her seat with tears in her eyes. Her mama had made that cake specifically for her, and she didn't want to share. She didn't care that he was fresh out of jail and eating like he was feeding three people; she was actually feeding another human and had cravings like crazy.

He frowned with his hands out and palms up. "What I say?"

Joseline shook her head. "Who knows. She cries about everything nowadays. Blame it on hormones, I guess."

Joi hadn't gotten around to telling Projex she was pregnant, nor was she ready to. When they hugged the first day he came home, she made sure not to press her belly up against him and wear loose clothing. She was doing all of that, and Joseline didn't see why. He was going to find out sooner than later, and she was hoping by then they at least knew who the daddy was. That was another thing Joseline hadn't gotten her to talk about. It irked her nerves, but she couldn't do anything about it.

"That's crazy," Projex said, shaking his head. "Kordell asked could you save him a plate."

"He better come in here and fix it himself. Ain't nothing changed. The only person I'm tending to is you and that one in there," she said, kissing his head.

Projex grinned. "Love you, Mama."

"I love you more. I'm so happy you're home. It still feels unreal."

She always got emotional when it came to her kids. Joseline didn't see how a parent, no matter the age, wouldn't.

"Man. It does. That time went by fast, though. It didn't even seem like I was in for three years."

"It felt like it to me. I know you trying to catch up and get back out here with your friends, but be careful and make smart decisions, okay? Everyone doesn't get a second chance."

Projex nodded his head. He couldn't help but agree with her more.

"I got you. I'm not even on that anymore. I'm trying to handle business with this music. That's where I'm headed in a little bit. Laurent said he got something for me."

Joseline smiled at hearing his name. "I like him. He stayed checking up on me, making sure me and Joi were good."

"That's what real niggas do."

"Language," she scolded. She didn't care how old he was.

"My fault. Who else checked up on you?"

"Mm. Wouldn't you like to know."

Projex chuckled. "See. There you go playing. Just tell me. I know she did."

"Nope. My daughter-in-law actually has a life of her own and wasn't worried about me."

"Yeah, a'ight. It don't matter if you tell me, I'ma find out."

"Now, don't go messing with that girl. She's focused right now."

Projex stood from his seat. "And I'ma focus on her. We both gon' be focused on each other."

"What if she has a boyfriend?"

"She don't."

"And how do you know that? You swear you know everyone's business." She laughed.

Projex just knew. He could feel it. "It's an intuition thing. We connected in a way. I'd know fasho if she had a man. Even if she do, I'm still not letting up."

"Lord." Joseline sighed. "Leave that girl alone, Bryshon."

He smirked and kissed her cheek. "Never. You talkin' crazy. I gave her that lil' space she wanted, and now I'm on her. She should've gotten married or something."

Joseline cracked up. "So only way you'd leave her alone is if she married another man?"

"Yeah. Cause that means she talked to God about him. We don't play that. Me and the big dog be talking too, so I know if she married someone, He approved. She didn't, so," he tossed his hands up and faked like he was shooting a jump shot, "I'm shooting my shot."

"Well, good luck." Joseline laughed. "I hope it's better than that airball you just shot."

"There's always a hater somewhere." Projex laughed.

When Kordell pulled up, he came in, fixed him a plate to eat, and they headed to meet Laurent. It felt like old times riding around the city, and Projex took everything in. He hated how they started gentrifying the hood with a bunch of upscale houses he knew his people couldn't afford. One street had $500,000 homes, and across from it were homes that were abandoned. The community had been asking the city to fix them up for years.

"Cuz, I'm happy then a mothafucka that you home," Kordell beamed with a grin, passing him a blunt to spark up.

"Nah. I'm good. I ain't trying to go in this meeting smelling like a pound of weed."

Kordell tucked it behind his ear. "I feel you. So, what's good, nigga. How you feeling?"

"For real? Blessed. Ain't no way I should be out right now, but I am."

"Yeah, that shit wild. So, they straight dropped the charges?"

"Yep. My lawyer presented the evidence or lack thereof. They couldn't believe it."

Projex could, though. Ross, his old lawyer, was fired. Thanks to Naaz recommending him his lawyer, Projex was free. It took a while, but three years was nothing compared to what he would've been doing. The judge had sentenced him to thirty years. Projex had Ross file an appeal before he had Grandpa Joe fire his ass. It was crazy how money moved in politics. There were people who'd been waiting for trial forever, and Projex came in with some money behind his name, and just like that, his case was moved up.

"I can't either. But fuck it, though. You out and we 'bout to fuck the industry up."

Projex grinned, not wanting to hype himself up, but he was feeling the same way. Once they pulled up to the address Laurent had texted him, they hopped out. After asking the receptionist where the meeting was, they rode the elevator up to the sixteenth floor. Two guards were posted up outside of the boardroom doors.

"Names?" one of them asked.

"Projex. I'm here to see Laurent."

"And you?"

"This my cousin. He good."

The guard knew to expect Projex, but not Kordell. He looked him over smugly and stepped to the side to let them in. Kordell sneered at him. Before stepping inside, Projex silenced his phone.

"I must've fucked his bitch or something." Kordell laughed, but Projex didn't.

He was focused right now and knew having guards at the door with big ass AK-47's meant there was a lot of money in the room. Spotting his boy, Laurent stood from his chair. The oval-shaped table had about thirty chairs, and they were almost all occupied.

"My nigga," Laurent said as they slapped hands. "How you feeling?"

"Like I should've worn a suit to this bitch. Who all these people?"

Laurent chuckled. "You good, bruh. This the team that makes shit happen and writes our checks."

"Our?"

"Hell yeah. What you thought, you weren't getting paid?"

Projex was stunned for a second. Laurent had been telling him he had him whenever he got out but never mentioned anything about a check. Not just one, but a bunch of them.

"Nah. I ain't really know what to think," Projex told him honestly. Being locked up had his mind everywhere.

Laurent tossed an arm over his shoulder. "I told you I had you, bruh. This shit with us for life. Let me give you a welcome home present."

Walking away from the group of people at the table, Laurent brought him to an office. It was decked out with plaques on the walls, pictures of Black Hip-Hip legend's in the game, and gold decor.

"This yo' office? You walked up in here like you own it," Projex said.

"Nah. It will be one day, though."

He opened up a safe with a key from his pocket and pulled out an envelope. Handing it over to him, Laurent had a big grin on his face.

"I feel like I need to record this moment," he said, pulling his phone out.

Projex's brows raised. "C'mon, cuz. You ain't gotta do all that."

It was too late. Laurent was already recording. He'd said the same thing when he received his first check that was worth something to talk about, and he wanted Projex to have this memory cause there'd be plenty more in the future.

Slowly, he broke the seal of the envelope. His heart fell to his feet, and he lost his balance. Thankfully, there was a chair right behind him to fall into.

"Yeeeeah, baby. I told you!" Laurent yelled out in a hype manner.

Projex's eyes misted. He wanted to break down and cry, but he held it together. "This real?"

"Hell yeah, it's real." Laurent laughed, then gave him an authentic smile. "That's all yours too. I already got my cut. One of the songs from the album I dropped in February just went platinum too."

Projex's eyes widened, and he stood up. "Get the fuck out of here! You for real?"

"Yeah. I got the word this morning."

Not knowing what else to do to express his gratitude, Projex hugged his nigga. He didn't care how he may have looked because he was overly grateful for him right now. All those late nights in the studio, him writing verses to send him, spitting lyrics over the jail phone, visits, and all had paid off.

He sniffled and pulled away. Laurent stopped recording. "Bruh. Thank you. You don't even know, man."

"Nah. I do. That's why it's always gon' be solid with us. We really came up together, no bullshit. Half the songs I got out you contributed to, so it's only right you see the benefits. I'd be less of a man if I played it any other way. Plus, you looked out with that camp yo' grandpa put on. That was really the start of it all."

Projex looked back down at the check in his hand. He'd never seen so many numbers in his life. His chest swelled just thinking about how he could really take care of his mama and sister now. His grandma didn't want for anything, but he was about to lace her pockets too.

"Aye. Did my girl get her cut of this?" Projex asked.

Laurent smirked. "Yo' girl?"

"Man, don't play with me. You know who I'm talking about. She should get a cut too."

"Yeah, man. I made sure of it. She's the one who was thuggin' it out with me in the studio when niggas were faking. She wouldn't take as much, trying to be humble, and said, give most of it to you. I'm signed and shit, so I had to make her understand the contracts and all, but she good."

He nodded his head. If anyone deserved some of this money, Loriana was the person. Regardless of them not speaking, she never lacked on making sure Projex's words were heard. His notebooks he'd left with her hadn't collected dust since he was gone and wouldn't. His words were powerful and worth a lot of money... seven-figures worth.

"A'ight bet. I'm just making sure. Damn. I can hardly breathe. This shit wild."

"It's gon' get even crazier. All them people out there want to discuss the record label we talked about starting."

"Aye. What you been taking since I been locked up? You really done tapped into a whole notha' level, bruh. On Chevy, this shit wild."

All Laurent could do was grin. They'd struggled long enough.

"Had to. I knew that street shit wasn't gon' last forever, so I got serious. Even with you locked up, I knew you was plotting, so I just did the groundwork, and now we on."

"I owe you."

Laurent shook his head. "Nah, nigga we owe ourselves. You don't owe me shit, but some more songs."

They laughed, slapped hands, and threw up their set.

"On SAG, nigga we on," Projex boosted.

"On the gang. Them niggas been waiting for you to touch down."

Projex couldn't wait to hit the hood and see his people. First things first, though, business. Second, he was pulling up on Loriana and dropping off some celebratory dick. In his eyes, that was the only way they should celebrate together. He'd wine and dine her ass another day. She deserved it.

Walking back into the boardroom, all eyes fell on him. Laurent's manager greeted Projex with a firm handshake and a pat on the back.

"Mr. Songwriter, himself. Welcome home. I'm Maxwell Mitchell, owner of MM Record Label."

"What's good. I've heard about you."

"All good things, I'm hoping," Maxwell chuckled, as did some of the people in ears reach. "Welcome to the team. That's if you trying to get this money…"

"Yeah, yeah, fasho. I'ma run my options down, though. I just got out and need to play the field for a little bit; get my feet wet in the studio again."

Maxwell understood completely. "No biggie. We can still talk business. Take a seat. Who's the guy you brought with you? He do anything?"

Projex looked at Kordell, who was sitting idly by, feeling somewhat out of place. "That's my cousin. We can find him something to do."

Maxwell waved him over. "Bet. Let's get down to business."

The first of the month was always busy at Aspire. Loriana was used to it, but some days her workload was ridiculous. She wasn't complaining, not about work anyway. As she trudged up her flight of steps to her apartment, all she could think about was the hot shower she was about to take and the nap that wouldn't come after, thanks to her friends.

"Don't be acting like you don't want us here," Trell said as she punched in her code on her door.

"I'm not acting. Why can't y'all come back tomorrow?"

"Because I already bought all the stuff to make tacos and margaritas," Candace told her.

In her hands were groceries for them to eat tacos while Trell carried the Tequila. They all slipped their shoes off at the door and placed them in the shoe rack. She hated for people to wear shoes in her place.

"Right. And it's called taco Tuesday. Not taco Wednesday. We go to Juvie's for wings tomorrow. Get with the program, miss ma'am, and stop acting brand new."

Trell acted like he was massaging her shoulders before walking away, but Loriana stopped him. "Wait, hold on. Give me a real one. That felt good."

"You just be using me. You lucky I love you."

"Mhm," she hummed as her eyes fluttered.

While they stood in the kitchen like it was a spa, Candace washed her hands and started prepping to cook. It was already seven in the evening, and she planned to be tipsy and full by eight or before that.

"I'ma go hop in the shower and get comfortable. Don't come get me if y'all need me," Loriana told them before making her way down the hall.

"That shower better wash that mood you're in down the drain, I know that!" Trell yelled after her.

Loriana didn't bother to reply. Stepping inside her bedroom, she stripped from her fitted dress pants, silk top, and loosened the ponytail in her head. To this day, she still rocked her signature style unless Moo could get her to try something different. The most she'd done was dye it a ginger color that she didn't see herself getting rid of anytime soon. The reddish-yellow shade made her tawny brown skin pop even more.

Going to her bathroom after grabbing her phone out of her purse, she cut the shower on. Sitting on the toilet to relieve her bladder, she scrolled through her unread texts. Keeping up with not only her work phone but her personal one as well wasn't something she'd mastered yet. People would literally have to double text and call her for her to pick up.

After replying to Mhy, Nyree, Greg, and Symir, who was asking how her day was, she locked her phone. Normally, she'd play music while in the shower, but today was one of those days where she wanted to decompress without noise. Just the sound of the water. When she flushed the toilet and washed her hands, her phone went off with another text. She thought to ignore it, but the text had her snatching her cell up.

816-555-2909*: What's up, ma.*

The unsaved number didn't need to come with a name; she knew exactly who it was. She could practically hear the three words coming from his lips. Licking her lips, Loriana went to type but stopped.

"Do I ask who this is?" she mumbled to herself, not knowing how to go about responding. She felt like she was eighteen all over again. Only this time, she was more guarded.

"No. I'm not going to reply. He's been out for how many days and just now texting me? Boy, bye."

She put her phone down on the counter and went to undo her bra, but the incoming Facetime call from that same number stilled her body.

"What the hell," she whispered. "Why is he Facetiming me?"

Hesitantly, she picked it up and answered. Being sure to show just her face on the screen, she sighed. When Projex's screen showed nothing but blackness, she rolled her eyes.

"You got an attitude already?" He chuckled.

His voice made her pussy wet and heart leap. *Damn, I missed his voice.*

"What do you want? And why are you in the dark?"

"Still asking a bunch of questions. You know the answer to the first one, though."

"Actually, I don't. I'm going to hang up if you don't show me your face."

Projex laughed. He had her flustered already and loved it. He took in her beauty and felt an overwhelming feeling of nostalgia greet him. Loriana was still his lil' baby.

"You so damn fine. Let me just stare at you without you getting all upset. Can I do that?"

She rolled her eyes. "Whatever. I'm busy, so get to the point."

He moved his thumb from over the camera, and Loriana gasped. Loudly. She didn't give a fuck about how thirsty she sounded. Projex had just snatched her soul from her body with his looks alone.

"Oh, my gosh," she squealed lowly, studying his features with expertise.

"I know, ma. I look good, huh?" He laughed, making her do the same. "Damn. I missed your smile."

"You look… you look so good. Oh my gosh, I can't even believe I'm telling you this."

She palmed her forehead and shook her head.

"I can. You ain't never been one to not say how you feel. What you doing, though? You ain't got no clothes on and shit."

"Oh," she chirped, remembering that the water for her shower was running. "I was about to shower. What're you doing?"

"In the car coming to see you."

Her lips parted, and her eyes blinked slowly. "Um. Yeah, no."

"What that mean? No, as in not right now? 'Cause I ain't trying to hear that."

"You still think everything has to go your way."

"It does." They stared at one another for a few seconds, and he added, "With you it does. Send me your address."

"Projex," she whined, and his dick hardened.

"Ma, please don't say my name like that. I ain't felt no pussy since I been home, and you know what saying my name like that does."

"Really?"

"Really what?"

"You haven't had sex yet?"

He shook his head no. "Nah. That's why I'm coming to see you."

"Boy," Loriana laughed, "you got me messed up. What you think I'ma just give you some?"

"I know you are. That's my pussy. I done wrote my name all over that mothafucka. Embedded my shit in yo' soul. This fresh out-of-jail dick is all yours, ma. I mean, unless you want me to give it to somebody else."

He smirked at the wrinkles in her forehead. She was contemplating too hard for him, but he'd let her live.

"That pussy wet, huh? Lemme see?"

Boldly, Loriana panned the camera over her body, stopping between her legs. Her fat pussy print in the black boy shorts she was wearing had his mouth watering.

"That pussy still fat," he said with appreciation and cleared his throat. "For real, though. Can I come see you? I don't just wanna have sex. We got some catching up to do. You ate yet?"

"No, but my friends are here cooking. Maybe we can link up tomorrow. I'm going to the studio, so we can meet there and grab dinner afterward."

"No."

She huffed. "Why ask me questions you're just going to say no to?"

"Because them not the right answers. I don't care about yo' friends being there. I ain't coming over there for them."

Loriana couldn't do anything but shake her head. Projex was still stubborn.

"Fine. I'll text you my address when I get out of the shower."

He grinned. "A'ight. Don't forget either."

"I won't, Bryshon."

"Don't be saying my name like you know me," he said, making her laugh.

Easily, he could still put a smile on her face, and Loriana loved that. She was scared of that, too. When they hung up, she undressed and hopped in the shower. What was supposed to be a peaceful shower turned into one where her mind was only thinking of what was about to happen. As she washed up, she willed herself not to play with her pussy. Projex was absolutely right about having her wet, and the slight graze of her fingers almost sent her over the edge. Her body was on fire, and he hadn't touched her yet.

"Maybe he can just eat me out," she murmured, needing a release badly. "No. I'm tripping. Let me hurry up."

She went back and forth on what to do her entire shower. Once out, she oiled her body down with her *Fairy Dust* body oil from Treasured Yoni. Normally, she wouldn't put on a bra, but she didn't want Projex to be any more distracted than she knew he would be.

Slipping on some grey leggings, a white tank top, and her house shoes, Loriana removed the ponytail holder from her head and shook her curls. Grabbing her phone, she headed into the living room. She'd texted him her address when she got out of the shower, and now her nerves were on ten just waiting.

"It smells good in here," she said, climbing onto one of her bar stools.

"Thanks. You feeling better?" Candace asked while chopping up some cilantro.

Loriana nodded her head. "Yeah. Let's take some shots right quick."

Trell's head twisted her way. "Oop. Okay, then. Let's pour up. I just knew you weren't down for the get down today but prove me wrong."

She flipped him off while grabbing the bottle of Casamigos. Breaking the seal, Candace slid her three shot glasses to fill.

"What we toasting to?" Trell asked, holding his shot in the air.

"It doesn't even matter. Let's just drink," Loriana said, tapping her glass against the countertop and throwing it back.

Candace and Trell looked at her with wide eyes before looking at one another.

"Well, okay then." Candace laughed, doing the same. Trell followed suit.

Fifteen minutes later, with three shots in her system, Loriana felt lovely. Trell had turned on some music that was blasting through her installed hidden speakers in the living room, and they were up dancing while Candace fixed her a plate. She wasn't about to wait on them.

"Ain't no hustle in you, baby, get ya money up. I been hustlin' for too long, just tell me what you want. The second phone my trap phone. Got two cribs, but always gone. I just bought my mama a crib so big, you'll never know who's home," Loriana rapped animatedly to one of Laurent's unreleased songs.

"The Patek on me two-toned, had to bulletproof the Lambo. Niggas ain't really shooters, they just say it 'cause it sounds good in they songs," Trell followed up, just as hype as Loriana.

"Y'all swear y'all some gangsters." Candace laughed just as a knock resounded through the apartment. The music was so loud, and they were in their own world; Candace had to get up and get it. Only then did Loriana realize Projex had shown up. He wasn't empty-handed either.

"Oh. Hey," Candace said, not recognizing him.

She looked over at Loriana, who was walking to the door. He grinned as soon as he saw her face.

"What's up, ma. You gon' let me in? I got all these bags and shit."

Designer bags were clutched in each of his fists as he crossed the threshold of her home. Projex was trying to make up for the missed birthdays and holidays he wasn't able to get her anything for. Candace was looking at her, trying to ask who he was, but Loriana was entranced. It was as if he'd magically casted a spell on her. She was unmoved as he placed the bags on her couch, moving about as if he'd been there before. Loriana hadn't even told him to take off his shoes.

"Un, un Mister. We don't wear outside shoes around the house," Trell told him.

Projex looked Loriana's way and smirked. "My bad."

Walking over to the door where she was still standing, Projex slipped off his Jordan's and placed them on the side of the shoe rack. Leaning toward her, he kissed her cheek.

"Introduce me to your friends," he whispered, snapping her out of her daze.

Realizing they hadn't met him, not Candace anyway, she did the honors. Trell was much too drunk the night Symir dropped her off at home, and he never saw him before getting picked up.

"Candace and Trell, this is Projex. Projex, my friends."

"Wait," Candace said, putting her second taco down. "I knew you kind of looked familiar. You cut your hair."

Projex smirked and ran a hand over his deep-set jet-black waves. They made Loriana feel woozy from just staring at them. They were the reason she gasped when he showed his face on Facetime. When she saw pictures that were posted on Facebook when he got out, he still had his hair. Now, it was gone. She loved him with it but was ready to sit on his entire face right now. He looked *too* damn good, and Loriana wanted to ask who his barber was so she could send a fat tip his way. His lineup was so precise, it wasn't fair.

"Yeah. Y'all in here turning up, I see," he acknowledged, peeping the liquor on the counter and Laurent's music playing at a low volume now.

"Yeah. Just a little Tuesday turn up. You wanna shot?" Trell asked, walking into the kitchen.

"Nah. I'm good. What's up, L-Boogie. You a mute now?" Projex asked, grinning.

"Whatever. Hey. Welcome home."

"Thanks. That dry-ass greeting. Can I get a tour?"

Candace chuckled under her breath. Niggas were always trying to get a tour, knowing all they really wanted to see was the bedroom. Projex was serious, though. He was proud of Loriana and knew she'd worked hard for her own spot.

"Uh, yeah. It's only two bedrooms, but it's mine."

"Fasho. Ain't nothing wrong with that. At least you got your own shit. I'm homeless right now."

Loriana knew he was joking, but her brain transmitted words before she could stop them. "You can stay here with me if you need somewhere to stay."

Projex's heart swelled at her generosity. That made him want to give her the world. "I was playing. I'm crashing at my mama's right now, but 'preciate you for looking out."

"Oh, okay."

She hated how she sounded so disappointed but didn't dwell on that for long. "You wanna bring those bags to my room?"

"Yeah. I can do that."

"Um, how you know we didn't want to see what was in them?" Trell questioned.

Loriana waved him off. "I'll show you later."

She'd convinced herself that having sex with Projex wasn't going to happen, but that was before the liquor got in her system and before he was standing in her place looking every bit of fuckable. It didn't help that he'd worn a pair of grey *MAG Co.* track pants that fit just right. The bulge behind them couldn't be missed at all.

Once down the hall and in her room, forgetting all about the tour he asked for, Loriana was back staring. Prison had done his body so right, it was sickening. His biceps were huge, neck thicker, and face fuller. She could spot his abs underneath the white shirt he was wearing. He had on no jewelry except his pendant chain of Chevy, and he smelled good. That was a given. He always did.

Projex had placed the bags on the black uphol-stered bench against her window and was now walking back over to her. He didn't want to be aggressive with her, but the savage yearning he felt in him had Projex yanking her to him. He hugged her tightly, letting her feel all of his emotions.

"Ooh," Loriana yelped, then giggled. "You're so rough, dang. Hi to you too."

He smacked her ass then caressed the sting. "Damn, I missed you. You got so fuckin' thick."

Projex jiggled her booty in his hands playfully. While she hadn't reached her complete grown woman weight, Loriana had gained some and in the right areas. Her stomach was still flat, so her additional weight resided in her thighs and ass. Her breasts had gone up a few sizes, too, while she'd only grew an inch in height. Projex, on the other hand, was towering over her at a good six-foot-two. Two inches taller than when he went in. Everything on him seemed and felt bigger now as she hugged him.

Pulling back some, she stared up into his handsome face. Her fingers rubbing at the patch of chin hair that finally grew in while away. The rest of his face was clean of hair, except for the dust of a mustache above his lip.

The pad of his thumb ran across her bottom lip. "I'm sorry."

Loriana blinked the sudden tears in her eyes away. "No. Don't do that right now."

"Nah. For real, come here," he said as she tried walking away from him. "Listen. I'm sorry for leaving you at the time I did and for how I handled you. When you needed me the most, I got locked up, and I still feel bad as fuck about that."

"There was nothing you could do. Don't blame yourself."

Loriana had learned to not blame herself as well. Asking herself what if was useless because the situations had already occurred. There was no turning back the hands of time. Once she learned to control those thoughts, life had gotten better. It wasn't great, but she survived one of the darkest moments of it and was grateful.

"I could've handled us better. Yeah, I was pissed but not calling you sooner or letting you come visit me was wrong."

Her pretty eyes rolled, and he smirked. She only wore her glasses now when she worked, so it was going to take some getting used to seeing her without them. He had to get used to seeing her, period.

"Yeah. That was wrong, but I got it. I wasn't there for you, so I can understand why you treated me cold."

"Did you get your mind right?" he asked, knowing that was one of the main reasons she'd broken up with him.

Loriana nodded. "Obviously." They smirked. "No, but seriously, yes. You ever felt like you had to reinvent yourself because the old you just wasn't working?"

"Hell yeah. That's how I feel now."

"That's how I felt. I wasn't giving myself enough of me. Was too busy focusing on everyone else."

Loriana had learned to give herself grace too. Not every day was going to be a good day. There were times where she simply could not get out of bed.

Having no energy to do anything but just lie there in her sorrows. She appreciated those bad days because good ones seemed to follow.

"And what you focused on now?" Projex asked, staring her in the eyes.

Her chest heaved, and her neck grew warm. Sliding her hands underneath his shirt, she caressed his six-pack. Her erect nipples pressed against the fabric of her lace bra into his hard chest. She felt his dick grow against the lower half of her stomach. With her lips almost touching his plush pink ones, Loriana whispered, "You," and dropped to a squat in front of him.

Projex grabbed her wrist. "What you doing? I told you we don't have to have sex."

"Shut up," she mumbled lowly, snatching his pants down. "I thought this was mine?"

Her palm massaged his dick as she looked up at him. Projex's eyes lowered. He knew Loriana had been turned out by him, having taught her how to suck his dick the way he liked, but this woman in front of him was new. He liked it and tried not to let his mind venture to a place that would for sure ruin the moment.

"It is," he spoke lowly while lowering his black briefs.

With time came growth, and Loriana was sure Projex's dick had grown. The way it bounced out of his briefs, damn near poking her eye out, she couldn't help but giggle.

"Mmm. I missed you." She was speaking to his dick, not him.

Projex shook his head, and his eyes closed as she caressed him. Loriana needed two hands to do the job. Freakily, she let her tongue lather his pole before her hungry, wet mouth engulfed him. Back and forth, she bobbed her head.

"Mmm, ma. Fuck," Projex hissed lowly.

That only motivated her more. Loriana took her time sucking him. The heaviness of his dick sliding in and out of her warm mouth was turning her on so much, she stuck one hand between her legs while the other was holding his thigh for support. She was struggling to take him all in, but she kept sucking anyway. Projex was a good teacher, and though it'd been years since she'd taken one of his courses, his lessons were never forgotten.

Breathe through your nose, she told herself and relaxed her throat. Projex felt the tip of his dick bump against the back of her throat, and he cursed.

"Fuck!"

Yanking himself from her mouth, he smacked his

dick against her pouty lips, rubbing the tip all over them. Greedily, she sucked him back in. Nastily, Loriana slobbered, slurped, and gagged on his pole. Projex was so close to nutting down her throat, he had to grab ahold of her head. It was feeling way too good and way too warm.

With a handful of curls in his hand, he fucked her mouth with determination. His hips pumped, making sure to dig deep. Her hands were placed at his hips and mouth wide open. Spit dribbled down her chin and out of the corners of her mouth. When Loriana acted as if she were swallowing or getting ready to hawk up spit, Projex's dick twitched, and he nutted down her throat. She'd literally sucked him soulless.

"Fuuuck, ma," he groaned loudly, not giving two fucks about her friends. Clearly, she didn't, so he wouldn't either.

As he came, Loriana stared up at him. She felt possessed, but in a good way. Pulling her lips off him with a popping noise, she licked her lips and smiled.

"Mmm. Now, that's how you welcome your man home."

Projex's nose flared. "Get up. Take these off."

He was rushing and instructing her but doing the job himself. He wanted her butt naked and bent over, and that's just the way she was seconds later. Ass high in the air, Projex admired the tiger stripes decorating her hips and ass cheeks. The arch in her back was so deep and pussy so wet, he had to taste her.

Projex didn't bother to remove his shirt. He went headfirst between her legs and coated his face with her pussy. Nastily, Projex moved his head around like he was trying to cover himself in her scent. In her juices. And he was. He'd missed the smell, taste, and feel of her plush lips in his mouth, on his tongue, and cumming for him. Her clit was his favorite. It stuck out the more aroused she became, and Projex flickered his tongue all over it.

"Ah! Ah! Oh my… ohmygooosh." Her words slurred as he ate her with no remorse.

His tongue danced along her folds, probed her ass, and suckled her clit before Loriana came undone.

"B-Bryshon!" she yelled out. Her eyes met the back of her lids.

Projex slapped her ass and kept going. "Mhm. This pussy so fucking good, baby."

His praises did her in. They always did. Climbing onto the bed behind her, Projex lifted her up at the waist some, then removed his shirt. The head of his dick smeared her slickness around. Loriana turned her head some to watch them in the mirror that was in the corner of her room. His body was ripped, making the tattoos she loved more pronounced. The deep v-cuts in his lower abs were a clear indication that he'd gone hard while locked up. Loriana wanted to drag her tongue in the creases of them both.

Running a hand down her back, Projex took a deep breath and slid inside—almost slid, inside of her.

"Ooh, wait," Loriana said, trying to run.

Projex pulled her back by her waist. "Quit running and take this dick. It's yours, ain't it?"

He slid back inside, this time successfully. His stomach caved, and his head spun upon entry.

"Mm. This shit way too fucking tight," he grumbled, but not complaining.

Taking deep breaths and measured strokes, he glided in and out of Loriana with ease. She was so wet, and besides her moans and his grunts, that's all you could hear.

"Why this pussy so wet?" He asked, not really wanting an answer.

Between her arousal for him and her SaltXo yoni bar she'd been using, Loriana was dripping wet. Tossing her ass back onto him, Projex became hypnotized at the way her ass rippled. She'd gotten thick, but her booty wasn't outrageous. It fit her frame, had the perfect amount of jiggle and was smacking loudly against him as she fucked him with everything in her.

"Yeah. That's it. Look how sexy you are fucking me."

Projex long stroked her with a firm hand placed on her back. Each time he dipped and swerved in her walls, Loriana leaked more. Her bed was saturated with her juices.

"Aaah yes! Yes! I missed this dick," she exclaimed loudly.

Smack!

"No, you didn't," Projex told her, now right up on her. He gave her no room to run, just take straight dick—all nine inches of him.

"I did! I swear I did. Oh my, Bryyyyshoon!" She was squirting. Only he had been able to make her do so, and Loriana felt like she was floating away.

Her body collapsed onto the bed, but Projex didn't move. He straddled her and held her cheeks apart. Watching as her pussy clamped around his dick, he couldn't help but grin. Even if she had been fucking someone else, they hadn't been hitting it right. Her walls curved to him like he'd made them himself.

Leaning over her body, Projex moved her hair from her damp neck. Kissing her cheek, he entangled their fingers. Loriana's eyes fluttered, and emotions peeked as she watched them in the mirror.

"I love you," Projex confessed.

A tear fell.

"I ain't ever leaving you again."

More tears came.

"You gon' be my wife. I put that on my life. You hear me?"

Her head rubbed against her comforter as she nodded.

"Tell me you love me, ma."

Projex's voice was low and heart back to where it belonged. His dick was gliding slowly inside her as he spoke into her ear. This wasn't just them fucking. It was deeper than that. Their souls were reconnecting.

Loriana's eyes closed as she came again. This was too much.

"Tell me, ma. I need to hear you say it," Projex urged. "You feel this dick all in you. It's yours. Tell me."

He craved those words from her and her alone. Projex needed her to stroke his ego. She'd slightly wounded it but knew she was the only one to mend it as well. Hating how she wasn't saying a word, Projex kissed her in the mouth, lifted her hips, and started fucking her roughly. That dick was so deep in her guts, Loriana had no choice but to try and use her words now.

"Aaah, baby. I love you! I love you so much! Don't ever leave me again," she cried as he held her tightly.

"I promise I won't," he declared, releasing deep inside of her.

They laid there for all of two minutes in silence before one of them said something. Loriana was too sleepy to even open her eyes.

"Ma, somebody knockin' on your door," Projex told her.

"Tell them to go away," she mumbled.

Chuckling, Projex sat up in the bed and hopped off. Finding his briefs, he slipped them on and went to the door. When he opened it, Trell didn't bother to hide his eyes from looking directly down at his member.

"Aye. Don't play with me, nigga," Projex spat. "What you want?"

"Um, tell Lo, Symir was just at the door."

Loriana popped up in the bed so quick, Projex's head jerked back. He went to say something but closed the door in Trell's face instead.

"Rude, sexy mothafucka." Trell smirked and walked away.

Barely able to stand, Loriana slipped her leggings on and searched for her tank top. Once she found it, she slid it over her mess of a head and grabbed her phone. The entire time, Projex watched her with a scowl on his face. He wanted to see how this was going to play out. What he wasn't doing, though, was leaving.

Dialing Symir's line, he picked up on the first ring. "What's up, baby. You not feeling good?"

She cleared her dry throat. "Um, no. Not really. I must be coming down with a cold."

Projex scoffed, and she looked over at him. *Yeah, her ass sick a'ight. Sick from taking all this dick.*

"Damn, you do sound a lil' sick. I was just at your door, but yo' friends said you weren't feeling good. Want me to bring you some meds?"

"No. I already took some. It might just be a stomach bug or something. Thank you, though."

"You know it's nothing. I can come take care of you. You know you spoiled when you not feeling good."

When she smiled, Projex walked over to her. It was time to get the fuck off the phone. She looked at him with wide eyes and scurried to the other side of her bed.

"Right. But I'm good. I'ma just sweat it out."

Projex held his hand up and started counting down from five.

"A'ight. Well, I'ma check on you later. Feel better. I love you."

Her body stilled, and words got clogged in her throat. Projex knew whatever he said on the other end had her shook to even say back... and he wanted her to.

"Say it. I dare you," he told her.

Loriana mugged him. She didn't care that they'd just got done having sex; he didn't run nor scare her.

"Thank you. I love you too."

She said the words quickly and hung up. Projex couldn't move. They simply stared at one another with a million thoughts running through their minds. Loriana saw the hurt mask his face before his head bobbed. He licked his lips and broke their staring contest.

"You can't be mad!" Loriana yelled.

Projex ignored her and pulled his pants and shirt on. Moving around the room, he picked his keys and phone up from the dresser. Loriana walked over to where he was standing and got in his face.

"So, you're mad?"

"Nah. I'm straight."

She crossed her arms. "We don't lie to each other."

"But you'll lie to that nigga, though. What you save his feelings for and not mine?"

Her chest ached. "It's not like that. I wasn't trying to hurt your feelings, but what was I supposed to say?"

"You wasn't supposed to call that nigga in the first place, but a'ight, Loriana. I don't even know why I'm tripping. You ain't my bitch no more."

The slap to his face came so damn fast, Projex's eyes crossed some. The rage in her eyes had him sucking his teeth.

"Fuck you. Don't you ever disrespect me and call me out of my name. Not your bitch? Not your bitch!? Who is then, huh? Who held you down while you were sitting in there doing time? Me! And you want to disrespect me?"

She was beyond pissed. Loriana was hurt. Did he not expect her to move on with her life? He was the one who cut her off, and she still had his back. She made sure that when he came home, he had money to his name and a platform to build from. Loriana didn't have to do any of that. She could've left him hanging like he thought she would.

"Damn, ma. I ain't mean to call you a bitch. I didn't mean it how you taking it."

"Yes, you did!" she screamed frustratedly. "Every time something doesn't go your way, you speak out of anger like a little ass boy. You love me and think that's love? It's not!"

He stepped into her face. "Who loves you then? That bitch ass nigga you was just on the phone with? Huh? He love you?"

"Yes! He loved and protected me enough to not push me away when I needed him most."

Her words split his heart in two. She saw it break through his eyes, but Loriana didn't care. He wasn't about to come into her world and try to blame her for his shortcomings. So, what she loved Symir. It was easy to do so. He made loving him worth it, but she couldn't help that her heart was in two places. It was playing tug of war with her past while making promises for so much more in the future.

Projex didn't even know what to say. His words were a jumbled mess in his head, and before he said some shit that would really end them for good, he backed away from her.

"A'ight, ma. You got it." His head bobbed, and he scoffed in a pissed off manner. "You confessing your love for another nigga, while my nut drippin' from your pussy and sliding down your legs. That shit crazy."

Loriana looked down at her leggings, and sure enough, there was a wet spot on them. When her head lifted, Projex was pulling her door open. She didn't bother to call him back, because honestly… what was there to say? This was life. It didn't come with an instruction book, and she'd learned that long ago. She only hoped that with what she knew now, it'd be easier to navigate through.

"Who am I kidding," she huffed loudly. "This love thing is never easy."

Chapter Fourteen

F ive in the morning in Atlanta on Labor Day
was nuts. Projex didn't even know how they'd
made it through the day, but they had. Wanting to
celebrate life, his freedom, and their song going platinum, Laurent had the team in Atlanta for the weekend. It was Tuesday morning now, but they'd arrived
on Friday and had been on go since.

Laurent had a club performance that sold out
within an hour of fans knowing he'd be in town. The
city, though he wasn't from there, came out and
showed nothing but love. Another well-known artist
from St. Louis named, Young Mel, had even pulled
up on him. Projex was taking it all in. He didn't
consider himself famous and preferred to be lowkey,
but he couldn't front like seeing a crowd of three

hundred plus people sing, and rap lyrics he wrote didn't affect him.

He wanted to take his phone out all night and call Loriana and show her what she'd contributed to, but he didn't. It was a week later, and he was still in his feelings. Hearing the woman he loved confess her love to another man did something to him. Seeing how his hard work had paid off did too. It made him want to go harder. He was ready to tuck his feelings to the side and put in work. There was nothing like hustling through your hurt. That pain would always turn into profit, no matter where it came from.

On the ride back to their Airbnb, almost an hour away from their venue, Kordell drunkenly rambled. Projex just smirked, knowing his cousin was fucked up, but it was all good. He'd brought him on the trip too 'cause as promised, Projex wanted to see all his niggas eat. Kordell was blood, so it was automatic with him. It wasn't like that for everyone, though.

"Yo, cuz. I love you, nigga. You hear that crowd tonight? And them bitches screaming your songs?"

Projex smirked. He wasn't nearly as drunk as him. "Yeah. That shit was wild."

"Man! That hoe was so live. I should've got me one of these freaks to come back to the crib."

"Hell nah. That's the quickest way a nigga gets set

up. We good. Our flight leaves in a few hours anyway."

Projex wasn't with letting people know where he rested his head. He never had been and wouldn't switch up because he had some money, or bitches threw themselves at him. He'd set niggas up the same way before.

"You right, you right. I'ma just sleep this shit off. My girl back at home anyway."

Projex laughed, whipping through traffic. "You girl? When you get in a relationship?"

"Nah. Not no serious shit. I just be fucking on her and taking her shopping sometimes."

"Aaah. You a trick then. Got it."

The cousins laughed. It felt good to do something simple like crack jokes and not through a jail call. Projex was never taking the simple things in life for granted again. As they pulled up to their Airbnb, Projex parked the Range Rover he was pushing and hopped out.

Once inside, Kordell headed straight for the couch while Projex went to the kitchen. He needed some water to take a BC powder. He hadn't drank much, but they were drinking dark and light, and he didn't want to have a headache when he woke up. Pulling his phone from his pocket, he went to check a text from his mama, and his phone died.

"Damn. I think I left my charger with Laurent's ass," he grumbled, walking into the living room. "Aye, Dell. Let me use yo' charger right quick."

Slumped and already knocked out on the couch, Kordell didn't hear a word he said. Searching for it himself, Projex looked through his bags that were next to him. Spotting it, he snatched it up and was about to go back to the kitchen when Kordell's phone vibrated and fell out of his hand onto the wood floor.

Projex froze when he went to pick it up. "Nah. I'm tripping," he mumbled. He just knew he didn't see this girl's name on his phone. When she called back, Projex answered.

"Kor—" Kelsi's voice got caught in her throat. "W-What you doing answering his phone?"

"Nah. What the fuck you doing calling his phone? You a rat."

Kelsi laughed. "And you're a killer. What's next? If I'm a rat, so is your cousin. Tell him to call me when he wakes up. That's if you don't kill him, too."

When she hung up in his face, Projex went directly to Kordell's text messages. He frowned, only seeing her name and another unsaved number in it.

Flipping the phone over, he realized it wasn't the one he normally saw him with; it was his second phone.

As he read their text messages, Projex became sick to his stomach. Kelsi had been the one to testify against him in court, claiming she was there when Austin's friend was killed. How the jury believed her fake ass tears was beyond him, but now he knew her motive.

Kordell had been communicating with Austin, Kelsi, and the cops to throw Projex under the jail. All this time, Projex had been kicking it with the one person who wanted him out of the game. Austin was in his text messages promising to give him ten G's to knock his own blood off.

"I can't believe this shit."

Standing up from the couch, Projex snatched the gun he had on him from his waist. Nudging his cousin under the chin with the barrel, it took everything in him not to blow his brains out. He wanted answers first.

"Dell. Dell. Wake yo bitch ass up, nigga." When he didn't move, Projex splashed water on him.

Kordell grumbled, and eyes squinted up at him. When he saw the gun, he sat up and tried sobering up. "Yo, cuz. What's good? What's going on?"

"What's one thing I hate?" Projex asked calmly with venom in his voice.

Confused, Kordell's wet brows furrowed. "Huh? I'ont know, cuz. Why you got that gun on me?"

"You know why, nigga! Why, cuz? Why you have to be a fucking rat, dawg," Projex was pissed. He was really about to have to take his blood out and console his auntie at his funeral.

It finally clicked for Kordell. "Cuz, those niggas was threatening me with crazy numbers if I didn't talk."

"But you don't even know shit! Who killed that nigga, Dell?"

Kordell shook his head. "Come on, man. We don't gotta talk about no murder. You beat the case."

"Nah bitch," he spat, smacking him across the face with the gun. "You been talking! Who killed Malcolm since you and Kelsi know so fucking much."

Kordell held his jaw and looked up at him. He was praying he didn't shoot him but knew Projex would've done so by now if he really wanted to.

"You did, cuz."

"Wrong. Chevy did. And he's dead, so my nigga can't serve time. Neither can a snitch."

Projex pulled the trigger, not giving a fuck that

he'd just gotten out of prison. A snitch would never live to see the light of day around him, blood or not. That shit wasn't thicker than the tears he'd shed in that cell.

Yawning, Loriana pulled into Joseline's neighborhood, hoping she didn't have to hear Joi's mouth. She offered to take her to her doctor's appointment this morning and was running a little late. Joi had yet to tell Projex she was pregnant, and every time Joi brought him up to Loriana, she got annoyed.

Just as stubborn as he could be, she could be too. They hadn't talked since he left out of her place that day, and they wouldn't if it were up to her. All week she'd been trying to make sense of their argument, thinking maybe she was wrong, but she knew she wasn't. It didn't help that Symir had been nothing but sweet to her.

He'd taken her out to eat and to a car show over the weekend, bought them a four-hour pass to one of the best spas in town, and listened to her express how she wanted to branch out with her own music platform one day. Symir was a listener, and a boss in his own right. They connected on a level that had matured Loriana, and she was so appreciative. He'd come into her life with pure, clear intentions, and she loved him most for keeping it real with her.

"I'ma get my shit together," she grumbled sleepily, turning down their street.

Once in the driveway, she parked and thought about honking her horn but didn't. Peaches had always told anyone who pulled up to her house honking that didn't no hoes live there. So, Loriana called her instead. As soon as the phone rang once, Joi was coming out of the house. The person walking out behind her had Loriana's eyes squinting and bottom glued to her seat before she was unbuckling her seatbelt and climbing out of the truck.

Nervously, Joi bit into her bottom lip. "Oh, hey. I thought you weren't going to make it."

"What are you doing here?" Loriana ignored her and questioned Symir.

Joi looked back and forth between them. "You know him?"

"Yes! Now, what is he doing here, Joi, and don't lie?"

She swallowed hard, looking to Symir for answers, but he didn't have any to give.

"He um. He was taking me to my doctor's appointment."

"Why would he be—" Loriana stopped herself mid-sentence.

Realization slapped her in the face. Tears pricked her eyes before she could stop them, and queasiness filled her empty stomach. The same man she'd just been silently praising and promising herself to be better to was a fraud. Joi had been so hush-hush about who her baby daddy was, and now Loriana knew why. It was her so-called man who'd clearly been keeping secrets from her since the beginning.

While she was busy trying to protect her heart from Projex, she should've been doing the same with Symir. Loriana wanted her heart back. Not just from him, from both of them. It was clear neither of them knew how to handle it with care.

To Be Continued...